A Shet

STAND-ALONE NOVEL

A Western Historical Romance Book

by

Hannah Lee Davis

Copyright© 2024 by Hannah Lee Davis

All Rights Reserved.

This book may not be reproduced or transmitted in any form without the written permission of the publisher.

In no way is it legal to reproduce, duplicate, or transmit any part of this document in either electronic means or in printed format. Recording of this publication is strictly prohibited and any storage of this document is not allowed unless with written permission from the publisher

Table of Contents

A Sheriff for Violet 1
    Table of Contents 3
    Letter from Hannah Lee Davis 5
Prologue 7
Chapter One 10
Chapter Two 17
Chapter Three 25
Chapter Four 34
Chapter Five 38
Chapter Six 48
Chapter Seven 56
Chapter Eight 65
Chapter Nine 73
Chapter Ten 80
Chapter Eleven 90
Chapter Twelve 100
Chapter Thirteen 110
Chapter Fourteen 118
Chapter Fifteen 126
Chapter Sixteen 134
Chapter Seventeen 143
Chapter Eighteen 151
Chapter Nineteen 160
Chapter Twenty 170

Chapter Twenty-One 178
Chapter Twenty-Two 185
Chapter Twenty-Three 193
Chapter Twenty-Four 201
Chapter Twenty-Five 211
Chapter Twenty-Six 217
Chapter Twenty-Seven 224
Chapter Twenty-Eight 233
Chapter Twenty-Nine 241
Chapter Thirty 252
Chapter Thirty-One 263
Chapter Thirty-Two 273
Chapter Thirty-Three 283
Epilogue 293
   Also by Hannah Lee Davis 317

Letter from Hannah Lee Davis

As my beloved husband, my school sweetheart Mister John Bennett would say:

"Life is like a bowl of soup—you've got to stir it once in a while, so all the good stuff doesn't settle at the bottom."

Hi y'all, I'm Hannah Lee Davis, a spry 65-year-old widow who's finally gotten around to doing what I've dreamt of for years—writing stories that touch the heart and soul. I was born and raised in the heartland of Indiana, where the cornfields stretch as far as the eye can see, and where folks still know the value of a hard day's work and a kind word. But these days, I find myself out in Colorado, sharing stories and sunsets with my darling sister, Janice.

Why did it take me so long to put pen to paper, you ask? Well, life happened, sugar. I spent most of my years caring for my family, raising kids—after years of trying, mind you—and looking after my aging parents. My husband's ailment needed time and dedication from my side. Don't get me wrong; I wouldn't trade those days for anything. But there were nights, oh yes, many nights, when I'd sit in my knitting chair, crocheting blankets or scarves, and my mind would wander. Each stitch was like a sentence, each row a paragraph, and before I knew it, I'd crocheted whole stories in my head.

Crocheting, you see, is a lot like weaving stories. You've got to have the right pattern, the right tension, and above all, the right yarn to make something truly beautiful. It's a labor of love, one stitch at a time, just like life.

So why now? Why have I decided to become a published author at this ripe old age? Well, darlin', it's simple. I've got stories in me that are yearnin' to be told—tales of love that burns like a prairie fire, and courage that stands as tall as a mountain. I write because I want to wrap you up in a narrative as comforting as one of my homemade quilts, a story that'll make you feel at home, no matter where you are. I write because this is what make sense for me, imagining worlds where my husband John would admire, worlds where brides find the love of their lives in the most unexpected ways.

I write because this is what John made me promise before he passed away.

So, grab a cup of hot cocoa, settle into your favorite armchair, and let's journey through the wild frontier of human emotions, one story at a time.

Until next time,
Hannah Lee Davis

Prologue

January 1885

"How could you do this to us?" Cornelia Thompson's eyes sparkled with tears as she glared at her daughter Violet, pure contempt twisting her features.

Violet took a step back. Her stomach dropped like a stone as she took in her mother's expression. She and her mother had never gotten along, always at odds with one another. But tonight, her mother's brightly flushed face and bared teeth summoned a disturbing thought. *She despises me. She always has.*

"Do what?" Violet exhaled, her voice trembling. "Refuse to marry the rake of Boston? Know what I am worth?"

"The rake of—" Father's eyes widened, and he slammed his glass down on the mahogany sideboard. "For God's sake – Isaac Wilson was our last hope! Without him, we will have nothing to our name. Without him, our family is *ruined*! This is how you show your thanks? After everything your mother and I have given you?"

Violet's lungs felt as though they might burst. "I don't care about *things*!" she screamed. "I don't care about grand houses, or pretty dresses, or China dolls. All I ever wanted was a mother and father who *love me*. I wanted parents who thought the world of me – not spending day in and day out picking me apart. But to *you*, all I'm good for is preserving your wealth! Are your social status and your trifling friends all you really care about ?"

Father stepped back, his hand raised. Even as Violet opened her mouth to continue, stinging pain bit across her cheek, sending her lurching backwards. She lifted her hand to her face, a sob rising in her throat.

Disbelief flooded through her. Father was standing directly in front of her now, the shadows of the hearth fire dancing across his white, tense features.

"You are to marry Isaac Wilson by June," he spat, his blue eyes hard and cold, boring straight through Violet. *"Do you understand?"*

Tears slipped down Violet's hotly smarting cheek. Her throat closed. Without uttering another word, she whirled on her heel and fled the room, slamming the door violently behind her. *I'd do nothing but waste more breath if I stayed...*

She rushed up the stairs, eyes blurry with tears, and jostled one of the household servants. The woman let out a surprised cry as Violet pushed past.

She nearly tripped on her skirts as she reached the top of the carpeted staircase...the same staircase she had once descended as a Boston debutante, desperate for her mother and father's approval. *I think I hate this home. You're not supposed to hate home, are you?*

But now, the thought of lingering another minute in this suffocating, soulless place made Violet's stomach turn. Her slippered feet padded softly on the thick brocade carpet until she reached her own bedroom door and flung it open, darting inside.

She slammed it shut behind her and pressed herself against it. Closing her eyes tightly, she slid to the floor, her knees refusing to hold her.

She pressed shaking palms to her temples. *What am I supposed to do?* Panic tightened her chest.

As if in direct answer to her plea, someone gave a faint knock on her door. "Miss Vi-Vi? May I enter?"

Violet's eyes flew open, and her heart leapt.

Lou.

Some of her stifling loneliness drained away slightly, replaced by a tinge of hope.

Violet scrambled to her feet and opened the door. Standing there was Lou her maid, her only friend in the world.

Violet reached out a hand and tugged Lou into the bedroom.

"Miss Vi-Vi, your cheek!" Lou gasped, clapping a hand to her mouth.

Violet shook her head. She reached out and grasped Lou's arm. "Never mind that. I need your help."

Chapter One

Miles City, Montana

June 1885

Violet Olivia Thompson stared in dismay at the inky, jagged stroke across her piece of parchment. A black stain bloomed on her gloved fingertip, and she grimaced.

Writing while sitting in a bumping, jostling stagecoach was proving to be a complicated task, but she needed to do something to distract herself.

For two different reasons. The first reason was sitting directly across from her, an unkempt gentleman who called himself Hank. He had a scraggly, patchy beard, and his mouth was twisted into something between a grimace and a smile. He was clutching the old carpetbag on his lap so tightly that his knuckles turned white. A greasy hat slouched across his forehead, and his clothes were sweat-stained and rumpled. A green bandana was tied around his neck, splotched with brown – presumably from liquor.

In the cramped coach's cabin, she could smell him too well, sour and stale, the same scent her father wore after one too many drinks of port or whiskey in his study. Clearly, Violet wasn't the only one who noticed. The other women in the coach were furtively pressing handkerchiefs to their noses in an attempt to stifle the man's unpleasant odors.

But the thing that unnerved Violet the most about Hank was how he had stared at her almost constantly since he had first boarded the stagecoach two hours earlier. Violet spared a cautious glance at him, noticing how his eyes raked over her from her coiffed hair to the pointed toes and button rows of her black Parisian travel boots.

Violet dropped her eyes to her paper again. The second reason she needed to write this letter to Lou right here, right now, in this rickety stagecoach, was to calm the anxiety fluttering in her stomach. With every mile, she drew closer and closer to Helena, Montana, a town thousands of miles from everything she knew. The letter would've been so much easier to write on board the train, but she'd been told that her train didn't reach Helena. She had been compelled to board this stagecoach.

Violet stared down at the letter with unfocused eyes, replaying the fateful night that had changed everything.

Even today, a fortnight later, she still keenly felt the pain of her father's blow across her face. Her heart had still been pounding like a funeral drum when she flung open her wardrobe doors, searching among the silk and muslin day dresses for her two plainest dresses.

After the dresses, a pair of leather boots, the ones she'd always worn to the park or the museums and art galleries in Boston.

And then Lou—ear, loyal Lou, who had done more for Violet than she could ever hope to repay—Lou had helped her pack the old carpet bag, now stowed atop the stagecoach. Lou hadn't even paused to question Violet's plan. Instead, she had flown into action along with Violet. She had packed the underclothes, the boar-hair brush and ivory comb, the bottle of lemon verbena perfume, and even Violet's Bible. And Lou was the one who had taken a pair of sewing scissors to Violet's hair, shearing off the silky black curls that had been one of Violet's vanities.

If it wasn't for Lou, Violet would already be married to Isaac Wilson, a cad with only his wealth to recommend him to the Boston socialites.

Isaac Wilson. She gave an involuntary shudder. She'd rather die a spinster than marry him. She knew that for certain the night she'd secretly followed him to the door of a brothel.

She'd stopped in her tracks the moment he went through the door. The smells of smoke, whiskey, and waste had nearly choked her. But none of that was as revolting as her final glimpse of him in one of the upstairs windows, tangled in the arms of *three* women.

Her heart had raced almost as quickly as her feet on the way home. Surely, surely, if Mother and Father knew of such an offense, they would change their minds about the engagement. But she had been sorely mistaken. To them, *she* had been the offensive one, speaking of unmentionable acts that ought to have been left in the shadows.

Ruefully, Violet rubbed the steel-tipped pen between her stained fingertips. She should never have been surprised that her parents didn't care.

What she had seen that night was utterly insignificant to Augustine and Cornelia Thompson. As far as they were concerned, Isaac Wilson's wealth made him the most respectable bachelor in the entire city. Then the stagecoach bumped, bringing Violet back to the present as she struggled to swallow past the lump in her throat. She might have enjoyed this ride, if it weren't for "Hank" with his soiled clothes and piercing stare.

The other four passengers in the coach were pleasant enough. One was an elderly gentleman in a bowler hat and a faded, pressed tweed suit. Wire-rimmed spectacles were perched on his long, pointed nose. He was thoroughly absorbed in a book by Washington Irving.

His name was Horace Bentley, and his spinster daughter Agatha sat beside Violet. Her clothes were plain, almost insipid, and her personality was much the same. But she had been warm and friendly nevertheless, and Violet found that strangely comforting as the stagecoach carried her deeper into wild territory.

The other two passengers were a middle-aged woman and her teenaged son. The woman was Colleen O'Neil, her Irish blood apparent from her faded red hair and the thick Irish brogue that tinged her every word. Her son Sean, his hair the same shade as his mother's, dozed with folded arms beside Mr. Bentley.

Violet glanced past him out the stagecoach window. Sweeping plains covered in rippling grasses stretched out as far as the eye could see. Faintly rolling hills rose above the horizon. *Lou would love it out here.*

Violet twirled her pen between her fingers, exhaling slowly to release the tension squeezing in her chest. *This teaching arrangement needs to work out.* It had been Lou's idea—she'd found the teaching position in the paper. And Violet had given every last penny's worth of her heirloom brooch to cover the significant travel expenses. This was her last chance at freedom.

I wonder what my future students will be like? How wild will Helena be? Violet might be well-read and schooled by the finest tutors in Boston, but she had not a bit of experience teaching children. And she imagined that the polished, wealthy Boston children she knew would be a far cry from the children in a frontier town like Helena.

Across from her, Hank cleared his throat, and Violet made the mistake of glancing in his direction. His mouth tilted in a wry smile, and he straightened a little in his seat. "You don't look like you're from this part of the country," he drawled, planting his palms on his knees as he leaned forward a little.

Violet's stomach turned. When she spoke, she was careful to use the slower, musical accent she'd been hearing at the train stops ever since Chicago. "Actually, sir, I am. Born and raised in St. Louis," she lied.

That had been her cover story from Boston to here. She didn't need anybody knowing she'd traveled from Boston, especially if Mother and Father were looking for her. Though, she was beginning to think they couldn't be bothered. She'd even planned her clothes to match the part—she thought she looked quite plain, but perhaps she wasn't blending in as well as she imagined...

"St. Louis, hm?" the man asked, frowning. "Got family out in Helena?"

Again, Violet lied. "That's right," she chirped sweetly, hoping he would drop the subject.

How much longer until Helena? She didn't know if she could abide another hour in the presence of this uncouth man. *Please let us be close,* she prayed.

"You're not one of them mail-order brides, are you?" The man let out a wheezing cackle, and Violet stiffened with distaste.

"No, sir." She wasn't lying this time. Of course, she'd heard about those opportunities as well. In fact, Lou had once jokingly suggested such an idea, but Violet had thoroughly vetoed it. *Could you* imagine *keeping house for a rancher?* she'd had wondered aloud. *Hopefully the dashing fellow wouldn't mind eating porridge for a while, at least until I learn to cook.* That had sent Lou into fits of laughter.

The man across from her cleared his throat again, and Violet nearly sighed aloud. When would he realize that she was merely being polite? *Doesn't he know how impertinent it is to ask such personal questions?*

"Say, you don't happen to be any relation to one of them Astors, are you? I must say, I ain't seen such an elegant lady this side of the Missouri." He clicked his tongue, winking at her.

Violet opened her mouth to tell him that no, she was not an Astor, when suddenly a piercing boom shattered the air, followed quickly by several more booms that sent Violet's heart leaping into her throat as her insides coiled tightly in horror. The other members of the stagecoach also jumped, and Agatha let out a loud cry, clutching at Violet's arm.

Shouts and pounding hoofbeats rose outside, and Colleen O'Neil choked out, "Highwaymen!" in a shrill, panicked voice.

From the number of voices, it sounded like several men were riding near the stagecoach. Violet tried to make out what they were saying. She kept hearing the word "green" again and again. Then, very close by, one of the riders bawled out, "Turn yourself in, you green devil!" A moment later, he appeared in Violet's window, mounted atop his galloping horse. He was brandishing a gleaming pistol.

Violet's heart pulsed wildly in her chest as the stagecoach picked up speed. She peered out the window, eyes scanning the road behind, and caught sight of several more riders. Then the coach plunged forward. Likely the horses had spooked. Agatha's grip on Violet's arm tightened as the coach lurched and began teetering sideways.

The last thought that flitted through Violet's head as the world careened sideways was that at least she'd die free, on her own terms, and not as an unwilling bride, especially the bride of a cad like Isaac Wilson.

Violet floated through the air, tumbling down onto her bed, its velvet blankets and goose-feather mattress rising to meet her. Only, when she landed, blinding pain lanced through her, as if she'd just collapsed onto the Boston cobblestones.

Hands were tugging at her, pulling, always pulling. Her mother's voice resounded through the air, an enraged cry: *How could you do this to us?*

Violet forced her eyes open. The cobblestone roads and feather beds dissolved, giving way to grass and dirt. Nothing but grass and dirt. The metallic taste of blood spread across her tongue. But the hands were still pulling her. Fingers were digging into her forearms with a bruising grip that caused her to cry out. *I'm not in Boston, am I? I'm going to die out here in the middle of nowhere.*

Then her body was lifted into the air, and the next thing she knew, she was hanging upside down, face crushed into damp cotton soured by sweat. Something as firm as iron wound around the backs of her knees, securing her in the dizzying position.

The last thing Violet heard was the wheezing, drawling voice of the man from the stagecoach…the man in the green bandana. "Don't you worry your pretty little head, Miss St. Louis!" Violet's insides knotted with revulsion, and she opened her mouth to scream. But no sound left her lips.

Something glittered before her eyes. There was a dull as something hard as a stone smashed against her head, and the world went dark.

Chapter Two

Gabriel Brooks loosened his forefinger on the trigger of his Colt pistol, watching the short man already several yards in front of him, who was bent beneath the weight of the woman thrown on his shoulder. "If you shoot or follow me, she's dead," he yelled across the prairie.

Damn it. He's getting away. Gabriel tugged on Apollo's reins to bring him to a stop as he squinted at the man. He'd never seen the Green Terror in person before...but it was impossible that this man could be anyone else. And the fact that he'd taken a prisoner for leverage was exactly what Gabriel would've expected.

Sure, the man didn't look like much. But Gabriel's information had been thorough, and all the other stagecoach passengers were accounted for.

At least, all except the woman being kidnapped. Gabriel squinted harder, confused. It *was* a woman, but her hair appeared to have been hacked short, tumbling in loose curls over her face as she slumped across the man's back. The whole scene was so absurd that Gabriel might have chuckled if it weren't for the fact that he was watching an abduction play out right before his eyes.

The man paused for a moment and pulled out a pistol, waving it haphazardly in the air. "No tails!" he yelled again. Gabriel clenched his jaw. He glanced behind at his men and gave a shake of his head, indicating that they stand down.

With a sinking heart, he watched as the short man and his captive vanished into the tall grasses. He marked the spot. They were headed for the tree line at the start of the Beartooth foothills.

They'd missed the Green Terror...again. *That devil.* Hank Logan was his real name. He'd had a chance to run before Gabriel's posse had reached the wrecked stagecoach, and he'd taken it, along with a captive, to make matters even worse. Next to being the most dangerous man Gabriel had ever hunted, the Green Terror was also the most evasive.

Sighing, Gabriel swung his leg over Apollo's back and landed in the dust, spurs jangling loudly. "George, you go ahead and trail him," he called to his deputy. The older man dismounted and handed off his reins to Timothy Hawkins.

Why he'd allowed Hawkins along, Gabriel couldn't fathom. Hawkins was an upstart of a kid who took himself too seriously. He tended to remind Gabriel of himself sometimes. But Gabriel felt no sympathy for him at the moment. In fact, he was about ready shake young Hawkins within an inch of his life. If Hawkins hadn't lost control of himself and started pursuing the stagecoach, those horses wouldn't have spooked, and Gabriel could have ordered the carriage to a halt...and they'd finally have the Green Terror in their grasp.

But Hawkins, impulsive and desperate to prove himself, had urged his horse into a gallop before Gabriel could stop him. And everything had spiraled out of control from there.

Gabriel ignored Hawkins pointedly and addressed George. "We'll go by the main road and meet you on the other side of the trees. But take care you don't push 'em too far south, else we'll lose him over the border."

He drummed his fingers impatiently against the grip of his pistol. He wanted to accompany George, pursue the Green Terror, shoot him the second he got a chance. His stomach boiled with impatience. *Good Lord, I almost had him.* He could barely refrain from shooting Hawkins a withering look. The boy's head was hanging, and a glance revealed that his face was crumpling.

Gabriel nearly rolled his eyes.

It was downright maddening to be so close to the man he'd been tracking for months on end. He'd watched Miles City dissolve into panic and paranoia, and he'd been nearly helpless to stop it. Until now—for the first time in weeks, he nearly had Hank Logan in his grasp. Nearly had him in the crosshairs of his pistol barrel.

And then, just like that, Logan had darted away.

Gabriel started as someone slapped his back. He turned to see his foreman Benjie Fisher. "Relax, Gabe. We've nearly got him," Benjie chuckled, shaking his head, blue eyes twinkling.

It wasn't the first time Benjie had used thos words, but right now, it sent irritation prickling hotly beneath Gabriel's skin. "Relax?" He clenched his teeth, re-mounting his horse in one fluid motion. "As if we had time for that."

Benjie remounted, following Gabriel, and Hawkins trailed behind as they carefully moved up the main road as it wove around thicket of trees at the base of the nearby hills.

"This is the first lead I've got in months," Gabriel muttered as Benjie trotted up beside him. "*Months.* And now that bastard's gone. He'll be over the Wyoming border before nightfall. Then we'll just have to wait like sitting ducks."

Benjie's smile faded, but he waved his hand dismissively. "Naw. He won't be able to keep himself away from the silver mines. He'll be back, and we'll get him then."

Gabriel dipped his chin in a curt nod. Benjie had a point. Even so, despair formed a pit inside him.

He'd happened upon the lead on Hank Logan's whereabouts by mere chance. Ma would call it Providence. He'd been about to walk into Miles City Saloon when a flash of green caught his eye. He turned to see the infamous green bandana, tied around the neck of a short fellow in a rumpled, grease-stained shirt. The man was talking urgently with what looked to be a stagecoach driver. There was lots of gesturing.

Just then, a gunshot rang out from inside the saloon, distracting Gabriel. When he turned back, the two men were gone. He began to run towards the stagecoach stop just down the street. But to his dismay, just as he approached, the coach pulled away at an urgent clip. Gabriel spurred his horse into a gentle trot along the dusty road, smiling humorlessly to himself. The only good thing about losing Hank Logan at the stagecoach stop was seeing how rattled he'd looked while he was talking to the driver. *He's scared, alright. He better be.*

Benjie must have noticed Gabriel's smile. "What's so funny, Gabe?"

"Looks like Hank Logan is finding out the hard way that he can only push people so far before they turn on him," Gabriel chuckled. "And now he's paying the price for it. I doubt his own henchmen will take it kindly that he's robbing them blind for his own ticket to freedom."

Benjie snorted. "Well, as far as we're concerned, his luck's nearly run out."

"God, I sure do hope so. I'm getting mighty tired of chasing him to kingdom come. There's only so much more Miles City can take. It's already precarious enough around here."

Gabriel should know. He was the sheriff...and the acting mayor. It was his duty to see that Miles City grow from a frontier village into a thriving town, one that would hopefully attract the railroad barons. But the railroads would never come to Miles City if it remained embroiled in lawlessness and poverty.

Hank Logan needed to be put behind bars. And Gabriel would be the man to do it.

Benjie's teasing words echoed through Gabriel's head. *Relax.*

Gabriel scowled anew. *How the devil am I supposed to relax?* There was far too much at stake to take it easy these days. The people of Miles City looked to *him* to instill peace in their township. "I'll be damned if I stand by and let Miles City become another ghost town," he growled. Already, two families had packed up and moved along to Helena. It was only a matter of time before others followed suit.

Benjie nodded, his usually cheerful expression waning. "I know we've got a ways to go before we're another St. Louis. But I don't think we'll become a *ghost town* anytime soon. There's people coming out here every other week these days. Sure, the Green Terror ain't our only problem. But we'll wear him down and get him behind bars in no time. One less thing to worry about."

Gabriel wished he could easily share Benjie's optimism. "He's as slippery as a fish in the Tongue."

"I can feel we're gonna catch him in no time...I feel it right here," and Benjie patted his stomach.

"That so? Maybe you're just hungry," Gabriel chuckled.

Benjie laughed, too. They rode in silence for a few moments before he spoke up again, a dreamy note in his voice. Gabriel knew that tone—Benjie sounded like that anytime he was deeply contemplating something. "What kind of stores do you think will come along and set up shop in Miles City?"

"Well...a real post office would be nice," Gabriel mused. "A bank, too. We need one of those. And a school, of course. Good for all those children running about, getting underfoot all the time. Sure would be nice to have those Lawrence kids busy with learning."

Benjie snickered. "Sylvia Lawrence better not hear you say her children cause mischief. She'd have a fit."

"She would," Gabriel snorted. "She thinks they're the sweetest little angels."

Sylvia and her husband Thomas Lawrence ran the general store, the Lawrence Mercantile, and their three young children raised hell whenever they could. Being one of the wealthier families in Miles City, the Lawrences tended to think highly of themselves. They always made it a point to air their opinions about the rest of the town, and Gabriel hoped fervently that another general store would spring up soon. That would put them in their places.

"She sure do put on airs, don't she?" Benjie grinned. "You recall when they first came to town?"

"When Sylvia thought I was her own personal security guard? How could I forget?" Gabriel muttered.

Sylvia had equated *sheriff* with *store guard*, and had told Gabriel that in no uncertain terms.

"What'd you tell her?" Benjie laughed. He knew as well as Gabriel, but he never got tired of hearing the story.

"I told her I weren't gonna to stand in front of her store all day like a damn footman."

Benjie laughed. "Boy, did she squawk up a storm after that! I certainly didn't want to be in your shoes. I think a highwayman would take one look at her and turn tail and run the other way. She don't need a guard."

Gabriel shook his head, smirking.

Of course, Sylvia Lawrence's concerns did have some merit. Nobody could rest easy with Hank Logan and his band of thugs at large. His small stature had earned him the name the "Miles City Napoleon," among the townsfolk themselves, but that wasn't nearly as threatening or as widespread as the "Green Terror."

These days, Hank Logan was doing less waylaying and more scamming of those eager silver miners desperate to strike it rich in the Beartooth mines. Unfortunately, that didn't mean the inhabitants of Miles City could let their guard down. The longer Logan's reign of terror continued, the greater number of people would flee Miles City for a more peaceful environment.

"I'd love to see Sylvia and the Green Terror face off in a duel of their own," Benjie mused. "Maybe we should've brought her with us."

"Lordy, what a sight that would be," Gabriel sighed. He pressed his lips together, staring at the trail ahead.

"Somethin' else is troubling you, ain't it?"

Gabriel glanced up to see Benjie eyeing him knowingly. He hesitated a moment before replying. "It's just...I can see what Miles City's supposed to be. It's already taking shape bit by bit. We already got more buildings going up for future businesses. Hell, my own ranch cabin's gonna be a real home now. Not just a shack on the prairie anymore."

It would be a real home with a fireplace, a water pump, a sink, and *two* separate bedrooms. "Miles City's growing fast, and I want to see it through. I want it to flourish. But lately...things have been so unsteady in these parts," he sighed. "What with the railroad situation and all."

"You fret too much. The railroad will come our way, just you wait and see."

"I sure hope so."

"Well, let's talk about somethin' a bit more cheerful," Benjie said determinedly. "Your ma still pestering you about givin' her grandchildren?"

Gabriel grimaced. "She sure is," he muttered. *Not exactly a cheerful subject.*

Benjie snickered. "She still tryin' to set you up with a lady friend?"

"Don't remind me," Gabriel groaned.

Benjie gave a lighthearted shrug. "Gotta distract you from moping somehow. Consider yourself lucky. I don't got me a ma who'll find me a girl."

Gabriel rolled his eyes, and Benjie dissolved into another fit of laughter.

He hoped Benjie wouldn't press too far. He could practically hear Benjie's cackle if he ever found out that Gabriel tended to avoid his new house these days. Gabriel would never admit it to Benjie, but the bare home did little more than remind him of what his ma called *loneliness*.

Their conversation was interrupted by a piercing scream, and then a furious roar. Apollo and Benjie's horse skittered anxiously beneath their riders, tossing nervous heads. Gabriel glanced at Benjie, his stomach cinching.

In the purple haze of dusk, George came thudding down the road towards them, motioning wildly. "Hurry, they're just up ahead!"

Chapter Three

"Wakey, wakey, sweetheart."

Violet jerked her face away from a calloused hand against her cheek. Her body went stiff with horror as she opened her eyes to see Hank's grizzled face. Her temples throbbed, causing her stomach to cramp with nausea.

She was on the ground, lying in prickly grass, and the shadows were much longer than they'd been when she was in the stagecoach. Nothing but fields, and her grimy kidnapper with his grimy bag.

She tried to move her hands, but rope bit into her wrists, binding her arms behind her back. Something warm was dripping down the back of her neck.

Hank bent over and smirked at her, wheezing heavily as he planted his palms on his knees,. "I needed to rest up for a moment. You're a luscious little thing—not so easy to carry across these hills."

His words made Violet's skin crawl. She flashed him her most withering glare. "Why are you taking me?"

Hank huffed, yanking the green bandana around his neck up to swab his shiny face. "Why would I leave a sweet strumpet like you behind? For someone else to snatch up all that finery? That wouldn't be no good, no good at all."

"Finery?" Violet choked. *He can't ever know who I am, or he'll never let me go.* "I'm just a boatman's daughter! That's all!"

Hank guffawed, pointing a dirty finger in her face. "Aw, you can't fool me, darlin'! I know a lady of stature when I see one.

And you're anything but lowly. Every inch of you says East Coast city slicker."

Violet's mouth fell open. "I'm afraid you're mistaken," she stammered, her cheeks burning. But Hank's eyes flashed triumphantly. "I'm many things, darlin'. But mistaken ain't one of them."

Then he reached over and grabbed her around the waist, and with a loud grunt, he slung her over his shoulder so that her head dangled upside down behind him.

Violet's entire body recoiled as he hooked his arm around the backs of her knees. "Please..." Her eyes began to sting as she stared down at the ground a few feet from her head. "My father's got no money, if that's what you're after. He hasn't got a penny to his name. These are my last fine clothes. I've sold everything else."

"Pshaw! You can fib all you like; it ain't gonna change nothing. I'm taking you along with me, and there ain't nothing you can do." Hank bent and snatched up his old bag, cackling gleefully.

Tears dripped down Violet's face as she tried to writhe. Hank's arm only tightened. "None o' that! Tell me, darlin', what's a sweet critter like you doing all the way out here in Montana? You and me is friends now, so you don't gotta fib."

"I told you—I've got family out here in Helena."

"Naw. Where your folks from? Philadelphia? New York? Boston?"

Violet's heart fell into her throat. "St. Louis," she insisted. "And Helena."

Hank ignored her. "I'll tell you what's going to happen, honey. And you get to decide if this is gonna be easy or not.

You're gonna to give me your pa's address, and I'm gonna sent him a nice little letter telling him that if he ever hopes to see his daughter alive again, he can send me a fortune of my own."

"My father is *bankrupt*," Violet insisted, repeating the lie. "He's got nothing, not even a *cent* to his name!"

Hank cackled. "Even so…I got more than one use for you, darlin'."

Violet dug her teeth into her bottom lip so hard that she tasted blood.

"This bag I've got right here–"Hank swung the bag into Violet's view. "–this bag's my ticket to a better life here in the Montana Territory. And now that I've got you, family fortune or not, I'm set to make a name for myself out here.! And wouldn't it be real nice for me get to Helena with a girl like you."

Violet tasted bile, and her gut knotted when he added, "It'd be a crying shame to not make you my wife – such a fair thing…"

Panic washed over her like icy water. She thrust out her leg and then jammed it forward, planting her knee right into Hank's chest with every ounce of strength she possessed. Hank gave a choking gasp and staggered forward.

Violet collapsed to the ground, knocking the air from her lungs. But before she could scramble to her feet, he'd grabbed her again by the hair. She cried out as he yanked her into him.

Goddammit," he snarled. "Maybe I need to use my pistol on you again." His sour breath puffed against her cheek. "You're a feisty little thing, ain't ya?"

Then a wild idea flashed through Violet's mind—wild, but worth a try. Anything's *worth it if I can escape this...*

She let out her shrillest scream. "*Snake!* There's a snake on you!"

"A snake?" Hank's hold loosened only for a moment, but it was all Violet needed. She twisted, planting her face into his chest, and dug her teeth into his sweaty shirt until she bit flesh.

Hank let out a howl of pain, releasing her instinctively, and Violet stumbled backwards, falling to the ground with a thud.

There wasn't a second to lose. She pushed herself up to her feet and began to run. Behind her, Hank bellowed, "Stop!"

Violet ran forward blindly through the tall prairie grasses, hair falling into her face. There was a steady trickle of something red dripping into her eye, but her hands were still bound – she couldn't brush it away. She tried to reach up to brush it away, but her hands were still bound. She did her best to shake it aside and kept running.

Footsteps pounded not far behind her. She pushed herself to run even faster. Her lungs felt as though they'd burst; her head was throbbing. Pain coursed from her temples to her feet. Her travel boots were no good for walking far, let alone running through fields.

Tears dripped down her cheeks, mingling with blood and dirt, as she careened forward—until suddenly she ran straight into something solid.

A person – a man; he gasped in her ear. *Hank!* Violet screamed and tore away from him, but he grabbed her bound arms behind her back. She tried to writhe out of the man's grasp, slamming her shoulder into him.

"Good Lord," the man shouted over the roar in her ears. "Hold up, ma'am! You're alright, you're alright!"

Violet reared backwards, sobs shaking her entire body as she managed a glance over her shoulder. A sheriff's badge was gleaming on the man's chest, just a few inches from her face.

Not Hank. Her knees buckled with relief, but the man—the sheriff—caught her before she could fall, gripping her waist in a gentle hold. "Hold still, ma'am," he said, and then she felt the rope loosen around her wrists.

As soon as she was free, she turned and looked up into the man's face, but she couldn't make out much in the dark. He was so tall that he loomed over her.

"There's a man," she choked out, wrists still stinging from Hank's tight knots. "A man dragged me out here, and he was just chasing me."

She whirled around and pointed into the darkening field, and then gave a start. Two other men were standing there with their horses, reins in hand. One was shorter, and the other was tall and gangly.

The sheriff behind her addressed them. "Benjie, George. Scout the area. Hank Green might still be at large."

"Will do." The two men saluted and mounted their horses before riding into the shadows, and Violet heard the thunder of their hoofbeats fading into the distance.

The sheriff took her arm again and guided her down to sit on the ground. Then he knelt beside her. "Come over here, Hawkins," he barked. More hoofbeats drummed in the air—another rider approaching. He trotted past Violet, reined in his horse, and dismounted. A lantern swung from his hand, sending light dancing over Violet and the man beside her.

"Good God," the sheriff whispered, and she turned to look at him. The lantern illuminated the most intensely blue-gray eyes she'd ever seen. He was younger than she expected, maybe thirty or so, with short auburn hair. No beard.

The rider set the lantern down, drawing Violet's eyes to the loose collar of the sheriff's dusty shirt. The few buttons were undone, revealing light brown chest hair. Violet tore her eyes away.

He studied her intently. "How does your head feel?"

She stiffened as he lifted a large hand, brushing fingers across her wet forehead. When he pulled away, she caught a glimpse of blood on his fingertips. Then the world began to spin, and she sagged sideways, floating out of consciousness...somewhere, someone was hollering, "No sign of the green devil!"

***

The first thing Violet noticed when she cracked open her gritty eyes was her head. It felt as if it might *burst*. Then a bright light shone into her eyes, and she heard several men talking around her. She lifted a trembling hand to her face and felt crusted blood beneath her fingertips. She moaned softly, closing her eyes again.

"Ma'am?" A deep, pleasant voice sounded somewhere close by. "How are you feeling?"

Violet slowly sat up, at least as much as she could. She squinted against the blinding light. The trees stood in a dark line in her periphery. A man was squatting next to her, arms resting on his knees. His sharp eyes pierced her. A sheriff star sparkled on the left side of his chest. *The man I crashed into...*"Where am I?" Violet whispered. Exhaustion weighted her down. Even turning her head hurt. A heavy saddle blanket was draped over her, and she ran her fingers over the rough, heavy fabric.

"You're just outside of Miles City, ma'am," the man said politely.

"Miles City? That isn't too far from Helena, is it?"

"Helena's over three hundred miles west of us, ma'am."

"Three hundred—" Violet's mouth dropped open. Not very ladylike, but that was the least of her worries. "That's days and days away still." Her eyes began to burn, her throat closing. *How can I possibly get there now...?*

"What's wrong? You've got family waiting in Helena?"

Violet stiffened and pushed herself into a sitting position, rough grass prickling her palms. She almost snapped that it was none of the gentleman's business. *He hardly looks like a gentleman, though. More like a backwoods rancher.*

Instead of answering his question, she asked him one of her own. "Did you catch that Hank fellow?"

A muscle under the man's eye twitched and he shook his head. His voice was low and terse when he spoke. "He disappeared before we could reach him. Did he mention anything about where he was planning to go?"

"Whoa, there, Gabe! Don't start interrogatin' the lady. She just woke up, and she's had a frightful evening." The tall, gangly man stepped forward into the lantern light, shaking his head.

He looked friendly, with red hair, freckles, and bright blue eyes, and he offered Violet a wide grin. "I'm Benjie, ma'am. A pleasure to meet you. Wish it were under different circumstances, though. Hawkins," he called, "come over here and say hello."

Violet peered around Benjie to see a boy sitting on the grass. Hawkins...the one who'd brought the lantern. He stood up and came closer, and Violet realized that he couldn't be more than sixteen.

Someone else moved behind Benjie, and she saw the third man, the short one who had ridden off with Benjie earlier. He was holding the horse's reins. The lantern light barely reached him. He peered at her curiously. A red cloth wrapped around his head, and he was wearing almost entirely buckskins. "That's George," Benjie told her.

Gabe—the sheriff, evidently—sighed and dipped his chin, but to Violet's relief, he didn't ask her any more questions.

The men looked at her curiously, and Violet glanced down at herself, suddenly self-conscious. She was covered by the saddle blanket, but she still wore her traveling dress. She peered awkwardly under the blanket to see that the skirt was torn somehow, probably in her flight from Hank. *And my hair must be a sight...not* to mention the blood that had probably dried in it.

Violet wanted to crawl out of her skin. She drew the saddle blanket further up her chest, digging her fingers into the heavy cloth.

The darker, shorter man smiled in an almost fatherly way. "We were worried about you. The Green Terror certainly didn't spare you, the bastard. How's your head?"

"What brings a lady like you all the way out to the middle of nowhere?" asked Benjie.

Violet dug her teeth into her bottom lip. They were probing too much for her taste. *Why are they so curious about me?* Could they have received a description of her from her parents? What if one of them telegraphed authorities that they'd found her? *I'd be forced back to Boston to marry Isaac Wilson.* Her stomach sank inside her.

"My stagecoach got attacked..." she said vaguely. She began the painful process of getting to her feet, but to her surprise, the sheriff stepped forward and grasped her arm, lifting her up effortlessly. Violet clung to the saddle blanket, wrapping it around her like a skirt, and relief surged through her when he stepped away.

She ran a down the front of her frock, smoothing her bodice. "Thank you for saving me from that unsavory character...Hank?"

"The Green Terror," Benjie supplied.

"Yes—him. But really, I should be on my way now." Violet glanced around and her heart lurched. Of course...no sign of her carpetbag anywhere. It was probably back where the stagecoach had crashed.

I guess that's that. She dipped her head to the men, and then she turned and began to walk into the night. But the sheriff reached out and grabbed her arm, holding her still. "Where are you off to?"

"Helena." She didn't care how far away it was—she certainly wasn't going to stay here. "Thank you very much for rescuing me, but I'll be on my way now."

The sheriff raised an eyebrow. "It's the middle of the night. And like I said, Helena's three hundred miles west. I'm not going to let you wander off out here. You're coming back to Miles City with us."

Chapter Four

Gabriel could have laughed when he realized that this young woman intended to march back out into the darkness. She was a study of contradictions. Her ridiculous haircut reminded him of his fifty-something-year-old neighbor Anna Mae, but this girl was far prettier than his surly neighbor.

Gabriel didn't loosen his grip, even when she tried to pull away again. But when she rounded on him, eyes wide with outrage, he hastily released her hand.

His face heated. Thankfully it was dark enough that he doubted anybody would notice his flush.

"Sir?" she asked, her jaw clenched, in that clearly affected country accent that didn't convince him for a second. There was no denying that this girl came from some big city in the East.

He cleared his throat and used his sternest tone. "Where are you planning to go, ma'am?"

"Go?" The young woman's pink mouth went thin. He could practically see her thoughts racing behind her eyes. Another laugh rose in his throat, but he swallowed it back down. "I've told you already. Helena, of course. I've been offered a schoolteacher's position there by a Mr. Julius Laramore, and so...here I am!"

Gabriel exchanged glances with George and Benjie. George stepped forward, clearing his throat. "Ma'am, I don't know how to tell you this any other way. Julius Laramore is nothing but a scalawag, I'm afraid."

The young woman's dark eyebrows lifted, her face paling slightly. "Excuse me?"

"He's a scam artist, ma'am. His 'bride and teaching agency' was dissolved by sheriffs in Ohio a few weeks ago. The villain lured girls out here and then forced 'em into...well..." George grimaced. "...harlotry."

The young woman's cheeks drained entirely of color, her lips forming a perfect "O.". She blinked, and then her face crumpled. Sobs began to rack her body as she pressed the back of her hand to her mouth.

Gabriel and other men shifted uncomfortably. They didn't often see a woman cry, at least not this up close.

The poor little thing had blood running down her cheek, a stark slash against her porcelain skin. Her black hair hung in a tangled mess around her face, and her eyes were almost doe-like in her oval face.

Something in Gabriel's chest twinged. He felt bad for her, out here with no one and nothing. He tugged a handkerchief out of his pocket, handing it to her.

She took it, gulping, and wiped her face. "That can't be true," she whispered, shaking her head. "I've been writing him for the last few months. He told me they needed teachers out in Helena and—and—"

George winced. "I'm afraid those letters can't be trusted. He was a lyin' scalawag."

"No," the young woman whispered. She turned away from them, wrapping her arms around herself. The lantern light flickered across her profile, illuminating her charming curves.

Gabriel's chest tightened as he stepped forward, clearing his throat. "Ma'am, it's true. But I suppose it's just as well that you find out now, rather than making the long trip out to Helena."

The young woman shot him a dirty look. "Of course, the silver lining," she choked out sarcastically.

Gabriel's face heated with a mixture of irritation and amusement. "What's your name, ma'am?"

The young woman closed her eyes, breathing shakily. A sparkling tear slid down her cheek, mingling with blood. Then she spoke, in a much smaller voice than before. "Violet. My name's Violet."

"Violet?" Gabriel prompted her, but her lips tightened.

"Just Violet." She wrung her hands, peering up at him from beneath sooty lashes. "I'm an orphan."

Gabriel didn't believe that for one second. *But why would she lie about such a thing?* Clearly, she was out here on her daddy's dollar, maybe trying to get her fair share of adventure before returning home to settle down as a socialite.

Another girl roped into some prostitution scheme. Gabriel always felt pity for them. Pa had always taken pity on them, too...maybe too much pity. He'd taken to leaving home more often, trying to save them all, like it was some kind of crusade. It had never been fair to Ma.

Gabriel didn't intend to do the same...but this girl was here, and she needed help. "Well, Miss Violet, I hope you don't really think it's wise to walk off into the night all the way across wild territory to reach Helena."

Violet sighed. "Well, be that as it may, I suppose I'll have to stay here in tonight. Is there a boarding house?"

"'Fraid it's full, ma'am," Gabriel sighed. "And the only other places that rent out rooms are above the saloon...but you probably don't want to stay someplace like that."

"There isn't *anywhere* else to stay?" Violet's face fell.

"There's a cot in the sheriff's office," George said, swatting Gabriel on the arm. "Ain't that right, Gabe?"

Gabriel barely refrained from rolling his eyes to the sky. *Just what I need. An uppity little rich girl whining in my ear all night.* The sheriff's office was his own space for the time being, at least until he finished his cabin. He'd been craving an evening alone all day, but now...

Violet's expression slowly brightened. "Can I stay there until I figure out something to do?"

Gabriel paused, eyeing her. He didn't love the idea of playing caretaker...but she was clearly a duck out of water out here. Pity pricked in his chest again. He jerked his head in a nod. "Why not?"

"Well, we'd best be getting back into town, then!" Benjie pulled himself up onto his horse, and the rest of the men followed suit.

Gabriel mounted Apollo and guided him closer to Violet. Then he leaned down and held out his hand to her. Her eyes widened, and she reached up and placed her hand in his grasp.

He swung her up into the saddle behind him and she gave a soft cry, arms immediately encircling his waist.

Gabriel's stomach tightened. His entire body warmed at the sensation of her body pressed against him, and he nearly sighed aloud. *This'll be a long ride home.*

Chapter Five

Violet blinked the sleep out of her eyes. Her temples were throbbing powerfully, and a soft moan escaped her as she lifted her hand to her head. Everything came flooding back. Last night's ride to the sheriff's office had lasted for what seemed like hours. It had been excruciating.

She opened her eyes to see black metal bars across from where she lay.

A jail cell? She gasped aloud. Her entire body protested as she sat up slowly, rubbing her eyes. The blanket slipped to the floor as she swung her legs over the edge of the cot.

Are they holding me in this prison until my parents arrive? Her heart lodged in her throat as she scanned the room beyond the bars.

It was mostly bare. There was a desk nearby, with a man slumped in, and a kerosene lamp was hanging on a hook by the door.

There was no sign of the surly sheriff Mr. Brooks.

The man must have heard Violet's gasp. He roused from his nap with a grunt and turned in the chair. It was the short, swarthy man from last night–George, she faintly recalled.

"Mornin', Miss Violet." He clambered to his feet and walked over to stand in the doorway of the cell, his arms folded. "How are you feelin' this morning?"

"I've been better." Violet offered a wan smile.

"Well, I was told to let you know that there's a filled tub for your bath in the back storeroom for your use, if you'd like it.

And your bag has been left right over here." George jutted his chin, and Violet saw the familiar carpet bag sitting next to the cell door.

Her eyes prickled. "That was awful nice of you." She just barely remembered to use her best impression of a girl who did *not* grow up attending finishing schools and who had not been taught everything she knew by a governess and private tutor. *St. Louis. I'm from St. Louis now.*

"Aw, it wasn't me. It was Gabriel—he woke up early this morning, rode out and fetched your bag. Some kindly folks brought into the post office from that wrecked stagecoach. He also asked me to draw a bath for you. Said you'd probably like one."

Well, that was certainly kind of him. *I wouldn't have expected that...he's a little prickly, in my opinion.*

"Well, I'll step out front," George went on, "and you can take that bath if you'd like, get a fresh change of clothes."

Violet thanked him and exhaled in relief when the door clicked shut behind him. She needed a moment to gather her thoughts, and perhaps have another good cry.

Why is everything going so disastrously wrong? She wanted to scream. She was supposed to be on the road to Helena, and there was supposed to be a nice room of her own waiting for her in a boarding house, and she was supposed to teach some sweet young children how to read and write.

But everything is going wrong now. I'll never be a teacher. I'll be sent back to Boston by tomorrow, surely.

Violet slowly stood, her head spinning. She walked out of the jail cell and picked up her bag. Then she peered around until she spotted another door – the storeroom.

She pushed open the door and peered inside. An old steel washtub stood there, filled with glassy water, and Violet felt a rush of excitement. More than anything, she wanted to wash off the dirt and grime that covered her from the day before. She just wanted to be clean, and curl up in a warm nightgown in a giant feather bed like the one she'd left behind her at her parents' Boston home.

But I'm here now...and I'll be grateful for what I have. She dug around in her carpet bag for a simple, light dress, something without lace and layers of velvet. She'd been melting in the stagecoach yesterday because of that stifling traveling suit.

Then she found a plain funeral gown—one of her simplest dresses that she owned. She pulled it out and examined it. It might be black, but it was also devoid of frills and lace and velvet. It was made out of cotton, with a perfect lack of bustle in the skirts.

That's the outfit...now for the towel. Violet went back out to the jail cell and plucked up the blanket she'd had on the cot. *That'll have to do.* Then she went back into the storeroom.

She closed the door behind her and then stripped off her clothes, finally discarding her corset and shift. She sighed, closing her eyes. *How wonderful to be free at last!*

The water looked so maddeningly refreshing. She draped the blanket over the edge of the tub before slipping down into the cool water. Her sore body cried out as she tilted her head back, closing her eyes, sighing.

I can't remember ever loving bathing quite so much as I do now. Perhaps she'd simply never appreciated it as much as she should. So many tiny things that she'd taken for granted back in Boston.

Violet knew she should bathe quickly, but she stretched out the bath as much as was reasonably possible, racking her mind for a plan. *Any kind of plan.* But she'd never been wonderful at planning things out. She usually just...acted.

And that's my problem. "Just acting" is exactly what landed me out in the middle of nowhere, Montana.

Once she felt clean enough, Violet clambered out of the bath, her skin raw from scrubbing. She wrapped her blanket around her to dry off, and then she unfolded the funeral dress. Before she put it on, she listened for any kind of sound...

Nothing, except faint whistling. George must still be on the front porch.=

Violet slid on her dress, pulled up a pair of stockings, and slipped her traveling boots. There was no looking glass in here, so she leaned over the tub and peered down at her reflection in the water. Her damp hair framed her face, plain and drab compared to the ways Lou used to style it.

If only she could have come with me. But instead, here Violet stood, utterly alone, in a tiny town on the brink of a vast frontier. Her stomach knotted.

She left the storeroom and hurried over to the front door to let George know that she was done and he could come back in if he liked.

He smiled. "Naw, I'll stay out here. It's near-perfect weather this mornin'."

Violet smiled back. Privacy was a welcome thing. *I think I'll write a letter to Lou.*

That was a good start to a plan. Violet didn't exactly want anyone following her when she slipped away, and the less people who knew where she was going, the better. Already she'd probably told these folks in Miles City far too much.

Violet went to her carpet bag and extracted a paper pad and her fountain pen. Then, she sat down at the desk, and she began to write.

Dear Lou,

I began a letter to you yesterday, but so much happened that you wouldn't believe! To begin with, I was nearly kidnapped by a wanted man traveling in my stagecoach. The stagecoach ran off the road, and he grabbed me and tried to carry me away. Apparently, he planned to make me his wife. I have never been so terrified in my entire life! Rest assured that I managed to get away, and I found help from the local sheriff and his men. They were kind enough to give me a ride into a small town called Miles City, where I am staying until I figure out what to do next.

But I have news that is even more grave than this. You recall Mr. Laramore, that man who offered the teaching position in Helena? Well, I found out that he is a truly dreadful man, intent upon luring me out west for unspeakable things. I am thankful that I know now, but I am at a loss. I write to implore for advice, as now I am in the middle of nowhere in a strange town with nobody I know. I don't wish to return to Boston, but what other options do I have? Mr. Laramore is now in possession of the only money I had to my name, and so I have nothing with which to pay for board. And there is but one place here that rents out rooms. And it is full.

Violet lowered her pen, eyes blurring as her throat grew tight. Her stomach knotted up in a way that made her feel positively ill, and she took in a deep breath to steady herself. *Compose yourself,* her mother would say, with that exasperated sigh she always used with Violet.

What would Lou *say?* Would she even believe Violet's letter?

She probably would, but it would also thrill her, since this was exactly how all their favorite novels began, with a damsel utterly out of her element, minutes before meeting the man who would sweep her off her feet.

But the only man Violet had encountered so far who could qualify as a romantic hero was Mr. Brooks the sheriff, with his sharp gray eyes and a humorless slash of a mouth. He was far too serious and brooding for Violet's taste.

She signed her letter, inserted it into an envelope, and sealed it with a small bit of wax that she heated over the hanging lamp.

Then she walked over to the front door and peered out.

George noticed her immediately and waved her over. "Is there anything you need, little lady?"

"I need to have this letter mailed out immediately." Violet held up the envelope in her hand, giving it a small wave. "Could you take it to the post office for me?"

"Well, the post office is right over there, ma'am. But I'm afraid your letter won't ge too far right now. The next stagecoach won't be arriving for another month."

"A month?" Violet's throat closed. "Why not sooner?"

George shrugged. "Lots of big, wide-open territory in these parts, I expect. The stagecoach got more ground to cover."

Violet clenched her teeth, willing her tears back, and nodded. "Very well. I'll drop it off, then."

"You take care now. If you need anything, just holler."

Violet set off down the steps of the sheriff's office. It was situated on a far corner of the town, and she followed the boardwalk down to Miles City's main street. Both sides of the street were lined with what looked to be several shops and storefronts, a saloon, and several small homes. There were almost as many construction sites as finished buildings, with most places on the main road still unfinished and in need of paint.

At the very end of the street stood a tall, burned building with a steeple, which Violet could only assume was once a church, although it was only a charred shell of a structure now. Altogether, Miles City was hardly a Boston, or even a St. Louis or Chicago. It was hardly more than a village with muddy roads.

But as she paused, peering down the road, she could catch the glimmer of a river running by, and beyond that, rolling hills. What had the sheriff said last night on their ride? How Miles City was between two rivers, the Tongue and the Yellowstone, which made it a fertile land for farmers.

Violet kept walking, eyes drawn to the rough signs posted at each construction site. One sign announced a new bakery in the works. Violet's mouth watered at the thought of a petit fours with pink and white icing. Those were her favorites at the parties in Boston, the only ray of joy that could relieve a suffocating corset.

Of course, eating baked goods anywhere always meant that Mother would descend later to lecture her for being careless with her figure. *No man will care to marry you if you let yourself become plump. Your waist is already twenty-five inches...*

Violet nearly rolled her eyes at the thought. *Mother will be happy to know that I don't have any money for food. Before long, my waist will be small again.*

She kept walking until she stood in the open doorway of the general store, stunned by the fineries showcased in the windows. There was a lovely silk evening gown and fine sets of China, along with bags of flour and barrels of nails.

But it was the dainty lace embroidery that drew Violet near—so much like the fineries she'd buy with Lou back in Boston. A wave of homesickness built in her chest, making it difficult to breathe.

She stepped forward into the shop.

"Good morning!" An older woman had appeared in a back doorway—likely the storeroom. She patted a loose strand of blond hair into place and hurried around the counter, scanning Violet up and down. "You must be Violet! You're all everyone's been talking about today!"

Violet opened her mouth to reply, but the woman rattled on. "You are an acquaintance of Gabriel Brooks, I've heard?"

"Well, yes. I mean, we—"

"Oh!" The woman clasped her hands, laughing shrilly. "I've never met a mail-order bride yet. Of course, you would think we'd see more of them out here, since there are so few eligible young women in these parts. But to tell you the truth, I never would have expected *Gabriel Brooks* to order himself a bride. He's so quiet, as I'm sure you've noticed. But, well, even the sheriff needs himself a wife. He's been looking lonelier these days, if you ask me."

"Oh, no—no, I'm not—"

The woman let out another squawk of glee. "I *knew* I wasn't dreaming when I saw him carrying you into his place last night! Now, Mr. Lawrence, my husband, *he* refused to believe me. Said I was seeing things." She flapped her hands in the air, and Violet was reminded of a frantic goose. "Now, will you

45

be having a ceremony out here? Or is the wedding already settled?"

Violet's head swam, and she took a step backwards.

The woman seemed to notice her confusion. "Oh, goodness. Forgive me!" she chortled. "I am Sylvia, Sylvia Lawrence." She dipped in a curtsey.

"It's good to meet you..." Violet's hand closed tightly around her letter. Every word from this woman's mouth had sent her into a panicked daze. Before Sylvia Lawrence could say anything else, Violet turned and rushed back out onto the boardwalk.

She picked up her skirt and flew down the walk towards the post office sign several doors down. She paused at the entrance, grasping one of the support beams of the awning.

Her heart pounded, and her knees threatened to buckle again. The world tilted. *People think I'm his* wife? *That prickly sheriff's mail-order bride?* Her head was spinning.

Gulping, she approached the post office's opened window.

The man sitting inside received her letter with a toothless smile. "That'll be a nickel, ma'am."

Violet's stomach sank. "I don't have any."

The postman sighed, squinting at her. Then his expression brightened. "You're Sheriff Brooks' new bride, ain't you?"

Violet couldn't even smile. She simply turned, abandoning her letter, and kept on, nearly running now, her skirt tangling around her legs.

Gasping for breath, she finally stopped in front of a store window painted with the letters *Carol's Bows*. An older woman was standing out front, sipping from a pewter cup. Steam rose from the cup, curling in the crisp morning air.

Something about her features and sharp blue-gray eyes was very similar to Mr. Brooks. Violet forced an uncomfortable smile, still trying to catch her breath in her pinching corset.

The woman's eyes crinkled as she returned Violet's smile with a gentle one of her own. "You must be the girl Gabriel plucked off the prairie last night."

Chapter Six

Gabriel's back protested as he strode down the street, scanning every building for a glimpse of Violet. According to George, she'd wandered off to mail something at the post office. *More trouble.*

He wasn't in the best of spirits that morning. He had tossed and turned all night. The fire in his cabin hearth had gone out, and he'd been shivering in the wee hours of the morning. And his quilt did little to keep him warm. It didn't help that he couldn't sleep from trying to guess the Green Terror's next move.

And now, here he was trying to babysit a young woman who by no means belonged out here in Montana, who might get herself killed if she weren't careful. The fact that she had been ready to strike out on her own made it clear just how little she understood how dangerous Miles City was. Especially for someone like herself. The clothes she wore and the way she carried herself put a glaring target right on her back. *And now she's waltzing on her own through Miles City. As if I didn't have enough to worry about!*

Gabriel stopped short when he spotted his mother across the street. She was standing on the boardwalk in front of her shop, with who else but Violet herself!

They were laughing together. Then Ma turned and saw him. She beamed and waved, and Gabriel offered a tight smile in return.

Reluctantly, he crossed the street to join them. For some reason, he found himself noting the way tendrils of Violet's damp hair clung to her cheeks and neck, the curve of her pink lips as she lifted her dark eyes to him.

"Gabriel, did you really let this girl stay in the *jail?*" Ma's gray eyes flashed as she shot him an outraged glance. "Why didn't you bring her over here? Or at least back to your place?"

Gabriel cleared his throat, shifting his weight from one foot to the other. "Last time I was upstairs," and he jerked his chin towards the apartment above the seamstress shop, "it was crammed full with your supplies. And we arrived in town late. Didn't want to wake you."

"Well," Ma huffed. "What about your place, then?"

Gabriel opened his mouth, but before he could answer, she drove on ahead. "Well, perhaps it's best that you didn't. You know how that Sylvia Lawrence loves to gossip." She shook her head with a sigh.

Gabriel scratched the back of his neck, heat rising to his face. He addressed Violet. "How did you sleep?"

"Very well. Yesterday was a...long...day." She lowered her eyes, her sooty lashes fanning across her cheeks.

"Carol! Sheriff Brooks!" A shrill voice rang out, and Gabriel nearly groaned aloud. *Sylvia Lawrence.*

And she wasn't alone. Behind her hurried several other townspeople, all wide-eyed and obviously curious as they clustered on the boardwalk in front of *Carol's Bows*.

Sylvia bustled up, clucking her tongue. She narrowed her eyes at Ma. "Aren't we friends? I had to hear from one of the *saloon* girls that your son brought home a mail-order bride for himself?"

"Give her a kiss, Brooks!" a grizzled man bawled out—Tom, an all-too-frequent saloon patron who often needed a good dunking in the horse trough to sober him up.

"Care to share her with the rest of us fellows?" another saloon patron snickered.

Gabriel grabbed Violet's arm at once and steered her through the doors of his mother's shop. Ma followed on his heels, politely bidding the crowd good morning, before yanking the doors shut and locking them.

One glance at Violet told Gabriel that she'd been shaken. Her eyes were wide, and her cheeks brightly flushed. She shrank away from the doors like a spooked cat.

Carol peered outside the front window with a tsk. "Heavens. Looks like Sylvia Lawrence has already done her due diligence, spreading word wide and far about the two of you."

"I am nobody's bride," Violet suddenly cried, whirling back to face them. "I didn't come out here to marry *anyone*! I came out here to teach! To be free of—" She cut herself off, covering her mouth with a trembling hand. Her eyes burned with furious tears. "But the next stagecoach doesn't come for another month? I don't—I don't have any money, or things! Just my bag. And this dress."

Ma clucked softly. "Honey, we oughtta fix that soon as we can. I'm afraid you won't get far 'round here without any money. And I know you ain't the type to sell yourself at the saloon." She walked over, grasping Violet's arm and rubbing her back.

"I'm—I'm not. But now—everything has gone so wrong, and I don't know what to do next."

A tear streaked down Violet's cheek, and something like sympathy twisted in Gabriel. Regardless of where she came from, she was certainly out of her element here. *That snake Laramore.* His stomach tightened into a hard knot of anger,

anger for Violet's sake. She'd been tricked and stranded by that good-for-nothing bastard.

Ma patted Violet's arm. "Why don't you come on upstairs and have a cup of tea?" She led Violet up to her rooms above the shop, jerking her head for Gabriel to follow.

Upstairs, Ma guided Violet over to the familiar old settee that had been around for as long as Gabriel could remember. Then she bustled into the neighboring kitchen , leaving Gabriel alone with Violet for the first time.

He walked over to the window, wishing he had his hat to knead in his hands, and leaned against the wall. A smoke would do. He tended to never know what to say exactly to young women. And anyway, there was no time to learn how. There was always too much to do.

He finally turned to face her with his arms folded. "So, Miss Violet…you want to be a schoolteacher? Why in Helena? Why not St. Louis? Don't they have plenty of schools there?"

Violet stiffened, lifting her chin almost defiantly. "I was looking for an adventure."

Gabriel raised his eyebrows. "An adventure?"

Before Violet could answer, Ma hurried back in with a tray of steaming cups and a teapot. She set it on the nearby dining table and began to pour cream and sugar in. "Gabriel?" She cast him a questioning look.

He managed a slight smile. "Any coffee?"

"Just tea."

Gabriel shook his head and watched as Ma placed a cup in Violet's hand before settling herself down on the settee.

"Now, I've been thinking. And I had an idea. Why don't the two of you get married?"

Violet sputtered into her tea, dissolving into a fit of coughing.

Gabriel blinked, a hot flush rising into his face. "Ma, what on earth…?"

Violet set her cup down on its plate with a loud clatter.

"Now, now," Ma said placatingly. "Listen to me real good. The coach doesn't come for another month, maybe even longer. Violet needs a place to stay. Saloons don't have room, and she doesn't have money to afford rented rooms for a month as it is. And as you can see here," and Ma gestured at the cramped apartment, "I've got no place to spare, unless you'll have the couch."

She gave Violet a kind smile, but Violet sat there, frozen, eyes wide and glassy.

Undeterred, Ma went on. "The only place that is safe enough, with plenty of room, is your cabin, Gabriel. But it wouldn't be proper for the two of you to live together unless you're married."

"Ma!" Gabriel took in a deep breath, hoping he didn't look as bright red as he felt.

"It would only be for a month! You'd both be better off, anyhow. Violet would be safe and have a place to stay, and she could keep the house instead of paying rent. And when the stagecoach comes, she can decide what she wants to do."

"—Ma—" Gabriel paused when Violet's eyes flickered to his, confusion written across her features.

Was she considering it? Or about to recoil?

God almighty, this is a crazy idea. Ma's lost her mind. But then the cabin crossed his mind, its empty rooms, the way they haunted him every time he stayed there alone.

Suddenly, an image came unbidden: Violet, flitting through the cabin, cooking and cleaning with him, warming every room. Making the cabin into a home.

He glanced over at Violet. She sat stiffly, knuckles white as she clutched her teacup.

He took in a deep breath. *You're crazy for even entertaining this idea, Brooks.* "It's your choice, Miss Violet. I won't hold you to being my wife if you choose to leave Miles City...but my ma's right. There's nowhere else for you to stay, unless you choose to camp."

"Camp?" Violet shuddered as she lifted her eyes to his. "You would really do this? To help me?"

Gabriel dipped his chin in a yes, working his jaw.

"Why?"

"You're an easy target for bandits. You are obviously not from these parts. And by the looks of it, your family has some money. It would make you desirable...prey."

Ma cleared her throat. "He's right, honey. You have clothes finer than anything we see in these parts, and already I'm sure word of you has gotten around. I'd be worried sick for you while you're here, and Gabriel can keep you safe at his place. And of course, there's your reputation to think of. We might be in Montana, but we ain't heathens."

"O-of course. But it's such a generous offer, and I—I don't wish to put you out, Mr. Brooks."

Gabriel couldn't help the smile tugging at the corner of his mouth. "Gabriel. Just Gabriel."

Violet swallowed and dug her teeth into the full swell of her lower lip. "Gabriel," she repeated. "What would be expected of me, in this arrangement?"

"Oh, I wouldn't—"

"Perhaps keep house for him? Lord knows that home of his needs a woman's touch," Ma piped up, earning a hard look from Gabriel.

"Just housekeeping?" Violet asked in a small voice.

Gabriel suppressed a smile. "We'd be married in name only, just so's to keep you safe till the stagecoach arrives."

Violet blinked and gave her head another shake. "Why would you expose yourself to talk? For instance, when I leave…"

Gabriel let out a bark of laughter. "I don't give a—"he nearly used the word *damn*"—a hoot what folks think of me. I'd just consider this part of my duty as sheriff. Keeping both citizens and visitors safe."

Violet took in another deep breath. "Well…" She closed her eyes, and when she opened them, she seemed more calm, less rattled. "I'll think about it."

Gabriel squared his shoulders. He walked back to the staircase, but before he went down, he paused and turned back, struggling to soften his voice. "Why don't you think it over for a night?"

"I—I will."

Gabriel offered her a slight smile goodbye. "Be back in the morning, Ma."

She trotted over and pulled him into a quick hug, pecking him on the cheek. "Don't you want to come by for dinner?"

"Can't. I'll be working late. Me and George and Benji need to track down the Green Terror. We might be at it all night."

"Well, take care and get *something* to eat. You're looking thin these days. Tired."

"I will, Ma."

Ma touched him on the cheek, leaning in to whisper, "You're a real good boy, Gabriel."

Gabriel forced himself to not look in Violet's direction, and he practically flew down the staircase and out the door, eager for fresh air and the space to think. Thankfully, the crowd had dispersed, leaving Gabriel to himself. *What the hell am I thinking?*

Chapter Seven

Carol Brooks let Violet sleep on her couch for a night, but it was a very cramped and uncomfortable sleep, somehow even worse than bedding on a cot in a jail cell. The lumpy cushions were too soft and too narrow to lie flat on her back. And she couldn't stop tossing and turning. She stared into the shadows of the room and tried to think of some other way to get through this. *There has to be some way around this…something better than marrying a prickly sheriff.* A sheriff who needed to learn to see the humor in life.

Of course, he seemed to have a close and sweet relationship with his mother, but other than that, he was stiff, and cold, and hardly the sort of man Violet envisioned herself marrying.

The only men she'd come close to daydreaming about were ones in those books she and Lou loved so much…those larger-than-life men, perfect gentlemen, often with a mysterious presence and a ghastly scar across their faces. Maybe even a hook for a hand.

In the morning, she woke up to the smell of frying eggs and bacon and baking biscuits. Buttermilk biscuits, Carol said, as Violet entered the tiny kitchen off the parlor.

Carol was an excellent cook. She had made a stew the night before, with cornbread, and Violet had been so hungry that she didn't even mind that the stew had been made with raccoon meat.

Thankfully, Carol made no mention of the possible wedding ceremony over breakfast. Violet picked at her food, her appetite faltering as she tried to come to a decision. Something inside her knew that Lou would tell her to marry this man. *If not for love, then for protection,* Lou would opine, practical as always.

"Lord, you eat like a bird," Carol chuckled, picking up Violet's half-eaten food. She shook her head. "We'll have to get you used to eating better. Out here, we work hard and eat well."

Violet swallowed a bite of buttermilk biscuit and pushed her plate away. "It's delicious, thank you," she murmured. "I'm full, though." Her stomach growled loudly, and she hoped Carol wouldn't hear it.

Her hope was short-lived.

"Now, Miss Violet, I won't have anybody under my roof going hungry. You hear?"

Violet nodded and slowly reached out for another biscuit.

Carol's eyes crinkled. "That's more like it."

As he'd promised, Gabriel Brooks returned to the shop that morning, hat in his hands, his hair glistening as if he'd combed it just moments ago. Carol bustled over to him and handed him a steaming cup of coffee, and then he sat down at the table across from Violet.

His mouth curved in the barest allowance of a smile. Violet wondered if he was even capable of a real smile.

"Did you sleep well?" His tone was quiet.

Violet dipped her head. "I can't complain."

Carol let out a throaty chuckle. "Lordy, that couch is hardly comfortable, but I just keep forgetting to order a new one at the general store. I find I never end up spending too long in there. That Sylvia drives me up the wall most days."

Mr. Brooks—Gabriel—took in a deep breath. "If you need more time to decide—" He eyed her closely.

Violet swallowed. *This is my only option if I don't want to return to Boston. I can either marry this sheriff, or marry Isaac Wilson.* The thought sent a chill through her. And it made her decision painfully clear.

"I'll marry you," Violet whispered.

Gabriel lifted his eyebrows, studying her as if he could see right through her. "As long as you're certain, that's enough for me." She couldn't quite tell if he was concerned or pleased by her acceptance.

"I am." Violet barely pushed the word out around the lump in her throat.

Gabriel gave a curt nod. "We'll be able to annul the marriage by the month's end when the stagecoach arrives."

"Very well."

Gabriel drained his coffee and stood up, his chair screeching across the wooden floor. "I'll go find the preacher."

"And I'll go find a lovely wedding dress I've got in mind for you." Carol stood up as well, beaming.

"Ma, this ain't gonna be a church wedding," Gabriel said. "We'll keep it small and be married behind my office."

Carol nodded. "'Course, but I'm a seamstress. Dresses are my specialty. And I've got just the thing for my future daughter-in-law. She's going to be a bride, so she oughtta feel and look like a bride."

Violet stared down at the lace tablecloth under her teacup saucer, a lump in her throat. *Is this really happening? Did I flee Boston and Isaac Wilson just to marry some stranger from Montana?*

She glanced up to find Gabriel studying her, his gaze intent, curious. The corner of his mouth twitched, and he dipped his head in a goodbye before heading out the door.

Carol turned to her. "Now, come on in here. I've got just the dress for you."

***

They met Reverend Samuels, the traveling minister, on a grassy hilltop just outside of town, since the old church was a pile of charred rubble. Violet stood stiffly, wearing the very silk wedding dress that Carol Brooks had been married in. The only people in attendance, after Carol, of course, were George, and Benjie, the lanky, freckled redhead.

She forced herself to look up at Gabriel. He stood beside her in front of the reverend, looking as stiff as she felt.

He met her glance with one of his own, his mouth a thin line, his expression serious and unreadable as usual, as the reverend proceeded through the matrimonial pronouncements.

Violet was in a daze. All the reverend's words ran together, a distant sound over the roar in her ears. No one had mentioned a thing about her wifely duties beyond housekeeping, not even Carol. *Is Gabriel expecting me to fulfill all my marital obligations?* A shiver trickled down her spine.

What's going to happen when it comes time to kiss? The bride and groom always kissed. Gabriel must be somewhat experienced—a handsome sheriff like him, out here in an untouched wilderness, with saloons nearby. Perhaps Gabriel visited the saloons for more than just a drink. If Isaac Wilson had taught her anything, it was that even the most respectable men could do the worst kinds of things behind closed doors. Maybe even her own father—

Violet veered sharply away from that train of thought. It was too nauseating to think about.

Then she heard Reverend Samuels say, "I now pronounce you husband and wife." He smiled encouragingly at Gabriel. "You may now kiss your bride."

And then, to her surprise, Gabriel stepped forward, leaned down and pressed a brusque kiss to her cheek.

Her heart leapt into her throat, but it was over quickly. The scrape of his stubble against her jaw lingered, sending strange tendrils of heat dancing through her. *I'd fall over if he kissed me on the mouth.*

"Now!" Carol clapped her hands, causing Violet to start. "I'm going to whip up a cake." She pointed at George and Benjie. "I expect the two of you for the wedding feast. I won't hear any refusals."

"I wouldn't think of passin' up a dinner cooked by Carol Brooks," Benjie chuckled, and George nodded in agreement.

"Especially not when it's celebratin' Gabe's wedding," Benjie added. "If I'd been told a week ago that Gabe was gonna be getting hitched, I'd have laughed till my sides split." He grinned at Violet. "You've made a happy man made out of my oldest friend."

"Benjie," said Gabriel in a warning tone.

Benjie ignored the warning and clapped him cheerfully on the back. "This one needs to learn a thing or two about relaxing. Maybe you teach him 'bout that."

Gabriel rolled his eyes skyward, his jaw tightening.

Benjie gave him another pat on the back and shot a wink at Violet.

The rest of the day passed in a blur. Violet joined Carol in the kitchen above her seamstress shop. She wasn't much help, having never cooked once in her life, but Carol showed her how to crack eggs, how to beat them with a whisk, and how to mix them with flour, sugar, and the rest of the ingredients for a cake. She also showed her how to fry up slices of ham on the cast-iron atop the small stove.

Before long, the kitchen table was set and laden with several platters of food, many of which Violet had never heard of or seen before in Boston homes. Mother would be horrified by the amount of butter and oil Carol used when making her food. The thought of Mother brought Violet up short. *What would she think of all this...?*

She heard footsteps on the stairs and loud male voices as George, Benjie, and Gabriel arrived for dinner.

The second Violet glimpsed Gabriel's face, the full force of what she'd just done slammed into her. *I just...married him.*

Gabriel Brooks was her...husband.

The room shrank in size, voices ringing too loudly in Violet's ears. Her corset was far too tight. She flashed Carol a weak smile, stammering out something about needing air. Then she pushed past the men and her husband and ran down the stairs blindly.

Someone called her name, but she didn't pause or turn. Instead, she pushed out the back door of the seamstress shop and stumbled into the back street, a loud sob bursting from her lungs. She pressed her hand to her mouth, sinking on wobbly legs onto the back steps.

She had only been out there for a moment when, she heard the door creak open behind her. Boots thudded on the ground.

"Violet?" It was Gabriel. Her husband.

"I just need a moment," Violet whispered, closing her eyes.

Gabriel sank down onto the steps beside her with two plates of food—"fixin's," as Carol called it. He handed her a plate, and Violet reluctantly took it.

But the thought of food turned her stomach, and she hiccupped, her throat swollen closed.

Gabriel propped his elbows on his knees, taking a bite of cornbread. The buttons of his collar were undone, and she saw tan skin fade to pale along his neck. Her heart squeezed oddly, and she looked away.

"I enjoy eating outside," Gabriel murmured. "Especially on evenings like this. I always think food's better under the stars."

"I've never kept house before," Violet blurted out thickly. She pushed around a cube of ham on her plate. Her face warmed, and she wondered if he'd regret this in a few days' time. *He'll find out soon just how little I know about cooking and cleaning. He'll know I can't keep up my side of the bargain.* "What are your expectations, as far as that goes?"

Gabriel turned, those gray-blue eyes cutting right into her. "Let's just take it a day at a time. I know it'll take you some time to settle in."

Relief eased the tightness in Violet's belly. She sighed, wiping at her wet cheeks. To her surprise, Gabriel reached into his pocket and withdrew a handkerchief. It was clean and crisp, folded into a neat square.

"Thank you," Violet sniffled. "It's just—I don't know what I'm going to do. I sent Mr. Laramore everything I had, and now...all I have is an old carpet bag to my name."

"Will you return to St. Louis? When the stagecoach returns?"

"St. Louis?" Violet frowned, and then remembered. "Oh, yes. Yes, I suppose I will."

She pulled her gaze from Gabriel, her heartbeat skipping—*Maybe he didn't notice my slip.*

But if he did, he didn't comment on it. Instead, he changed the subject. "Listen, if you are in need of money, then would you be willing to teach the children here in Miles City? There's plenty of 'em. Though, we don't have a proper schoolhouse yet."

"Teach..." Violet stared at him, stunned. "Why...I would love to." Her heartbeat quickened as she turned the idea over in her head. It wasn't exactly what she had planned. *Besides, what happens when the stagecoach comes? Will I just teach for a month and then leave? If I stay, will I have to stay married to Gabriel?*

"And I don't know when we'll have it finished," Gabriel added. "But I aim to have it rebuilt in the next few weeks."

Violet chewed her lip. After a beat, she asked, "How did it catch fire?"

Mr. Brooks sighed. "Some drunken fools nearly burnt down the town on New Year's. Threw some burning tar on it." Violet's jaw dropped and he huffed out a humorless laugh. "We've got a long way to go, but I hope to make Miles City the next stop for the railroad."

He paused for a moment, jaw working. "Listen...there's something I've got to ask of you. The Green Terror is still out there, and he's the type to hold grudges. I don't want you outside after dark until we get him behind bars."

A chill rushed down Violet's spine. "You really think he'll come after me?"

"I don't know. Like I said, he's unpredictable. And he's desperate now. It's clear you come from money, and he might see that as a golden opportunity."

"I don't come from money," Violet said hurriedly. Her heart began to pound heavily again. "I'm a boatman's daughter."

Gabriel's eyebrow lifted again, but he didn't argue.

Violet swallowed. "You think this...Green Terror might try hold me for ransom?" That was the kind of thing that happened to heroines in novels. Not to girls like Violet.

Gabriel's mouth curved in a small, grim smile "I'm afraid so."

His gaze lingered, flickering over her face. Violet tried to swallow again but found her mouth had gone dry. His eyes darkened, and he glanced down at her mouth. Only for a second. But it sent Violet's heart pitter-pattering so fast she lost her breath.

And then, it was over—he stood up with a soft grunt.

"I'm going to stay out here a little longer. To compose myself," she said weakly.

He jerked his head in a small nod. "'Course." That low, deep voice of his reverberated through her. She turned away, staring at the tips of her shoes beneath her dress. Then the door creaked shut behind her, and she was alone with her thoughts.

Chapter Eight

Gabriel was up early that morning, feeding Apollo and the chickens in the coop out back. As soon as he pushed open the front door of his cabin, the foreign scents of talcum powder and roses washed over him, sending him into a daze. There was another smell, too, tangy and sweet. *Some kind of perfume?*

It was the morning after Violet had moved into his home following their nuptials...and already he was beginning to regret his impulsive agreement to this arrangement. For one thing, he didn't do well with change. He was set in his ways, and he suspected Benjie of calling him "Bachelor Sheriff" behind his back.

And there had been a lot of change yesterday. When Violet first arrived at his cabin, she'd stared wide-eyed around the cabin in dismay. Thankfully, Ma had come too, and she'd cleaned out the second bedroom in the cabin and made the bed for Violet. She'd even dusted a little. And she had George, Benjie, and Gabriel drive over an old wardrobe from her own home. "It's not much, but it'll do for the time being," she'd told Violet.

Still breathing in the perfume, Gabriel closed the door behind him and turned around to find Violet already awake, sitting at the kitchen table, absorbed in a small book.

He froze. She still hadn't looked up from her book—a small recipe book Ma had given her last night.

This, of course, was the biggest change...a second person. At least he didn't have to share a bedroom with the young woman. It was difficult enough having her in his home, but the idea of sharing a *bed* with her? A shiver went through him. The idea of Violet in his bed, her arms around him... He clenched his jaw.

Then Violet lifted her head, cupid's-bow mouth curving into a stiff smile. "Good morning." She stood and ran her hands over her flour-covered apron.

"Morning." He crossed the room to wash his hands in the bucket of water on the sideboard. The new washbasin had just been installed there. All that was left to be done for the kitchen was to finish setting up the water pump. Briefly, he wondered if the home she'd left behind had running water, or electricity? Perhaps even a telephone? *How does she feel about living* here?

He dried his hands with a rag, then turned to face her again.

A crease had appeared between her dark brows as she studied the recipe book. She was working her lower lip between her pearly teeth. She seemed to do that a lot when she was quiet. And every time he noticed it, something inside him drew taut, something low in his belly.

"What are you fixing to make?" Gabriel finally asked.

"Buttermilk biscuits." She lifted her dark eyes to him, her mouth curving into a pout. "I tried yesterday, when you were out. But I burned them." Her cheeks darkened.

Gabriel prided himself on keeping a straight face, but he could have laughed out loud. "Ah...I suppose that's why I didn't see them at dinner."

He crossed the room and searched the larder for something he could take along with him while scouting today. Benjie and George were probably already waiting at the sheriff's office, ready to go over any new information about the Green Terror.

There was only a single piece of cornmeal left in the larder—but Gabriel hesitated, realizing that his new…bride…would likely get hungry, too, here at the house. He left the cornbread and opted for a piece of jerky from the smokehouse out back.

That should tide him over until dinner…if dinner wasn't burnt. Ma had promised yesterday to come by today to teach Violet how to cook.

"See you tonight," he murmured, placing his hat on his head. He opened the door, but before he stepped out, Violet called out goodbye. He turned, and her dark eyes gave him pause mid-step, if only for a moment. And then he turned, tipping his hat, and closed the door behind him.

Safe outside. He exhaled heavily and hurried to the small barn where Apollo waited, stamping impatiently.

He guided Apollo out of the stall and saddled him up, but he paused for a moment to stare up at the smoke curling from the chimney. Soft, sweet singing filled the air…Violet. She had a beautiful voice, so beautiful it made something in Gabriel ache.

He tugged gently on the girth, testing it with a finger. Then he slid the bridle over Apollo's nose. He mounted, but he lingered, his throat tight. Violet's voice carried on the early morning breeze, wrapping around him like an embrace.

***

Benjie and Hawkins whooped as Gabriel walked through the sheriff office door. "Gabe, how was your first night with your bride?" Benjie winked and leapt to his feet to jab Gabriel with his elbow. Hawkins guffawed across the room. George, leaning in the storeroom doorway smoking a pipe, let out a loud chuckle.

Gabriel nearly groaned, his face going hot. Instead of responding, he strode over to his desk and sank into the chair. He flashed Benjie and Hawkins a warning look, but of course, they ignored it.

Benjie shook his head and whistled. "Just think, only a week ago, your ma was pestering you about being alone. Now, here you are, married to a pretty girl from St. Louis." *...Is she really from St. Louis?* One more question he couldn't answer...

Gabriel pulled a whittling stick from his desk drawer. He began to work away at it. Time to change the subject. "Any news?"

Benjie shrugged. "You tell me. So, how do you like sharing your place with a lady?"

Gabriel shot Benjie a withering look before turning to George. "Anything?"

Struggling to keep a straight face, George nodded. He crossed the room, thumb tucked in his belt as he blew out a puff of smoke. "Sure do, boss. Believe it or not, the Green Terror was seen over in Elk Crossing in town last night. We just heard it this mornin'."

"He was in Elk Crossing?" Gabriel echoed faintly. He slapped his hand down on his desk, swearing. *He's still here, right under our noses! I should have stayed out last night and looked for the bastard.*

"He was carousing, so we've been told. In the Elk Crossing saloon. He was meetin' up with silver miners, talking about investors who've been buying shares from him. Looks like he's back on that ruse again."

Gabriel sighed through his teeth. "Well, make sure to keep up with the Elk Crossing sheriff. Tell him to keep his eyes and ears peeled for any news about the devil."

"'Course."

Gabriel hesitated a moment before his next request. "And...try to see if he's made any mention of Violet. I'm worried he'll come after her, use her for ransom."

George nodded, blowing out a ring of smoke. "Haven't heard anything about Violet. But there's lots of talk about some posse of Logan's own men trying to hunt him down."

Benjie's eyes went wide. "You suppose the Green Terror will have a shootout with his own men?"

Gabriel set down his whittling stick. "*Former* men. And I sure wouldn't be surprised. It's going to get to that point. He'll keep swindling folks blind. And the more people he angers, the more of a target he'll put on his head. His own men are likely ripe and ready to turn him in."

George waved goodbye and swung out the door, Hawkins on his heels, leaving Gabriel and Benjie alone.

Gabriel glanced up to see Benjie shaking his head, chuckling to himself.

He sighed. "What?"

Benjie snorted. "I just never thought I'd see the day. You gettin' married and all. You're just so set in your ways, that's all I'm sayin'."

Gabriel rolled his eyes. "I'm not that much of a stick in the mud, am I?" he muttered.

"Well, I wouldn't go far as sayin' that. But you have your routines, and you ain't partial to change. Your ma's been trying to set you up for years, but not until now do you give a hoot about women."

Gabriel scowled. "What do you mean, I never gave a hoot?"

"Since when have you been so keen to up and marry?" Benjie squinted at him.

Gabriel caught his breath. *Well, Benjie isn't wrong. It wasn't so hard to marry Violet.* He liked the way her scent filled his cabin. Maybe a little too much. He felt himself turning crimson. "It was just my civic duty, for God's sake."

"You know what I think? I think you're sweet on her." Benjie grinned.

Gabriel scoffed, picking up his whittling stick again.

"I'm serious!" Benjie folded his arms, looking a bit too pleased with himself. "We've grown up together, so I oughtta know when you're sweet on someone. Remember Lucy?"

Gabriel winced. "Benjie." He raised his eyebrows, using a warning tone.

Benjie waved his hand. "You can't fool me."

They were interrupted by a knock on the door. Someone came in to report stolen chickens—one of the local troublemakers, no doubt. The interruption was a welcome relief. Gabriel headed out to Apollo and rode out to the culprit's farm.

The day dragged on, filled with task after task, and throughout it, Gabriel's thoughts continued to wander back to his cabin, where Violet waited for him. Last night, in bed, he'd glimpsed her through the crack of his bedroom curtain as she slipped out to go to the out-house. Her nightgown billowed softly around her legs, and her dark hair tumbled down her shoulders.

What is she hiding? What is she running from?

She lacked the skill to lie. That much he'd figured out on their wedding night, when she fumbled her answer about returning to St. Louis. *She's not from there.* It was painfully obvious to Gabriel.

...And it had been painfully obvious to Hank Logan, too. Why else would he kidnap Violet from the stagecoach?

Gabriel dropped by the sheriff's office between tasks. Benjie was manning the desk inside. He decided to take the opportunity and sound out his thoughts with Benjie as an audience.

Benjie was happy to comply, and tossed him the trusty whittling stick while Gabriel collected his thoughts.

"It's strange that the Green Terror would hang around a saloon for so long. Especially when he knows we're after him. The man's pompous, but he's never been this reckless." Gabriel ran the blade of his knife up his stick. A wood shaving fell to the floor.

"He *is* getting a mite careless, ain't he?"

"I just imagined that he'd be more leery, what with his own men and *us* hunting him down," Gabriel muttered.

Benjie shook his head. "It's been said that he might be a little—" He whistled as he spun his wrist. "A little loose in the head. Some kind of infirmity."

"I've heard that rumor, too. Well, it might be his undoing." Gabriel pushed himself to his feet, stretching. "I'm going for a ride to the hills."

Benjie smirked. "You gonna be back home in time for dinner with your wife?"

Gabriel shot him a hard look. "It's just a technicality, at best. Temporary."

"Tell that to the reverend. I heard him tellin' your ma that he was sure delighted to have the honor of marryin' her son."

Gabriel didn't dignify that with a response. He swung out the door, letting it slam shut behind him, but he could still hear Benjie chuckling loudly inside.

He strode over to the hitching post in a huff and swung himself up into Apollo's saddle. He just needed to ride. Every time he breathed in, he could almost smell the scent of roses, and that other strange but sweet perfume. He thought he could take a stab at what it was. Violet had brought in a little bottle yesterday to put on her bedside table, and the label read *Lemon Verbena.*

He rode for several hours, returning to the Gallatin Forest and scoping for any sign of the Green Terror. But he wasn't really there to look. He needed to clear his head. His thoughts kept streaming back towards Violet. *It's just a technicality. That's all.* Though Violet seemed like the kind of girl who deserved better than this farce of a marriage.

It was dark when Gabriel finally rode back to his cabin, and when he entered, the place was dark except for the dying fire in the hearth. He walked over and picked up the poker, stirring up the embers, and then turned to head to bed.

But as he passed the curtain of Violet's room, he caught sight of a disheveled shape on the bed. Violet...fast asleep, not even under the quilt, still in her day dress and shoes.

She'll be cold...

Gabriel went to his own room and grabbed the blanket off his bed. Then he returned, entering Violet's room with all the reverence of a parson in a church, and hesitantly draped it over the young woman. He paused, just for a moment, to stare down at the thick fringe of her lashes against her cheek, the soft flush in her face.

And then the moment was over, and he backed quickly out of her room, pulling the curtain shut behind him.

Chapter Nine

Violet wrung her burn-covered hands as she paced back and forth across the cabin. Then she hurried over to the stove for the fourth time to check the biscuits in the cast-iron pan. Her fingers and hands were covered in red welts from accidentally touching the hot cast-iron pan or the stove, and she had even sliced her finger by accident when peeling some potatoes one evening. This morning, however, she swore to herself that she'd bake *unburnt* biscuits, finally.

Not that Gabriel would care. He was never home, always out patrolling or working. A week had come and gone since Violet's wedding to Gabriel Brooks, and already, her loneliness was suffocating. Gabriel always arrived back late, never in time for the dinner she labored over for hours.

But he was trying—a little. She had woken up one morning with his blanket draped over her.

Why does it matter that he's gone, anyway? At least Carol was taking care to make Violet feel at home. Carol had visited twice that first week to check on her, which Violet appreciated. Her new mother-in-law was as attentive as Gabriel was absent. The recipe book she'd given Violet was highly detailed, with step-by-step instructions. Even so, Violet still managed to burn almost everything she cooked.

There was a shuffling sound outside the door, and Violet paused to listen . She kept hearing that noise...or was it just her overactive imagination? She'd become jumpy and restless, every bump and creak of the cabin or the wind banging the barn door sent her heart racing. What if the cabin door swung open to reveal the Green Terror? She sometimes woke up during the night, sobbing after nightmares of his arms around her, dragging her into the Gallatin forest.

Then someone rapped on the front door, and Violet gave a jump and a gasp. She tiptoed over to the front door, pressing her face against the wood to peer through the crack between the panels. A young woman stood outside, with a basket hanging from one elbow and a child from the other. Her stomach was swollen with child.

Violet reached for the latch and opened the door, and the young woman smiled brightly. "Good afternoon. I'm Martha Woodard—my husband Jeff and I are at the ranch just over the hill yonder." She jerked her chin to the west of Mr. Brooks' cabin. "I suppose that makes us neighbors, don't it?"

Slowly, Violet opened the door wider, returning Martha's smile. "It's a pleasure to meet you," she said, just barely remembering to use her Western drawl. She stepped aside, waving her hand. "Would you like to come in?"

Martha thanked her and bustled in, setting down the young child on the floor. "This is Georgie," she told Violet. "Named after my pa."

Violet suddenly recognized that the young woman's smile. It reminded her of Gabriel's foreman. "You—you're George's daughter?"

Martha grinned, nodding. "That I am." She held out the basket she'd been holding on her elbow. "I brought some cobbler and some sweet bread."

"Thank you. I'm Violet. Violet...Brooks." Violet's eyes began to sting again.

She and Martha sat down at the table together, and Martha fixed her with a curious gaze. "So, you're the girl who caught our bachelor sheriff's eye, hm?"

Violet's cheeks heated. "Bachelor sheriff?"

"That's what we call 'im. Plenty of folks round here have tried and failed to set 'im up with their daughters, sisters, what have you. But it's clear he's married to his work first and foremost. Don't get me wrong, it's wonderful to have a sheriff with that kind of dedication. But we all worry about 'im. Worry he's running himself into the ground."

Violet lifted her eyebrows. "I see that he's well-loved around here," she said politely.

"He's a good man, decent to the core. Why, when it was my time to have Georgie here, Gabe brought Carol to help me. The circuit doctor was over in Elk Crossing, and me and Jeff, we were desperate for help. Carol's got some midwifin' experience, so she came to see what she could do. Gabe kept Jeff calm."

"Both of them have been very kind to me, and very generous." Violet played with the lace cuff of her sleeve. "I owe them both so much. For helping me settle into Miles City."

"Well, it's clear to everyone in town that he's smitten with you. Mrs. Lawrence says he couldn't keep his eyes off you when she saw the two of you in town last week."

Violet's stomach twisted. Gabriel smitten? With *her*?

Martha giggled. "Look at you blush. I'll tell you though, 'fore long you'll have three of your own little Georgies running around here." She placed a hand on her belly. "Jeff and I haven't been married a year and I'm already on my second."

Violet flushed and hurried to change the subject. "What does Jeff do?"

"Oh, he's a carpenter—does most of the building you see around Miles City. He and his men are out all day, working away at turning this place into a real city."

Violet could hear the pride in Martha's tone, a dreamy look in her eye. "He's gonna build me a big house one day, when we're rich, after more folks move out here with the railroad."

"How long do you think it'll take for the railroad to reach Miles City?"

"Another year or so, I think. We can hardly wait. Just you wait, we'll be as big as Chicago one of these days." Martha stood to pick up Georgie, who had begun to crawl towards the stove. "So, where do you come from? I heard word you're from St. Louis. Is that so?"

Violet nodded, guilt piercing her. "Yes, St. Louis." Her stomach knotted. *I wish I could tell her the truth. But Mother and Father might hear somehow and come find me.* She couldn't take the chance.

"You from one of those big St. Louis fur-tradin' families?

"Yes." Another lie. Violet tried to ignore the guilty prickle in her chest. "I came out here to teach."

Martha's eyes widened. "How wonderful! I've always wanted Georgie here to go to school, but I was beginning to think I'd have to school him at home, 'specially since the church went up in flames."

The smell of something burning distracted Violet from the conversation. She leapt to her feet, groaning. "Oh no!" Racing over to the stove, she picked up some oven pads to retrieve the cast-iron from the fire.

"What's the matter?" Martha hurried over to watch.

The biscuits in the pan had turned black, and the burnt smell hung in the air. Violet flounced her skirt, sighing. "I can't seem to stop burning everything I cook."

Martha bent to peer into the stove. "Looks like you've got it too hot in here. All you need is the embers. They make enough heat to cook anything, slowly." She picked up the poker beside the stove and poked it inside, pushing embers over the flames.

Violet watched, fascinated.

"You know what? Let me show you how to make my mouth-waterin' buttermilk biscuits that Jeff can't get enough of. Let's toss these out for the chickens."

"I don't think even the chickens would like those," Violet sighed, earning a laugh from Martha.

They spent the rest of the afternoon baking biscuits. Before Martha headed home with little Georgie, a plateful of warm, golden-brown biscuits sat on the table in time for dinner. Martha invited Violet to come visit anytime she liked. Violet's heart swelled with gratitude, some of her anxiety fading as she watched from the window as her new friend, baby in arms, walk back up the road.

She had just finished frying up some ham in the cast-iron when someone else knocked on the door. She took the pan off the stovetop and hurried over to greet her new visitor. Benjie stood there on the porch, his blue eyes twinkling. He'd come by every evening this week to check on her and let her know that Gabriel would be late due to his sheriff duties.

Benjie took his hat off in greeting. "Evenin', Mrs Brooks. You're a sight for sore eyes. Doin' some baking today?"

Violet glanced down at her flour-covered apron and wondered if she'd accidentally smeared any on her face. She stepped aside, motioning Benjie in, but he shook his head with a smile. "Can't stay long. I just came to let you know Gabe's gonna be late again. He's over in Elk Crossing— George got a lead regardin' the Green Terror's whereabouts."

"Oh," Violet hoped her disappointment didn't show on her face. She'd been eager to see what Gabriel thought of the biscuits she'd made with Martha. He needed to see that she was trying to hold up her end of the bargain. *I don't want him to think of me as just a helpless damsel from a big city*...even though that was exactly what she was. Not for the first time did she wonder if he was avoiding her, and the thought for some reason sent a pang through her. "Well, thank you for letting me know."

"'Course. My pleasure. You take care, Mrs. Brooks!"

Mrs. Brooks.

After Benjie left, Violet sat in the rocking chair on the couch, nibbling absently on a piece of cobbler. Disbelief coursed through her, drawing her into a daze. Was she really a "Mrs." now?

Even if it was all in name only... *The idea of being that silent, unapproachable sheriff's wife.* Violet clenched her jaw, wringing her hands. She listened to the squeak of the chair as it rocked back and forth.

The cabin was so empty, dark. Almost soulless. She shuddered, blinking away tears. *If I stay here in Miles City, will I have to remain married to Gabriel? Will I be doomed to spend every evening like this?*

***

Sleep descended gradually, and then all at once. Violet floated into a dream. She was back in her parents' Boston manor...but in this dream, she was a princess on a vine-covered balcony, draped in silk. And a stoic giant peered over the balcony railing...blue-gray eyes piercing her...

Violet leaned over the balcony's edge, and pressed her lips to the giant's, freeing him of a wicked witch's curse. He transformed a second later into Gabriel Brooks, looming over her, with a smile on his usually grave face.

And then he wrapped her in a tight embrace—burying his face against her neck—running his lips along her collarbone.

Violet awoke with a gasp, only to find herself lying in bed in her room, under the quilt. She climbed out of bed and tiptoed to the curtained doorway and peeked out.

Gabriel was leaning on the kitchen table, asleep. A forgotten cup of coffee steamed next to him.

Violet crept out. She slipped into his bedroom and grabbed his blanket off the bed. Then she went back into the kitchen and draped the blanket on his broad shoulders.

She paused, breath catching in her throat, as she studied his chiseled profile, his mouth slightly open.

Then he stirred, and Violet went flying back into her room, butterflies coming to life in her belly.

Chapter Ten

The next night, Gabriel returned home late again. And once again, he found Violet asleep on top of her covers. This time, she had a light satin robe over her nightgown.

Once again, Gabriel grabbed his blanket and walked back to her room, pushing the curtain aside and pulling the blanket over her. His fingertips brushed the nape of her neck, and a shiver going through him.

Her skin was so soft.

A sigh escaped his lips as he paused, hovering over her, studying the soft swell of her lower lip, the pretty column of her throat. He breathed in, and her scent filled his lungs. Something deep inside him pulled taut, and he closed his eyes.

God almighty.

But just as he released the edges of the blanket, Violet stirred. Her eyes fluttered open, and then she started, writhing away from him with a cry. She flailed her arms as if to push him off her.

Gabriel froze. *I scared her—*

"Leave me alone," she wailed, beating out at him with her fists. He grabbed her arms gently, trying to still her.

"Violet, it's me," he told her, tightening his fingers when she continued to writhe.

He gave her a small shake to snap her out of it—and then suddenly, it was over. Then the tears came. She began to cry softly, her body going limp, and suddenly, she was in his arms, her cheek pressed against his chest. Her entire body shook with sobs.

Without thinking, Gabriel reached for her, gently patting her back.

Why was she so frightened?

...Most likely because she'd been left alone here in his cabin all day. *I've only been thinking about myself, staying away from here so much, leaving her all alone..* Come to think of it, had they even shared a real conversation since getting married? *Don't think we have.*

After a few moments with Gabriel holding her, trying to not breathe in her sweet scent, Violet pulled away, still sniffling.

"I'm sorry," she whispered. "You scared me."

"Forgive me for that," Gabriel whispered. "I just didn't want you to get cold."

Violet nodded, using the hem of her robe to wipe the tears away. Without thinking, Gabriel reached out, brushing his thumb against her cheekbone.

He realized what he'd done when Violet went still, her eyes widening as she stared at him. Her nightgown hung loosely on her, leaving the skin of her collarbone and upper chest exposed.

Violet seemed to realize this too; she turned away, pulling his quilt up to cover herself.

"You shouldn't be in here," she said in a stiff tone. "I'm hardly decent."

Gabriel cleared his throat, scrambling to his feet. "Of course. Right." He turned and hurried back out into the main living area. *You're being a fool, Gabriel.* He pulled the coffee pot off the stove and filled it with grounds and water to heat over the fireplace. *What are you doing?*

His hands were shaking as he hung the pot on the hook over the glowing embers. Suddenly weary, he dragged one of the kitchen = chairs over to the fireplace to keep an eye on his coffee.

Violet didn't emerge from her room.

Her hair had been so soft under his fingers, her body soft and warm as she pressed against him, crying.

He exhaled heavily, running a hand over his face. *That stagecoach can't come soon enough.*

Already, his cabin was brimming with Violet, the scent of her overshadowing the smoke of the fireplace and stove, the signs of her presence everywhere he looked. A novel on the shelf over the hearth, a bouquet of wildflowers hanging on the wall, an apron she'd been using draped over one of the chairs.

If she stayed too much longer, he'd be in trouble.

It's just a technicality. That's all. He closed his eyes, taking in a deep breath.

The coffee perked, and he poured himself a cup. It didn't matter whether Violet stayed or left. He'd do his best to ensure her safety. And he'd see to it that the Green Terror didn't touch her again. It was merely his duty as sheriff.

But the next morning, he found his heart lodging in his throat when he awoke to the sound of her stirring in her bedroom. Her presence was deeply comforting, in a way that scared him. And the thought of her leaving caused him to ache. He'd expected to be sick of her by this point, to want her gone so that he could have the cabin to himself again.

He considered leaving before she emerged from her bedroom, as he usually did. But today, he lingered, his body a bit sore from sitting in the chair all night instead of sleeping on his own bed.

After a few minutes, Violet pushed her bedroom curtain aside and emerged, her dark hair curling charmingly against her jaw, a shawl around her shoulders.

Her eyes widened when she saw him. "Mr. Brooks!" she gasped.

Gabriel dipped his chin in greeting. "Morning."

Violet's cheeks darkened as she crossed the room to the table, lowering herself into the chair, and Gabriel joined her. It was about time he spent the morning with his wife. *Though I really should be heading out soon...and she's not my wife. Not really. Just in name only.*

"You can call me Gabriel," he reminded her, watching as she fidgeted with the cuffs of her dress sleeves.

Violet smiled slightly, turning pink. "Oh. That's right. Gabriel." Her eyes sparkled in the low firelight. "You're still here...I thought you'd be gone."

"I wanted to apologize. About last night. I didn't mean to spook you."

Violet let out a humorless laugh. "Of course. It wasn't as if you were watching me sleep or anything."

Gabriel blinked, heat rising into his face. "I wasn't."

Violet closed her eyes and gave her head a little shake. She went to the pantry and began shuffling around inside. "Will you be home for dinner?"

"I don't believe so." Gabriel drained the last of the coffee from his cup.

Violet poked her head out again, pinning him in place with those dark eyes, a small crease appearing between her brows. "Can I ask you something, Mr. Broo—Gabriel?"

Gabriel dipped his chin in a nod. "Go ahead."

She took a deep breath, squaring her shoulders. "Why—why did you agree to marry me? This whole arrangement benefits me far more than it benefits you."

"It's like Ma said...I need someone to keep house for me. Cook, look after things around here." *It's purely an arrangement of convenience.*

Violet ducked her head, scuffing the toe of her shoe on the wooden floor. "I just—I suppose it seems as if you've been avoiding coming back here...because of me."

Gabriel stiffened. "My duties around Miles City keep me busy. I'm not *avoiding* coming back here."

Violet dug her teeth into her bottom lip. She nodded. "Your mother told me that your father was a sheriff, too. Is that why you became a sheriff?"

Gabriel paused. *Now she wants to talk about Pa?* He scarcely spoke of that with *Ma,* much less...

Violet's dark eyes cut into him, searching for something. He stood awkwardly, picking his hat up off the table, and began to walk to the front door. Now, he was only a few steps from her, and she watched him with those unnerving eyes, waiting for him to reply.

He settled his hat on his head. "I don't mean to be rude, ma'am. But this is just a temporary arrangement. That's all.

Before long, we'll be going our separate ways...there's no need to get personal."

"I wasn't trying to pry. I just—it's a little strange, to be living with someone I know nothing about." Violet's voice lowered, as if she was speaking to herself. "Whom I never see."

That string in Gabriel's stomach drew taut again.

Violet's frown deepened. "And anyways, you've asked me several times about where I'm going, and why I'm out here. I'd call *that* prying."

Irritation prickled in Gabriel's belly. "Well, as the sheriff, it's my duty to know when people are lying."

"You think I'm lying?" Violet's face drained of color.

"I can't say I'm sure." Gabriel swallowed, his mouth dry. He should step away, but he could smell her. *Lemon verbena.* His thoughts slowed. "Like I said. It's best if we just keep to ourselves till this is done."

"Perhaps you're right," Violet whispered stiffly. Her eyes flashed. "Have a good day, Gabriel." And then, without another word, she stalked through the kitchen and disappeared into her room, the curtain swishing in place behind her.

Gabriel stood there for a long moment, trying to steady himself, and then he hurried out of the cabin. He paused on the porch, grateful for the cool morning air against his hot skin.

The stagecoach is a few days away. Then this will be over. The sooner the better.

But no matter what he did that day, he couldn't escape Violet.

To begin with, Sylvia Lawrence cornered him before he could get into his office. "How is your bride, Sheriff Brooks?" she beamed, bustling up the boardwalk to him, wearing the most frills and laces he'd ever seen on a woman.

His heart sank, but he managed a polite nod, reaching up to tug the brim of his hat in acknowledgement. He didn't pray much, but he prayed right now that he wasn't turning red. "She's faring well, ma'am."

"Oh, Sheriff Brooks," Sylvia cackled. "Always so serious. But don't you play coy with me. It is so wonderful to know you aren't over there in that big house of yours alone." She wagged her head back and forth. "I always knew that sooner or later a lady would catch your eye. Why, I told Mr. Lawrence just a month ago, 'I can feel it in my bones that our dear sheriff is going to marry soon.' I have a sixth sense about these kinds of things, you see."

Face burning, Gabriel tipped his hat again and began to turn, but Sylvia followed him. "Before you go, I wanted to extend a dinner invitation to you and Mrs. Brooks. We would love to have the two of you over."

Gabriel just barely refrained from rolling his eyes. He pushed open the office door and was dismayed to find Benjie, George, and Hawkins inside. The way they were fighting smiles, he could only assume that they'd heard the whole conversation.

"Thank you for the invitation, ma'am," he told Sylvia curtly.

"Let me know when," she trilled in an unbearably sing-song voice. As soon as the door clicked shut, Gabriel strode over to his desk. *Maybe the others could pretend this never happened.* He tried to not look at any of them.

"You gonna take the Lawrences up on their offer?" Benjie chuckled.

"The stagecoach gets here next week. There sure as hell won't be time." *Thank God.* Gabriel changed the subject even faster than usual. "Any word about the Green Terror?"

"Nothing about him this morning," George sighed. "Just another chicken burglar. And another fight around three last night. Folks was complainin' about gunfire."

Gabriel swore. It had been barely a month since the last gunfight in Miles City. He'd been hoping for a longer streak. "Did you find out who it was?"

"Some fellows from Elk Crossing," Hawkins spoke up. "One of 'em got shot in the leg. There was blood everywhere." When the others turned to peer at him curiously, he flushed and hurried to add, "A friend told me."

"'Course. A *friend*." Benjie's blue eyes crinkled. Hawkins scowled and threw a cleaning rag at him. "Come to think of it, I thought I saw you there."

"Why wasn't I called?" Gabriel demanded.

"Benjie got it handled." George took another draw from his pipe. "Besides, you're a married man now. We thought we'd leave you and your missus Brooks be."

Gabriel brushed past this. "Did you get any names? Why aren't they in there?" He gestured at the cell along the opposite side of the room.

"We didn't get to them in time," George sighed. "They high-tailed it out of there before we arrived."

"Hawkins!" Gabriel barked. "Did you get any names? What did they look like? Maybe they were some of the Green Terror's men. Did you catch what this fight was about?"

"I told you, I wasn't—"

"'Course you were," Benjie coughed.

"Hawkins. Names? Descriptions?"

Hawkins sighed resignedly. "It was these two fellows. They was arguing about something in the alley next to the saloon. Then they began to fight, and all of us rushed outside. One of 'em started to run, and the other pulled a gun on 'im and shot 'im in the leg. I don't know how, but the wounded fellow got out of there fast."

Benjie met Gabriel's eyes and spoke as if he could read Gabriel's mind. "It wasn't the Green Terror. He wouldn't be so stupid as to come back here to Miles City."

Gabriel pressed his lips together. "He's been more reckless than usual lately. First the stagecoach incident, and taking Violet, now this..."

"But why would he get out of there so fast? Even if he was injured?" Benjie frowned.

They all looked at Hawkins, who held his hands up. "I didn't see him! It was too dark in that alley."

Gabriel started for the door. "Was he tall or short?"

"I didn't see." Hawkins' face fell at Gabriel's scowl. "I'm sorry, Sheriff."

"Gonna go check for witnesses." Gabriel strode out the door to Apollo, who was waiting outside at the hitching post.

"I'm coming with," Benjie hollered, right on Gabriel's heels. They mounted their horses, and then George and Hawkins emerged from the office, following suit.

First, Gabriel rode to the saloon to see if Mattias the bartender could say who had been present the evening before. Mattias, a German fellow, hemmed and hawed as he tried to remember. He tucked his thumbs in his belt loops. "There was Tom, of course. He's always here. All my usuals. Hawkins there...Lawrence. Some miners. And a couple of the fellows staying at the boarding house. A couple of injuns, too."

Impatience prickled in Gabriel. "Names, Mattias? Anyone you didn't recognize?"

"Hell, it was all a blur. I was having trouble with one of my girls, so I was taking care of that all night. Someone tried to hurt her, see, and—"

"Which of your girls were there last night? Maybe one of them saw something."

"It was Missy, Beth, Carrie, and Hannah. Carrie and Hannah are at their boarding house, and Missy and Beth are upstairs gettin' ready."

Well, it was a start. Gabriel would have to find Tom, too...though Tom had probably been drunk out of his mind by three in the morning.

He began rattling off orders. "George, Hawkins, you check with Missy and Beth. Benjie, you find Tom, and I'll go over to the boarding house."

"Sure thing, boss." Benjie nodded. Everyone scattered, and Gabriel strode back out, mounted Apollo, and rode up the street to the boarding house.

It stood a little way back from the main street, apart from the in-town bustle. He met one of the saloon girls as she was coming down the steps, already bedecked in some kind of red corset. She smiled as he approached her with a polite tip of his hat. "To what do I owe the pleasure, Sheriff Brooks?"

Chapter Eleven

It was a breath of fresh air to get outside and walk. For the past three weeks, Violet had stayed around the cabin, mostly on the porch, sometimes taking small walks around Gabriel's property. She wrote letters to Lou, but she kept forgetting to put them out for Gabriel to take into town. So now, she carried a small, heavy packet of letters in her coat pocket, and it was soothing to run her fingertips over the melted wax seal as she strode along.

It was a beautiful summer morning, the birds singing all around, the air cool, the sunlight gleaming on the prairie grasses that swished in the wind.

Violet had only gone into town twice in the past three weeks, since it was such a drive. Once, to visit with Carol, and the second time to mail Lou a letter and buy groceries—as much as she could carry home, although Carol ended up driving them home for her in her trap.

And today would be her third visit to town. Her heartbeat quickened at the prospect of seeing people. Martha visited, and Carol did too, but if Violet stayed in that cabin too much longer, she'd lose her mind. *Cabin fever,* Martha called it.

That stagecoach can't come soon enough.

Her skirts would probably be all dusty by the time she reached main street. But she didn't care. She paused on the bridge that ran over the Tongue River on the road leading to town. The river was wide and majestic, its rushing waters taking Violet's breath away. She hovered there for a few minutes, leaning against the railing, just trying to let herself be.

Then she continued on, the cool breath of wind kissing her cheeks, and she hummed softly to herself, an aria she'd seen once at the Boston opera house. *Is it strange to not miss Mother and Father even a little?*

She pulled out a biscuit she'd stashed in her other pocket, and she nibbled on it. What were her parents were doing this very moment? Were they looking for her? *Very likely not. They're probably relieved I'm gone. They never wanted me, anyway.*

What would Mother think of Gabriel? She'd probably find him very stoic and unpolished. The exact opposite of Isaac Wilson. Violet closed her eyes, scrunching her nose as she tried to imagine Gabriel in a beaver hat and Boston finery. She couldn't quite picture it.

All she saw in her mind's eye was Gabriel with his usual furrowed brow, the rare half-smile. His rolled-up sleeves. His tall, sturdy frame. The way he practically had to stoop to pass through the doors in his cabin. And then his voice echoed through her head, deep and low, drawling, "It's best if we just keep to ourselves till this is done."

Violet took in a deep breath. He was right. But her mind wouldn't stop replaying the way he'd held her last night when she'd woken up, terrified, her heart pounding so hard he must've heard it. The way his fingers had slid up into her hair, the way his hand cupped the back of her head. His quiet voice, reassuring her gently. The warmth of his firm chest against her cheek.

It had all been over so fast, but for some reason, it sent heat flooding into her face. *Don't be foolish, Violet. Before long, you'll be leaving Miles City. You barely even know this man.* He was so serious. Too serious. A veritable closed book.

And anyway, I don't plan to be anybody's bride. This will all be over soon, and I'll be a teacher in Helena before long.

Violet rounded a bend in the road and stopped short at the sight of the town sprawling out beneath the gentle slope where she stood. After a moment's admiration, she hurried along down towards the cluster of buildings, the boardinghouse looming close on the corner of the boardwalk.

Several men hung around by the back door, smoking and washing clothes. They nodded to Violet in greeting, and some of them whistled as she passed. Violet quickened her pace and turned the corner of the boarding house to step onto Main Street.

Then a familiar figure caught her eye. She froze and took several steps back. Sure enough, there was Gabriel, standing at the bottom of the front porch steps to the boarding house.

And he was talking with a young woman—one of the saloon girls.

Violet couldn't hear what they were saying. She held her breath, trying to listen, but they were speaking in low voices, as if they were in the middle of a private conversation.

Then the saloon girl tilted her head, sashaying closer to Gabriel. Violet's mouth dropped open as the girl plucked something off of Gabriel's shirt, tracing her fingers down his chest.

Violet's stomach twisted into knots. She tore herself away and kept walking, feet practically pounding holes in the boardwalk. *Men. They're all the same. They just can't stay away from those saloons.* She exhaled shakily. *Why should I care what he does? He's not really my husband. He can do what he likes.* She'd leave this place for good in just a few days.

But her stomach remained in a ball, sinking lower and lower, and she turned, hurrying the other way, back past the smoking men, just so that she wouldn't have to pass by Gabriel and that saloon girl.

Finally, she reached the boardwalk that ran along the shopfronts.

"Oh, Mrs. Brooks!" cried a shrill voice just as Violet passed the mercantile, and Sylvia Lawrence stepped into her path. "How perfect! I spoke with your husband earlier. I mentioned to him that we'd love to have the two of you over for dinner. It seems like we've barely gotten to know you, and you've already been here for *weeks*."

"Thank you." Violet managed a bright smile. "That's too kind of you."

"Of course. Now, where did you say you were from again? St. Louis? My, what a big city. And it would be wonderful to have a truly educated young woman teaching my children when the church finally gets rebuilt. They just started on it yesterday. Your husband has been overseeing it." Sylvia's voice rose as she chattered on.

Violet's eyebrows lifted and she leaned over to stare at the church down the street. Sure enough, several men were nailing fresh boards on the roof. The rubble had already been cleared away, and only the salvageable parts of the structure remained.

"Excuse me, Mrs. Lawrence," she murmured, and hurried onward until she reached *Carol's Bows*. The corset around her waist began to feel too tight around her chest, every breath making her lungs burn.

After pausing to steady herself, Violet pushed open the door of the shop and nearly tripped on the way inside.

"Violet!" Carol appeared from the back room, spectacles settled on the bridge of her nose. The door swung open behind her, revealing an old mannequin draped in gingham. Violet spotted an edge of lace around the hem and at the throat. *She must be sewing...*

"I didn't know you was comin' into town," Carol said brightly. "Everything alright?"

"Yes," Violet gasped, holding her side. "I'm quite fine." She paused again, gulping in more air. "I've made up my mind, though. I won't stay here in Miles City and teach." *Or watch Gabriel flirt with saloon girls.*

Carol studied her with sharp gray-blue eyes, so much like Gabriel's. "Well," she said at last, "you're free to go when the stagecoach comes. Nobody's forcin' you to stay."

Violet closed her eyes, a tangle of emotions whirling faster and faster through her head. Her stomach wouldn't stop flip-flopping. "I know. It's just...I saw them repairing the church, and...it doesn't matter." *I won't tell her about her son and the saloon girl.*

"I've got a question for you, Violet." Carol returned to the back room, gesturing for Violet to follow.

Violet watched as she went to the mannequin and continued pinning a sleeve to the shoulder. "You seem to always be running from something. What are you running to?"

Violet tried to laugh, but it sounded hollow in her own ears. "I'm not running. I'm just trying to find a place to start a life of my own."

"Now, I'm not going to pry. But," and Carol fixed her with an intent gaze, "you're welcome to talk to me 'bout anything that's troublin' you."

Violet sighed. "Let's just say that everyone I left back home—they wanted to tell me who to be. What to do. And I just couldn't be that daughter for them."

Daughter. She hadn't meant to say that aloud. She turned, blinking away hot tears.

"What's the matter, dear?" Carol asked gently, and the floor creaked as she walked over, turning Violet back towards her. She pulled her into a hug.

"Nothing. It's just...I don't like feeling trapped."

"Well, Gabriel isn't going to force you to say, and nobody else will, either. You don't need to worry about that." Carol drew back slightly, fixing Violet with a searching look. "But I will say, it's been nice having you around. And I think Gabriel thinks so, too."

Violet couldn't help but scoff. "He's barely around the cabin to eat any of the food I've been cooking." Then she sighed. "Well, not that I can blame him. The only thing I know how to cook right is biscuits. Thank you for that cookbook."

Carol laughed, returning to her mannequin. "Gabriel is just like his daddy, in more ways than he'd like to admit. He works hard—too hard. He can be stubborn, too. Stubborner than a mule." She shook her head. "He tried to run from being sheriff, but he couldn't escape it. It's a big responsibility."

"I know."

"'Course, if you talked to him about being gone so much, he'll listen, I'm sure. He always wants to do the right thing."

The right thing, my foot. What about him and that girl? Does Carol know her son consorts with women of the night? "It doesn't matter." Violet forced a smile. "I'll be leaving soon, and I know he's busy with trying to find the Green Terror."

Carol pushed her tongue into her cheek, pausing in her work as she studied Violet again. *What is it?* Violet nearly asked, her stomach flipping. *What is she thinking?*

"I think Gabriel is scared of how much he cares for you."

"Cares for me?" Violet repeated thickly. She shook her head. "This is purely a business arrangement. For my safety. And for his convenience."

"Maybe. But that don't mean feelings aren't involved. I've raised that boy, and I've seen the way he looks at you, the way he talks about you. Never seen him like that before. He cares for you."

Violet's face heated, butterflies erupting in her stomach.

But Carol didn't know what Gabriel had said this morning, and she didn't see what Violet had seen this morning. Gabriel had certainly been generous to let her stay in his cabin, but that didn't mean anything. Especially not if he was busy looking elsewhere for female companionship. *He's just another Isaac Wilson.*

"I can't stay here," she whispered. "I ran away from an arranged marriage. And I never wanted to walk right into another one."

Carol pursed her lips. "Arranged or not, that don't matter. Some things are meant to be. And I sometime wonder if you were meant to end up here in Miles City. Providence, perhaps, had a hand in it."

"I don't think Providence had anything to do with it," Violet murmured.

Carol lifted her eyebrows in surprise, and Violet added hurriedly, "Providence has never cared much for me." *He could have given me parents who actually loved me. Who didn't just see me as a tool to ensure their way of life.*

She changed the subject. "I'm going to take these letters to the post office. You don't think the post rider's left by now, do you?" She needed to walk again, clear her head. Her thoughts kept spinning faster. Too fast.

"He usually leaves after lunch."

Violet swallowed and forced herself to offer Carol a cheery smile.

"You take care now." Carol followed her to the door. "And next week, I'd love to have you over for a goodbye dinner—the night before the coach arrives on Monday."

"Thank you," Violet whispered. "Thank you for everything, Carol. I owe my safety to you and your son. I'm sorry. I was wrong to speak in such a way to you."

Carol gave her a soft smile. "It's been a pleasure having you around. I'll miss you when you go on to Helena."

Violet hesitated, and then threw her arms around Carol's shoulders, a lump in her throat. How strange, that she'd found the mother she'd always wanted out here in Montana.

***

Gabriel returned home early that evening—earlier than he ever had in the past three weeks. Violet nearly dropped the pan of biscuits she'd just pulled out of the oven when he swung open the front door and entered the cabin, hat in his hands.

She set down the biscuits on the table with a clatter. "Gabriel!" she gasped. She was a mess, flour all over her arms, and probably all over her face and dress too. She hadn't expected him to return until after she'd fallen asleep tonight, as he usually did.

He dipped his head in that succinct way of his, like he couldn't spare the words. "Good evening." He hovered there across the room, leaning his shoulder against the mantle, his gaze roaming over her. More butterflies beat to life in Violet's stomach, and she reached up, wiping at her cheeks, pushing back several loose tendrils hanging in her face. A glance down at her skirts brought dismay; she was covered in white floury smudges.

"I just finished up dinner," she managed. "Fried ham and eggs and...biscuits," and she pointed at the pan in front of her with the dark brown lumps, for once only slightly burned instead of coal-black.

He gave a curt nod. "Got done a little earlier today. Benjie and George are keeping an eye on things in town."

Did Carol tell him what I said at her shop earlier? Did she make him come out here?

Violet's stomach turned as she remembered that saloon girl sashaying close to Gabriel, running her fingers down his chest.

She stiffened. "Well, you're just in time to eat." She gave him a cool smile. "Have a seat?" She waved her hand at the chairs.

Gabriel met her gaze, his throat bobbing. A muscle under his eye twitched. She half-expected him to say he'd take his dinner in the barn. But instead, he pulled away from the fireplace and strode across the room, pulling out one of the chairs.

He gestured at it, and Violet's throat closed. "Thank you." She lowered herself down into the chair, pushing back another stray strand of hair.

"'Course," she heard Gabriel murmur, right above her. Warm rushed beneath her skin, and she focused on the checkered tablecloth Carol had brought that first day here at the cabin.

Why am I blushing?

"I didn't burn the biscuits today. Well, maybe I did a little." She didn't miss the amusement in Gabriel's glance as he heaped some of the ham and eggs onto her pewter plate.

"They look good to me."

"Martha taught me," Violet blurted. "She's very kind."

His glance lowered to her mouth, lingering for one heartbeat, then two.

What does that mean?

Chapter Twelve

"I saw men working on the church." Violet pushed her eggs around on her plate. "Do you think it will take them long to repair it?" Why she asked, she didn't know.

Gabriel went still across the table. "I hope not. Shouldn't take but a couple weeks." There was another long pause before he cleared his throat. "Do you think you'll stay and teach here in Miles City?"

Violet's throat closed. "I—I don't think so." She stared down at her plate. *I don't intend to be married to another Isaac Wilson.* She'd thought Gabriel was nothing like Isaac. But she'd been so wrong.

Not that it mattered.

Another long silence dragged on. Finally, dinner was finished, and she stood to gather the dirty plates, wash them in the sink. She went stiff when Gabriel stepped up to the sink next to her. He was so close she could smell him—smoke and sweat. Heat pooled low in her stomach.

"What's this? Coal?" Gabriel picked up one of the blackened biscuits she'd made last night for dinner.

Violet's mouth fell open. "That's a biscuit!" In spite of herself, a laugh tickled the back of her throat. And suddenly, she couldn't hold back from dissolving into laughter, her resolve to remain aloof collapsing.

To her astonishment, Gabriel's mouth curved into a smile and he began to chuckle as well, setting the blackened biscuit down. "This belongs in the fireplace," he told her, his eyes twinkling. "Or I could skip it across the river. It's as hard as a rock."

Without thinking, Violet gave the water pump a jerk and splashed water in his direction. "Maybe by the time I leave, I'll make biscuits *once* without burning them."

She leaned against the sink, trying to catch her breath. And then she blurted out, "I don't think I've seen you laugh before." *I'm supposed to be angry with him. But it certainly is difficult to stay that way.*

Gabriel's eyes crinkled with mirth as he smiled down at her. But then, his smile faded, his laughter gone as soon as it came.

Violet's chest squeezed. She liked his smile, the sound of his laugh. It was low, pleasant. Warm. She wanted to make him laugh again. But he hovered there, just inches away, looming over her, his attention fixed on her. She tried to take in a breath, but she found it difficult beneath his gaze.

"You have something there—on your face." He lifted his hand to her cheek. His eyes once again flickered to her mouth as he smoothed the pad of his thumb against the curve of her jaw. "Flour."

Violet's stomach flipped. She should move away now. Escape his touch. But she couldn't do anything except stand there, trying to not lean into his hand.

Her heart thundered louder and louder between her eardrums, and her head became fuzzy, and sweat broke out on her skin. This dress was far too hot, the collar tight enough to choke her. Or maybe it was just Gabriel's nearness, making it hard to breathe or speak or even think.

"Violet," he breathed hoarsely. He lowered his head, so that his mouth was inches from hers. His breath was warm against her lips.

The memory of him and that saloon girl flashed through her head, sending a chill down her spine. She jerked backwards, catching herself before she stumbled. "I forgot to feed the chickens today," she whispered. And then she rushed for the door, pushing it open and shutting it with a loud click behind her. The cool air soothed her hot skin, ruffling the loose tendrils of her hair.

Gabriel's touch still burned into her cheek, like she'd been branded by a hot poker.

Maybe I should spend my last few days at Carol's... She tried to swallow, but her mouth was too dry. *No, you'll hold up your end of the bargain. Just a few more days.*

***

Gabriel didn't come home early again after that, and Violet told herself it was for the best. She did not understand whatsoever what had happened that night by the sink. Why had he caressed her face? Did he want to *kiss* her? Three weeks ago, she might have shuddered. But now, her face blazed at the thought.

The next few days dragged on, Violet's head spinning from morning till dusk, leaving her distracted as she attempted to tidy up the cabin and cook. She'd keep up her side of the bargain until the end.

Finally, Sunday arrived, the day before the coach was set to arrive. Gabriel came to the cabin to give her a ride in his wagon into town for dinner at Carol's.

The drive there was quiet, and Violet tried not to mind. *I wish I knew what he was thinking.*

Benjie, George, his daughter Martha, and her husband and children were already at Carol's place to say goodbye. The stagecoach would be departing fairly early the next day, at ten.

As soon as Violet set foot on the ground in front of the dress shop, Carol rushed forward, pulling her into a tight hug. "I'm going to miss you, sweet girl."

She led Violet up the steps, where Martha hugged her, too. "You've been a mighty fine neighbor," Martha grinned. "You made Gabriel's cabin into a real home."

Gabriel cleared his throat behind them. He'd tied the horse and wagon to the hitching post, and he removed his hat as he joined them on the boardwalk.

"Oh, you know as good as anyone that your cabin was a cold, heartless place before Violet got here," Martha snickered at him.

He didn't deign to respond. His brow knitted into a frown, and Violet wished again that she could read his mind.

"Oh, before I forget!" Carol reached into her pocket and pulled out a letter. "This came today. The postman gave it to me to give to you."

"Thank you." Violet took the letter, her legs trembling. A single word on the front of the envelope sent her heart galloping. *Lou*. It was the first letter she'd received from her friend since she'd left Boston, and her throat tightened.

She stopped herself from opening it and pushed it into the pocket of her dress. "I'll read it later," she managed, as steadily as she could.

When she looked up, she met Gabriel's eyes. He studied her intently, as if curious.

She brushed past him, following Carol and Martha inside.

Everyone climbed the stairs to Carol's quarters above the shop, where a hearty dinner had been laid out. Violet chose a seat next to Carol, and Gabriel sat down across from her. She tried hard to not look in his direction. The letter was burning a hole in her dress. She itched to open it and see what Lou thought of her current situation, her marriage to Gabriel. Would she advise her to go, or stay? Violet didn't like the way her chest ached at the thought of leaving Miles City, Carol, Martha, and everyone else who'd been so kind to her. As for Gabriel...

I can't stay married to someone like him.

In the blink of an eye, dinner was over, and Carol cleared the dishes away. The rest of the guests took their leave until only Carol, Gabriel, and Violet remained.

"Well, I suppose this is your last night as man and wife," Carol smiled, glancing between the two of them.

"Ma." Gabriel's voice was low, tense.

"What? I'm simply statin' facts. Violet, how do you know there's an opening for you in Helena. Wasn't the teaching position a scheme? Why not stay here in Miles City where there's a real need for you?"

"Ma." Gabriel set down his pewter cup a bit loudly. "What are you getting at?"

Carol ignored him, staring Violet down. "Why don't you give it another month? The church will be finished soon, and you can see what you think of teaching..."

"I can't." Violet's heart began to pound. She tried to steady herself with a deep breath. "It wouldn't be right. And anyways, I've got nowhere to stay here. No money..."

"Well, if you stayed married to Gabriel—"

"Ma. Stop. Leave it be." Gabriel's voice lifted slightly.

"I don't want to stay married to him. I don't want to be married to anyone," Violet blurted, too loudly. She leapt up, her chair nearly toppling backwards. She picked up her cup and rushed into the adjacent kitchen.

Gabriel's muffled voice reached her. "I'm going to wait out by the wagon."

"I'll talk to her," Carol replied.

The minutes dragged past, and Violet's eyes blurred as she pumped water into the sink, rinsing her cup. "Violet," Carol said gently from somewhere nearby.

Violet didn't turn, furious with herself for crying again.

"I'll pay you and Gabriel back for the stagecoach fare," she choked out.

"Now, don't you worry about that." There was a pause. "Where do you think you'll go?" Carol stepped up to the sink, grasping Violet by the arms and turning her.

"I don't know." Violet hiccupped, a sob rising in her throat. "I don't know. Maybe—maybe to Helena? Perhaps I could still be a teacher there. Or, if not, Chicago?"

"You're not one for planning, are you?"

"Not really," Violet whispered.

Carol chuckled. "I'm sorry I upset you just now. I just hate to see you go."

"I want to be a teacher. I've always wanted to do something like that, to feel like I have some kind of purpose. But now...I feel so lost. And confused. What if I do go out to Helena? What if there's nothing for me?"

"Tell you what. I'll give you a little more for the train ticket if you decide to go back east. Back to Boston."

Violet's throat closed. *Lou's letter.* Had she put her address on it? *She promised she wouldn't...*

Carol must have noticed her panic. "The post man told me where it was from."

"Oh."

Carol reached into her pocket, pulled something out, and pressed a dollar into Violet's palm.

Violet glanced at her, openmouthed. "Carol, you don't need to do this. I'll figure something out."

"Please, you'll be doing me a favor. It'll help me not to worry about whether or not you got where you needed to go."

"Thank you."

What are you running to? The question hung heavy in the air like smoke.

***

The next morning, Violet woke early, before it was light out, and began to gather her things, stuffing them into her carpet bag. When she was finished, she paced around her tiny room, wringing her hands and trying to not bite her nails.

She tried to distract herself by watching the sunrise out the window. When she grew too restless for that, she finally lay back down on her made-up bed. Tried to not think about the ride home last night, how deafeningly silent it had been. Gabriel didn't seem in the mood to talk, and she didn't see any sign of his sunnier side she'd caught that one night, the moment after dinner when he'd teased her about her biscuits.

She'd kept her eyes glued on the passing landscape, even if it was too dark to see anything. Something heavy hung in the air, thick enough to cut with a knife. Thick enough to make it hard to breathe. Gabriel's shoulder kept jostling hers, sending sparks of heat through her.

Is he hurt by what I said? And then annoyance swept aside her guilt. *Your ma might not know what kind of man you are, Gabriel Brooks. But I do. I know your type.*

At least Carol would drive her to the station this morning, which brought Violet some relief. She didn't have it in her to stomach another long ride into town beside Gabriel. She didn't like the way he made her insides turn upside down, the way each brush or glance sent her mind and heart spinning out of control.

After what seemed like hours upon hours, Violet sat up at the sound of rumbling wagon wheels. Gabriel must have left early, before she'd even woken up. There was no sight of him in the cabin or out the window, where a golden morning glow now washed over the farm.

Violet ignored the twinge of disappointment in her chest and grabbed her carpet bag, carrying it outside to where Carol waited in the yard.

It looked like Gabriel didn't even care to stay around and say goodbye. *Oh, well. It was all a pretense, anyway.*

Violet set her carpet bag in the back of the wagon and climbed up beside Carol, who was wearing a blue gingham bonnet and dress that matched her blue-gray eyes perfectly.

"I've made something for you to remember us by." Carol pulled out a brown backage from under the seat.

Violet gasped. "Thank you."

To her surprise, Carol leaned over and pecked her on the cheek. Her eyes were shiny. "Good Lord. I'm going to miss you. It's been wonderful having you here."

"Thank you." Violet swallowed hard. "Thank you for everything."

She tugged at the string binding the package and pulled the paper away from folded lavender fabric. When she held it up, the dress tumbled loose, with a full skirt and lace cuffs. The same dress Carol had been sewing the other day.

Violet caught her breath, her mouth falling open. "Carol! It's beautiful!"

Carol waved her hand as she snapped the reins, urging her horses forward. "I thought that color matched your name, sort of."

Violet hugged the dress to her, eyes stinging. "I don't know what to say. It's perfect."

"I reckon it ain't as fine as any dress you'd find in Boston."

"It's better," Violet grinned, blinking away tears.

"I didn't see Gabriel. I suppose he's already left?" Carol peered at Violet carefully out of the corner of her eye.

"I think so. He must have left early."

Carol sighed, giving her head a small shake. "He should've at least said goodbye."

I'm glad he didn't. I don't know what I would've said to him. "It doesn't matter." She managed a smile.

At last, they arrived in town, and Carol guided the team towards a big building that was supposedly intended to be a future train station. Violet tried to imagine a train running through the town, a train that would help Miles City grow and flourish. But right now, that was hard to imagine. Main Street was a far cry from a bustling city. Hardly any of Miles City was more than a handful of finished buildings and muddy streets that slowed down Carol's wagon.

Carol pulled the reins and brought the wagon to a stop at the steps of the train station. Violet climbed down, folding the dress and grabbing her carpet bag so she could pack the dress inside it.

"The stagecoach will be here in thirty minutes," Carol said. "I can wait with you if you'd like."

"No, no. It's okay. I know you must be busy. Thank you for driving me here."

"Happy to." Carol leaned forward and kissed Violet on the cheek, pulling her into a tight hug. Her blue eyes twinkled with a tender smile before she said goodbye one last time and walked back to the wagon.

Violet's vision blurred again as she watched Carol drive away, and she took in a shaky breath. Then she entered the station. It wasn't finished yet, and a singular bench was the only furniture. No paint had yet been added to the walls. Now all there was left to do was wait. And read Lou's letter.

Chapter Thirteen

Only after Ma's wagon pulled out of his yard did Gabriel stride back down the hill to his cabin. Something was amiss. When he pushed open the door of his cabin, he paused, catching his breath. Violet might as well have never left. Her scent lingered in the air—roses and talcum, and that lemon verbena perfume of hers. It made his head swim, and he nearly gasped aloud, as if he'd been struck in the stomach. He'd been gut-punched before, but this was different. Worse. *I should've at least been here to say goodbye.* But how would he even do that? He'd just be at a loss for words, fumble his way through it.

It was always just temporary. And he shouldn't forget that, either. He walked slowly over to her bedroom door—though it wasn't really *hers*. Pushed aside the curtain and paused, staring inside at her narrow bed, the covers drawn and straightened.

That lemon verbena scent was the strongest in here. His knees went weak, and he stepped over to the bed, sinking down onto the edge. She'd left his handkerchief clean and folded atop her bedside table.

His eyes lit on something peeking out from under the bed. A bottle. Her perfume. It must have fallen there without her notice.

Gabriel bent down, picking it up. The cool glass bottle weighed heavy in his palm, and he turned it this way and that, his mind slowing down to a sluggish pace.

That tangy sweetness embraced him, until all he could picture in his head was Violet. Her lips, her lashes, her sweet smile. That dark soft hair framing her face. Her comforting presence. Her laugh as he'd held up that burnt biscuit.

I should've spent more time with her. I should've said goodbye. Even if it meant he'd never see her again.

Well, maybe the stagecoach hadn't left yet. She'd likely want her perfume. Gabriel ducked out of the bedroom to check the clock on the mantle. It was only nine-thirty. Thirty minutes left.

He hurried outside to the barn, saddled and bridled Apollo, and swung himself up onto the horse's back. A tap of his heels sent Apollo cantering out of the barn towards town.

Just as Gabriel arrived at the beginning of Main Street, he spotted Ma steering her wagon back towards her shop. He snapped on the reins, urging Apollo into a trot.

Of course, Ma spotted him as he rode past. "Gabriel Brooks, where were you earlier? You couldn't even say goodbye to Violet?"

He patted his pocket, his face warming. "She forgot her perfume."

"Well, go on. She's waiting inside the station." Ma's eyes twinkled, though Gabriel didn't know why.

He dismounted and tied Apollo to the hitching post before hurrying up the steps of the coach station.

Violet was sitting on the bench inside, her carpet bag beside her. She was just unfolding a letter—the letter Ma had given her a few nights ago.

"Violet."

She jumped at the sound of his voice. "Gabriel?" She stared at him, cheeks flushing, and she stood hastily, smoothing her skirts. Her forehead furrowed. "What are you doing here?"

"You forgot this," and he withdrew the perfume bottle from his pocket and held it up. Her eyes flashed, and he wondered if he was imagining the way her features clouded like she was disappointed.

"Oh." She let out a soft, embarrassed laugh. "I thought I'd grabbed that. Thank you." She stepped forward and held out her hand.

Gabriel set the bottle in her palm, his fingertips skating against hers, and something like lightning arced through him. He swallowed thickly and stepped back, pushing his hands into his pockets.

"Have a safe journey," he managed, his throat tight. Violet nodded, digging her teeth into her bottom lip.

"I will... just as long as the Green Terror doesn't board my stagecoach again."

Gabriel's mouth twitched. "I'll see to it that he doesn't."

The distant sound of thundering hooves filled the air, and Violet turned with a gasp. "The stagecoach!"

Gabriel nodded. "It'll be here before long. Goodbye, Violet."

She turned back to him, her dark eyes wide, her lips parting. "Goodbye," she whispered.

***

Back at his own barn, Gabriel unsaddled Apollo and began to brush him down. But the memory of Violet at the station kept flitting through his head on repeat, and when Apollo snorted and whinnied with annoyance, he realized he'd been brushing Apollo's flank in the same spot for at least ten minutes.

Then the distant sound of rumbling wagon wheels filled his ears. A visitor to his farm?

He strode over to the barn door and leaned there, keeping his eyes on the end of the drive. Ma's wagon appeared. He could just barely see her in the driver's seat, and someone else beside her. Was that...

Violet? His heart leapt into his throat.

Before long, Ma steered her team into Gabriel's yard and drew them to a stop. Violet clambered down, picking her carpet bag out of the wagon bed.

She turned and spotted him, but Ma called before she did. "She's decided to stay! Isn't that wonderful?" She trotted up laughing and grasped Gabriel's arm, pulling him forward. "She wants to be the teacher for the children here in Miles City!"

Behind her, Violet shuffled her feet as if nervous. Gabriel met her eyes. "Are you sure?"

She nodded, taking in a deep breath. "If you're willing to let me stay here a little longer. I just—I didn't know where I was going to go. I need more of a plan, I suppose. But in the meantime, I can teach, once the church is rebuilt. And once I earn enough doing that, I can go from there. That is, if you don't mind me acting as your wife a little longer."

"You're welcome to stay as long as you need," Gabriel managed after a pause. He tried to catch his breath, tried to swallow. But his mouth had gone dry.

"Thank you," she whispered.

"We've got to celebrate!" Ma cried. "Miles City has a teacher now!" Before she left, she told them to ride into town that evening for dinner. She promised them she'd bake a cake and added that she'd invite Benjie and George if they were able to come.

Gabriel carried Violet's bag back inside and set it on her bed. When he turned, he found her standing in the center of the cabin, her hands clasped tightly. "Just another month or two," she told him, her words nearly tumbling over each other.

He gave a curt nod. "That works fine for me." His pulse thudded, heavy and fast. He didn't like the way relief unfurled inside him, warm and heavy like too much whiskey.

You look beautiful. But he couldn't say that. She wasn't his wife. Never had been, not *truly*. Just in name only.

Violet's expression turned serious. "Is there anything more I can do, to better hold up my side of the arrangement?"

Gabriel froze. What could she do? His mind was still sluggish, his thoughts in chaos and all over the place. But an idea began to ring through his head, and before he could stop himself, he blurted, "Dinner together…once a week. I know I've been coming home late since you moved in here. But I think…if you're going to stay here as my wife…we could at least get to know one another better." He cleared his throat, wondering if he was bright red.

Violet blinked, and she looked down at the floor. "If that's what you'd like…"

Gabriel hurried to clarify. "Just dinner. That's all." Now he must really be red.

"Oh, I know that's what you meant." Violet blushed too, keeping her eyes on the floor. "And yes. I can do that. Dinner once a week."

Gabriel dipped his chin in a curt nod. "I need to head to town now. But I'll come by and pick you up for Ma's dinner tonight."

Violet offered him a tight smile, wringing her hands. "Have a good day."

Gabriel forgot to move, hovering there before her for a moment longer, fighting the impulse to lean down and kiss her on the mouth. But instead, he turned on his heel and strode out the door of his cabin, letting it fall shut behind him.

***

George brought his fiddle that night, and there was a little dancing in Ma's parlor. Benjie, Martha, her husband Jeff, and their children had joined them once again, and this time the mood was less somber and more joyful. Benjie asked Violet to dance with him, and she accepted. Martha and her husband danced too, briefly, since Martha was fairly far along in her pregnancy.

Ma patted Gabriel on the arm. "Dance with me," she smiled. He sighed, fighting a smile of his own, and stood, letting her pull him to the middle of the room where the other pairs swirled. Gabriel had only danced once or twice in his life—he'd always been clumsy at it, and it was a surprise that he hadn't stepped on anybody's feet yet.

But Ma's eyes twinkled and she asked, "Who taught you how to dance so well?"

Gabriel raised his eyebrows. "Nobody. I never dance."

"Well maybe you should." Ma gave his chest a pat, fixing him with a playfully stern look. "Now, why don't you dance with your wife?"

And then she stopped them, jerking her head to motion over Benjie, and he swung towards with Violet in his arms, grinning from ear to ear.

"Your bride," he teased, and passed Violet off to Gabriel. And then, she was in his arms, her eyes big and bright, sparkling with laughter, her smile fading as she stared up at him, as if unsure.

He managed to smile at her shakily and together they circled around the room, a bit slower than the music and the others. She fit perfectly in his arms in a way that scared Gabriel, and he wasn't scared of much. Her hands were warm and soft in his.

He ignored the prick of disappointment when it was over, when she eventually stepped out of his arms and went to sit next to Martha. The music went on, but he stepped outside to smoke a pipe—he usually found it calming, and for the first time he wished for a glass of whiskey to soothe his frayed nerves.

He ran a hand over his face as he breathed in the spice of the tobacco and peered up at the stars over his head. They winked down at him, brilliant and breathtaking.

"You alright?"

Ma's voice startled him. He turned, lowering his pipe, and nodded.

"You wanted her to stay, didn't you?" Ma stepped up beside him.

He let out a hoarse bark of laughter, shaking his head, and pushed his pipe back into his mouth.

"Gabriel..." Ma grasped his arm, her blue-gray eyes piercing into him. "Why are you fighting it so hard? Is it because of me and your Pa?"

He scoffed. "It's because this is only temporary. Just for show."

"Is it?"

"Ma."

"You know what I think? I think it was tearing you up inside to see her go." Ma straightened her shoulders and drew back, walking back to the door. "But what happened between me and your pa...that still weighs on you, even after all this time. Though I know you'll never admit it. You can't fool me, Gabriel Brooks."

Gabriel couldn't speak. Instead, he kept drawing on his pipe, staring out at the brightly lit sky. Even if he was relieved that Violet had stayed—which he wasn't—it didn't matter. She sure as hell didn't want to stay married to him longer than necessary. And he didn't hold it against her. She was a determined little thing, and he could tell she had her heart set on something, though he couldn't be sure of what. *What would her family back east think of this whole arrangement?*

Chapter Fourteen

Dearest Violet,

I can't even begin to tell you how delighted I was to hear from you! I've been praying day and night that you made it to your destination safely, and I was beginning to worry that something had happened. I can't believe you were nearly kidnapped! And now you're married to a sheriff? He sounds exactly like that Count in The Mysteries of Roberto. *Do you remember? Our first Gothic novel? That brooding man locked in his castle, the one Elizabeth fell in love with...so romantic.*

Miles City sounds like it is growing quickly. Do you really think the railroad will reach it soon? I'm beginning to wonder if I should travel out to join you. Perhaps there will be work for me, at the boarding house, or maybe somewhere else. Things are going madly around here. I must tell you some grave news regarding your parents. They are the talk of Boston society right now, I'm afraid. Things are strained between them.

Your father left the house, and I've heard he's staying at Young's Hotel. The word is that they mean to divorce. *Your mother is trying to convince Isaac Wilson to marry her once their divorce is final, but of course, he doesn't seem pleased by the prospect. The gossip is that he means to take a mistress rather than pay suit to your mother. But of course, who is surprised by* that? *He is such a scoundrel.*

Well, I had better end this letter, but you must tell me if you mean to stay in Miles City or not. If you do, will you remain married to him for long? What do you plan to do? I must know! This is better than any novel! I pray that soon, I'll have enough for a ticket of my own. I will go mad if I have to stay in Boston any longer.

Affectionately,

Lou

Violet was rereading Lou's letter for the fifth time. *Count Roberto.* Of course. Lou was right—Gabriel was exactly like him.

Unease twinged in her as she tried to push out the image of Gabriel and the saloon girl from her head. She might be here another month, and she'd do her best with the situation she'd been dealt. But that didn't mean she'd have to enjoy it. Dread and anticipation warred in her chest, seeking the upper hand. Tonight would be the first of her and Gabriel's weekly evenings together. He'd hastened to assure her that it would only be dinner. Of course it would be, Violet told herself sternly. *Why would it be anything else?*

A shiver ran down her back as she added chunks of ham to the stew. Carol's stew recipe called for onions, potatoes, and of course, this ham. A little salt and flour, and some thyme.

She'd picked some thyme in the garden earlier, and she added it now, just as the front door creaked open. She turned to see Gabriel stride in, removing his hat. He hung it on one of the pegs near the door, his eyes darting to her almost nervously.

He gave a nod in greeting. "Evening." He was certainly a man of few words.

She offered him her brightest smile and pointed at the stew pot. "I just have to set it on the fire for a little while and it'll be ready."

The corner of his mouth twitched in a responding smile. "I'll go feed the chickens."

"I already fed them," Violet told him, smoothing the skirts of her lavender dress.

"Ah. Well, then. I'll wash my hands." He moved to the sink and began to pump out water, picking up the dipper and bringing it to his lips as he took a long drink.

Violet paused, unable to tear her eyes from the way his throat moved, his chiseled profile, the way his auburn hair lay wind-blown across his forehead. She turned away hastily and carried the now-ready pot to the fire.

Now, all that was left was to wait. She slowly returned to the table and sank into one of the chairs, and to her surprise, he joined her. She half-expected him to return outside rather than stay in here, trying to converse with her.

What was there to talk about with him? Surely they'd have nothing in common. It was strange, how they'd lived under the same roof for so long and still knew next to nothing about each other. *Did Carol tell him that I'm not really from St. Louis?*

"New letter?" Gabriel nodded at the folded sheet of paper on the table.

"Yes. From my friend back in—"

"St. Louis," he supplied, his eyes crinkling slightly.

"Yes, St. Louis. My friend, Lou. She's my only friend back home."

"Only friend?" Gabriel echoed, studying her again in that unnerving way of his.

Violet nodded, biting her lip. She studied the checkered tablecloth beneath her arm. "She and I both love books. We've read ever so many romances—lots of them set out here, actually. Out west. Though, some of them are also set in

Europe. Places like Italy, or France. Even the moors of England."

"Have you ever been overseas?"

"Oh, only once. When I was very young. My mother and father—" She stopped short. She'd never mentioned her parents to anyone here yet. *What would Gabriel think of them?* Their apoplectic lives in the height of society? "My parents took a trip to London once. It was a long ship ride—that's all I remember."

"London," Gabriel echoed. "So I expect you saw that queen of theirs?"

"Oh." Violet couldn't help but laugh. "No, no. Apparently we saw Buckingham Palace, though." She changed the subject. "What about you? Do you ever read?"

Gabriel gave a wry smile. "No time."

"Have you ever read any books?"

"Except for the Bible...no."

Well, there goes that topic of conversation. "Do you own any? I haven't seen any in here."

"No. But Ma does. She has a handful that I know of. What is your favorite book?"

"My favorite?" Violet's head spun. What a question! *How would I even begin to choose one?* "I suppose there's this one—it's an English novel. *The Pirate's Bride.* Margaret, the heroine—she is captured by pirates, and she is kept by their leader, a terrible ruffian named Drake. They fall in love and marry in the end. Lou thinks it's a little gruesome, but I love it." She caught herself before she rambled on too much. She could talk for hours about all the books she loved.

"Did you bring it with you?"

Violet's chest tightened. "No. I was in too much of a rush. I forgot to grab it. I should have, though."

Curiosity sparked in Gabriel's eyes, like he wanted her to elaborate. But he didn't say anything. Instead, he fidgeted with one of the napkins on the table. At least he wasn't trying to pry, even if he did think she was lying about everything.

She chewed on her lip. "It must be a lot, being the sheriff of Miles City."

"It can be. Sure isn't easy. But it has its rewards, I'd say."

"Rewards?"

"I think Miles City has plenty of promise. Prime farmland with the two rivers running by. The mines nearby. Just need to get the railroad out here. Before long, it will be a real city." There was a dreamy look shining in his blue-gray eyes.

He truly loves this town. "So, I suppose you've always wanted to stay here?" Violet asked softly.

Gabriel nodded. "'Course. I couldn't imagine living anywhere else."

"The Green Terror—have you gotten closer to finding him?"

Gabriel gave a grim smile. "Not as much as I'd like."

A hissing sound startled them both, and they turned to see the stew boiling over the top of the kettle. Violet rushed over and reached for it.

Gabriel shouted her name, but it was too late. Her fingers closed around the handle, and she jerked back with a cry as pain shot through her hand. The pot clattered, tipping precariously on the hook, but thankfully it didn't upset.

Violet squeezed her eyes shut. Another burn.

Gabriel took her by the arm, guiding her to the sink.

"Are you alright?" he demanded. He grasped her burnt hand, gently guiding it under the faucet. He pumped out cool water onto her stinging skin, and Violet let out a soft gasp.

"Lord's sake. Why'd you grab it like that?" he sighed, his forehead knitting.

Violet ducked her head, her face going hot. *How could I have been so stupid?* "I'm always burning myself," she whispered, trying to laugh.

Gabriel wrapped the handkerchief around her hand, tying it into a neat knot. Violet glanced over at the pot to see most of the stew boiling over into the fire.

She covered her hot face with her apron. "Oh, heavens. I wonder if there'll ever come a day that I won't burn something."

Gabriel chuckled. "Stew is stew. It'll be good." He was so close to her again…her hand was still in his. His throat moved as he swallowed, his cheeks darkening.

Violet's heart began to pound louder and louder, faster and faster. If she didn't move away, she might collapse into his arms. She might let him kiss her…

Something in her constricted and she backed away. "Thank you," she whispered. "I should—I should keep stirring the stew. Or else it'll boil over again."

Gabriel nodded and returned to his chair, his smile fading.

***

Violet was dressing. It was the dress Carol had made for her, and it was for a meeting Carol had invited her to—a women's group, a club called *Miles City's Second Chance*. "Lord knows we need it," Carol had huffed, rolling her eyes heavenward. She promised to pick Violet up that afternoon and take her into town for the meeting.

Wagon wheels crunched in the yard outside just as Violet finished fastening her last buttons. She trotted outside with a friendly wave as Carol pulled her team to a stop. Once Violet settled into the wagon seat beside her, Carol snapped the reins and steered them out of Gabriel's yard toward town.

The meeting was hosted by Sylvia Lawrence, of course, in a parlor in which she clearly took great pride. Martha Woodard was also present, as well as several other women from the community. One of them brought her young daughter, and another brought her baby son. Martha told Violet that she'd left Georgie with her husband. "Though, I'm worried he'll forget to feed the boy," she grumbled.

Sylvia Lawrence emerged from the kitchen with a big silver tray laden with little sandwiches and an assortment of other foods that reminded Violet of Boston luncheons.

"My silver collection is the only one there is in Miles City," she declared, with a pointed look at Violet. She seemed to singularly admire Violet for the sole reason that Violet had come from a big city.

Throughout the meal, Violet picked at her food, more interested in watching the women around her talk and visit. She could tell that they all knew each other well, the way they asked one another questions about their lives and families. She was realizing once again just how much of a tight-knit community Miles City was. Something in her ached to be a part of it.

"Everyone ready to begin?" Carol spoke up once everyone had finished eating. She got to her feet. She was just as much of a natural leader as her son. More than ever, Violet admired the woman. She was steely, resilient. A widow with her own dressmaking shop in a town like Miles City? Her strength must be incredible. *Like Gabriel.*

"First of all," Carol beamed, "I'd like to introduce my *daughter-in-law*, Violet. Violet Brooks. She has agreed to be Miles City's schoolteacher!"

The other women broke into applause and Violet's face warmed.

"Before long, they'll be finished rebuilding the church. But," and Carol held up a finger, "we don't have any books, or chalk, or tablets. We'll have to raise money for those items. Violet, since you are to be the schoolteacher, would you be willing to be in charge of gathering the supplies?"

Violet blinked, surprised. Then she nodded. "Yes, of course."

So, this is really happening. I'm going to be a teacher.

Chapter Fifteen

Hank's cough rattled loudly in the dusty cabin. He barely managed to reach the chair by the crumbling fireplace before his knees gave out and a wheezing gasp escaped him.

The cabin was a stroke of luck. The old dunce who used to live there was easy prey. He didn't even question that Hank was a government agent, that the cabin mortgage had never been paid, or that Hank was entitled to seize the land. The fellow had been stricken—too stupid to see past Hank's fancy way of speaking, the neat suit he'd stolen from one of those boarders in town.

The cabin was the perfect spot. It was far enough from Miles City that Hank didn't have to worry about seeing too many folks passing by the house, but it was close enough that he felt comfortable. It was always his belief that the best place to hide was right under the sheriff's bed, so to speak.

Gabriel Brooks would never think to search *this* close to Miles City, right within his jurisdiction. Maybe it was risky, but Hank didn't really care right now. These days, he could barely sleep thanks to his aching, feverish joints, and his cough kept getting worse. In the past few days, he'd even begun to cough up blood. It was a trial to get out and hunt, and most days, he just snatched a chicken or two from unsuspecting neighbors.

The cabin had been his base for a month already while he worked on forming a plan. He'd need men, and guns. Lots more guns if he wanted to take Miles City by storm.

Faint laughter floated outside, and Hank froze as someone knocked on the door. He listened closely. *Women's laughter.* He cursed and bounded out of his chair, trying to think. Likely they saw the smoke from his chimney and decided someone was home. But why were they here? *Is this some kind of plot to lure me out of here?*

He stumbled over to the sink, pumped out some water and splashed it on his face. Then he took a long drink, hoping it would wash the stench of vomit from his breath.

"What do these goddamned women want?" he grumbled, stalking over to the door. Maybe if he waited long enough, they'd leave.

But they didn't. Instead, they knocked again. "Mr. Beau?"

Mr. Beau don't live here anymore. Hank swallowed a chuckle, and with a grimace, he tugged the door open to find two women waiting on the step.

"You aren't Mr. Beau," one of them stammered.

"Mr. Beau's my brother. But he picked up and went back east to Minneapolis." Hank offered them his most charming smile. "Let me have his cabin here."

"Oh. Well, it's a pleasure to meet you, Mister…"

"Jim. You can call me Jim."

"Well, Jim. I'm Mary McNamara, and this is Emily Jones. We're here on behalf of the Miles City's Second Chance club. We're raising money for the new school. We've finally got a teacher here, and she'll need books, tablets, and chalk, and pencils, and plenty of other things for when school starts."

"Aw, well, ain't that nice?" Hank considered slamming the door in their faces. "A new schoolteacher?"

"She came all this way from *St. Louis.* It's clear she's very well educated," Mary told him, her eyes sparkling excitedly.

"St. Louis?" Hank's ears perked up. "You don't say?" *Wasn't that little snake of a girl on the stagecoach from St. Louis? She sure left me with a nasty scar.*

The skin she'd sunk her teeth into was still tender to the touch, maybe even infected. Hank knew a fellow who had been bitten once on the arm and lost the arm to infection...

Hank shook the grim thoughts away and kept his grin pasted on. "What'd you say her name was again?"

"Oh—Violet. Violet Brooks. She just married Sheriff Brooks," one of the women piped up.

"Is that so? Well, ain't that *lovely*." *Married the sheriff, eh? Isn't that just* wonderful? Sure would make things more interesting when he found the little lady and showed her what happened when she messed with Hank Logan. *And of course, the good sheriff wouldn't mind sharing his bride, now, would he?*

The girl obviously came from wealth. The way she carried herself, the way she spoke. Even her clothes whispered "money." *I'm not called the Green Terror for nothin'. I'll get my green, one way or another. She'll be able to take care of me. And once she gives me children, that'll be my ticket to her daddy's pockets.*

Sheriff Brooks would be a complication—a stumbling block, maybe. But the man was just like his pa—head so far up his rear that Hank would have no trouble whisking Violet away. Take her to San Francisco, maybe. Send her rich parents a telegraph and let them know that if they wanted their daughter to live, they'd be wise to send some cash.

Even if they didn't agree, he'd find other ways to make money off her.

"Sir?" *Oh, yeah.* One of the women was talking to him. Both of them stared. *Have I been muttering aloud again?* Hopefully nothing they could understand. He didn't need anybody learning his plans.

"I'm afraid I don't got nothin' to give you but this silver coin here." He shoved his hand in his pocket and fished out one of the coins he'd melted down from the silver he'd stolen last month.

"Thank you?" The woman stared down blankly at the coin he set in her palm.

"You two have a real nice day, you hear?" And Hank closed the door in their faces.

He leaned against it, listening to the sound of their footsteps as they moved off his porch. And then he hurried over to the back door, flung it open, and hobbled down the steps as fast as his constricting lungs would let him.

He stumbled up the hill behind the cabin. He'd need to find the sheriff's cabin and devise a way to wrest that St. Louis chit out of the sheriff's arms.

A tow-headed farmer's kid pointed him in the right direction. "Say, you've got blood on your face, Mister," the kid drawled.

"Shut up." Hank spat a clot of blood onto the ground as he shoved past the boy and started walking west. According to the kid, the sheriff's house was on the opposite side of Miles City, so Hank had to make a big curve around the town to be sure and steer clear of accidentally running into the sheriff himself. *That would spoil things, wouldn't it?*

He could barely walk by the time he reached the slope behind the sheriff's cabin. He hunched down in the grass beside a tree, leaning on it heavily as he reached up to mop the sweat from his face.

And there he stayed and kept a lookout for a glimpse of the little lady. Presently what looked like a woman emerged from the cabin, her hair cropped short, just barely brushing her shoulders.

There she is. She certainly had a fine, lush figure, and he could still feel her soft body in his arms. Yes, she'd do. *She's certainly easy on the eyes, isn't she?*

"Mmmm," he hummed to himself. "Good hips. Perfect for bearing sons."

"Watcha doin', mister?"

Hank jerked, tumbling backward on his rear. That towheaded kid from earlier was standing just behind him, staring down at him with round eyes.

Hank rolled onto his stomach, scrabbling his hands for purchase. "Get out of here, ya hear?" he hissed, reaching out to shove the boy.

But the boy stepped away out of his reach. "Are you friends with Sheriff Brooks?" he asked, tilting his head.

"Sure am. Real good friends. We go way back."

"Oh."

"Now, you run along, boy. Shouldn't you be home for dinner?" Hank sputtered out a bit more blood, hoping it would scare the boy away.

But he didn't budge. Instead, he folded his arms, squinting.

"Get!" Hank tried to shove him again.

"You're a mean old devil, ain't you?"

"Shut your trap! Go!"

Finally, the boy turned and sauntered away. Hank grunted, pushing himself to his feet, and started the long hike back to his cabin. *I'll come up with a way to get Violet alone, away from town. And then I'll take her.* If there was one thing Hank Logan wasn't, it was a quitter.

***

First of all, he'd need a horse. Two, maybe. He wasn't exactly in the best state to carry a plump creature like her across miles and miles of territory.

That would be another tricky part of his plan. He could buy a horse or two, but he'd need to do it secretly, somehow. Didn't want to catch anybody's notice.

The next day, he set out on the long hike to the Crow camp. Surely they'd have some horses he could buy. And they'd be foolish enough to take his silver, of course.

The hike took a full day, and he had to stop several times to rest. A shame he wasn't as sprightly as he used to be. Whatever was going on with his lungs, it sure didn't do him any favors.

Finally, he came to the gentle rise that overlooked a large Crow village with their round lodges dotting the plain. Sure enough, he could spot several mustangs from where he stood. He needed some sturdy ones for the escape with Violet. He'd have to find something to wrap around her mouth, and maybe some chloroform. He didn't want to beat her with his pistol again. He needed her sound of mind enough to care for his sons.

A young Crow brave met him halfway across the field to the village. Several more warriors emerged from the nearby thicket of trees, and they all stared Hank down, watching his every move.

He held up his hands, wheezing out a laugh. "Relax. I ain't here to take your land."

One of the warriors raised a double-barrel gun.

"No need for that," Hank grinned. He held up a small bag of his silver and rattled it around, hoping they heard the jangle of the coins. "I was wondering if I could buy a couple of horses off you. For some real bona-fide Miles City silver." *Do they even understand me?*

The first young warrior held up his hand as if to order the gun-holder to stand down.

Still grinning, Hank poured a couple of the coins into his palm and held them up. "Horses," he shouted, and pointed towards the corral set up nearby where several of the Crow horses grazed.

The rest of the warriors clustered around their leader, and they conferred with one another.

"How much?" one of them called out.

"Two horses," and Hank held up two of his fingers, "for thirty pieces of silver."

"Thirty?" the leader echoed. He walked forward until he was only a few feet from Hank and held out his hand.

"Let me see one," he ordered.

Hank rolled his eyes but tossed him one of the coins, smiling with glee when it fell into the dirt and the warrior had to bend and pick it up.

"Silver?" Several of the other warriors approached, and Hank handed another coin to one of them. The warrior tried to bite it and seemed satisfied. He gave a nod and handed it back to the leader, saying something in their language.

"Two horses?" The leader narrowed his eyes, scrutinizing Hank.

Hank nodded. "Yes, yes."

An hour later, he was riding back towards Miles City on one Crow horse, with the second in tow. He chuckled gleefully to himself. *Won't be long now before I have myself a bride. Her parents will wire me her dowry, and I'll be a wealthy man. They might also send something if I ask 'em for a ransom. Surely they'd hate to imagine their precious daughter the Green Terror's captive!*

Chapter Sixteen

Gabriel rapped on the open door of Ma's seamstress shop and walked inside, leaning his shoulder against the jamb. "Hey, Ma," he called inside. "You seen Violet anywhere?"

He'd returned to his cabin after finishing a day of work, only to realize that she was nowhere to be found. His heart pounded hard in his chest. The sun had just set, and pretty soon it would be completely dark out. He'd only waited an hour before he rode out to see about Violet, and even that might have been too long.

Ma turned, breaking into a smile at the sight of him, and hurried over to plant a kiss on his cheek. "She's over at the church. They only just finished it, and already she's been working over there for *hours* to get it ready. You won't recognize the place."

Then she paused, finally noticing his expression. "What's the matter?"

"I was worried," he exhaled, rubbing the bridge of his nose. "She wasn't at the cabin when I got home and...and it's almost dark." He squared his shoulders, trying to release some of the tension in his spine. Trying to act calm and collected. "I got a little worried, that's all."

Ma's smile widened. "Well, no need to fret. Your wife's gettin' ready to be a teacher, that's all."

Gabriel nodded, chewing the inside of his cheek. "I suppose I'll stop over there and see if she needs anything."

Irritation spiked inside. He left Ma's shop and strode down the boardwalk towards the church.

It had been three weeks since Violet decided to remain in Miles City and give teaching a try. She'd spent the last couple of weeks helping to collect donations while construction on the church continued. *But this is the second time she's forgotten our weekly dinner.* The first time, she'd been out with some of the other women in that club Ma had started, collecting donations from folks in town.

Gabriel arrived at the bottom of the church steps and paused to listen. Violet's sweet voice filled the air, carrying on the night breeze. He pushed open one of the new doors of the church and peered inside. The place smelled of pine and cedar. He had to round the corner to see the rest of the room. The ceiling was high, supported by sturdy rafters, and pews had already been set up, facing the pulpit. Violet was sweeping the floor vigorously, her hair clinging to her cheeks and temples. Her singing filled the church with song as she worked.

Gabriel hesitated before calling her name. Ordinarily he would find her graceful movements, her singing, charming. But tonight, he was tired, and more than a little irritated.

"Violet."

She turned, her eyes wide, and clapped a hand over her mouth, the broom clattering to the floor. "Did I forget again? I'm so sorry. I just—I got so caught up with everything here…"

Gabriel strolled closer and leaned against the back of the last pew, running his fingertips along the polished top of it.

"Martha's husband built the pews. Aren't they beautiful?" Violet took in a deep breath, closing her eyes and wiping her forehead with the back of her hand.

Gabriel sighed. "I wish you would've left me a note. Besides, it's going to be nightfall soon, and it's best if you're not out past dark."

Violet set the broom down, a crease appearing between her brows. "I know—but I just got carried away. Next time—"

"There might not *be* a next time," Gabriel snapped. "We talked about this last week. It's dangerous for you around here. The Green Terror—"

"The Green Terror!" Violet bristled. "Nobody's seen him around here lately, have they?"

Gabriel clenched his jaw. "No, but that's beside the point. The man nearly kidnapped you a little over a month ago. And yet, you just waltz around town, reckless."

"Gabriel—" Violet's eyes went wide at his tone.

"For God's sake, Violet."

Violet recoiled from him, eyes flashing. "All you do is wait around for that Green Terror. It's all you seem to care about."

Gabriel could roll his eyes at her dismissive tone. "It's my *duty*."

"Oh, of course. Your duty," Violet sniffed. "And was it your father's duty, too? Seemed like that's all he cared about as well."

Gabriel froze. *She knows about Pa?* Ma must've told her. He strode towards her and leaned in, his stomach churning. "You don't know anything about me or my family."

Violet glared back at him. "Maybe it's best if we just keep our distance from one another. Before long I'll start teaching, and I'll earn enough to get a room at the boarding house. Then I won't have to worry you anymore."

Gabriel's jaw ached from clenching his teeth so hard. "Maybe it would be for the best," he said stiffly.

"Fine," Violet spat.

"Fine."

But he was no more than a foot away from her now. He caught his breath, unable to move. It was as if he'd been locked into place, her dark eyes blazing into his.

The knot in his chest loosened, anger giving way to longing. The past two weeks had been agonizing, the entire cabin drenched in Violet—her sent, her voice, her things...he barely slept these days. Maybe that was part of his quick temper.

Her breath hitched, and she seemed frozen in place as well, her brows still knitted into a scowl. If he moved forward just a little, he'd be kissing her.

She's not your wife.

He shook the heaviness away and reeled backwards, spinning on his heel. As he strode for the door, he called, "I'll be waiting outside. Finish up here and I'll give you a ride home."

"I think I'll sleep at Carol's tonight," Violet said hotly.

Gabriel stiffened. "Fine."

He barely refrained from slamming the church door behind him. Then he walked across the street, down the side road where Benjie lived in his little clapboard house.

Benjie sat on the front steps of his place, puffing on a pipe. He straightened when he heard Gabriel's footsteps, and he broke into a grin when Gabriel waved a greeting. "I thought tonight was one of your dinners with Mrs. Brooks," he said.

It was too dark to see, but Gabriel could just imagine his smug grin. Instead of responding to the comment, Gabriel sat down on the steps beside him.

"What's the matter? Quarreling with the missus?"

Even though Benjie was probably joking, Gabriel cleared his throat and muttered, "Yes."

"A big one?"

Gabriel lifted one shoulder. "I suppose. Sure felt like it."

Benjie snickered.

"She's just so...impulsive. Careless. And mule-headed, too." Gabriel pounded his fist into his hand. "Drives me wild. Last week she forgot and stayed here in town, well after sunset. And I told her the dangers of that. But here she is, doing it again."

"She does drive you wild, don't she?"

Gabriel ran a shaking hand down his face. "'Course she does."

"Because you're sweet on her."

"For heaven's sake, Benjie..."

Benjie thumped him on the shoulder. "Honest. And she's sweet on *you*."

Gabriel snorted. "The hell she is. She's staying at my ma's tonight."

"I saw the way you two danced that night. You were beside yourself—you could barely contain it. Hardly recognized you. And you were mopin' all around town before the stagecoach returned. And now, you're terrified of somethin' happenin' to her. Ain't you?"

"I'm the sheriff. I worry about everyone."

"But not like you worry about Violet. You can't stop smiling around her. I caught you sniffin' your handkerchief last week. You put some of her perfume on it, didn't you?"

Gabriel rolled his eyes, face burning in the cool summer night. He wouldn't deign to dignify Benjie's comment with a reply. Because his old friend was, unfortunately, correct. *I'm a fool.*

"She's not sweet on me. And regardless of what I feel, I know better. This will all be over before we know it. She'll move out, our marriage will be annulled, and that will be that."

"Well, maybe if you talked to her about it, see what she thought…"

"She made it clear tonight."

Benjie sighed. "You won't even try?"

Gabriel pursed his lips, studying the patterns of the stars over their head.

"You owe it to yourself, Gabe. I think you've loved her since day one when she ran headlong into you. You've got her stuck in your head."

"We're too different." Gabriel tried to laugh but the sound came out all wrong. "Far too different. She comes from a different world."

"What about all them mail-order brides who come out here every day? Those kinds of arrangements work all the time.

And I'm sure they don't have anything in common at first, but then they build it into something real."

"That isn't the same as this." Gabriel gritted his teeth.

"What is this, then?"

Gabriel exhaled heavily. "I don't know."

***

For the next two days, Gabriel kept his distance from his cabin and from his mother's shop. He didn't want to run into Violet, though he wished he could somehow apologize—wished he was more eloquent, wished he could somehow express that it had been wrong of him to snap at her like that.

Then George got a lead on the Green Terror, and Gabriel tried to put Violet out of his head.

"A little boy saw someone odd," George informed them all at the sheriff's station that afternoon. "A man spitting up blood. He was short, wheezed a lot, according to the kid."

"Who's the boy?"

"One of those Donner kids."

The Donners lived just outside town, on the other side of Miles City from Gabriel's farm. "I'll ride out there," he said. "See if the kid remembers anything else."

He glanced up as he unwound Apollo's reigns from the hitching post, and then he saw her down the street, just in front of Ma's shop.

He fumbled the knots, unable to tear his eyes ayaw. He'd recognize that haircut anywhere.

Violet.

Heavens, he missed her. In a way that wasn't right for a man married to said woman in name only.

Then she turned, and her eyes met his. He shook himself and mounted in a hurry, urging Apollo out of town at a gallop.

At the Donner farm, Gabriel tracked down Patrick Donner just outside the barn and asked to speak with his son Daniel for a moment. "It's about the short fellow, the one who spit blood," he explained.

"Daniel!" Patrick hollered.

A young boy appeared in the door of the barn, a chicken in his arms. "Yeah, Pa?"

"C'mere. This man wants to ask you something about that sick feller you met a week ago."

"He was awful mean. Kept muttering something about horses," young Daniel told Gabriel.

"Horses?." *Why horses?* "What did he say his name was?"

"Jim."

"Did he say anything else at all?"

"No, he just tried to push me in the dirt a few times. He was really sick, though. Weak."

"Did he say where he came from? Where he's staying?"

"Nope."

"Well, where did you first see him?"

"The big hill behind old man Beau's place."

Gabriel barely thanked the boy before he was on Apollo and riding off to Beau's cabin, mind churning.

Could it really be the Green Terror? Right under my nose this whole time? Finally, the cabin came into view. He reined in Apollo, trying to make out any sign of smoke rising from the cabin chimney. But there wasn't a trace.

He tied Apollo to a tree and hurried up to the cabin door, rapped on it. It swung open the moment his knuckles touched it, revealing a dirty, unkempt cabin within.

Beau was a native to Miles City. He'd lived in this cabin for over a decade, though it was still a mystery to anyone how he could afford it, what with his addiction to cards. *I wonder if that's why he's gone now...?*

Gabriel poked around the cabin for a bit, inspecting every inch of the place for something, anything. A clue. A sign that he was on the right track. But nothing stood out. The whole place looked disheveled and long-abandoned. His stomach twisting, he headed back to town.

Chapter Seventeen

Violet hadn't slept in a week. There was just too much to think about. Before long, the school would open, and she'd be its teacher. Now that the books had arrived, she spent all her spare time poring through them, trying to forget about that terrible argument with Gabriel. Her chest squeezed whenever she thought of him, but it didn't matter. He couldn't make it clearer that he was uncomfortable with her being in his life, that he would rather not have to worry about her. *It's all just a burden to him, a duty.*

And she truly didn't care. Life was going wonderfully for her. She'd made new friends through Miles City's Second Chance club.

She especially refused to let their skirmish interfere in her friendship with Carol. Carol had been the first person to truly welcome Violet to Miles City, and she loved the woman more than her own mother.

And on top of all that, another letter from Lou had arrived just yesterday. Lou had given an update on Violet's parents. Mother and Father had officially divorced, apparently, and sold their Boston house. Mother went to live with family in Cape Cod, and Father had run off to New York City. And Lou was no longer working at their house, but at a cotton factory.

Violet could still hardly believe that her parents had truly decided to part ways. It was as if everything had imploded since she'd left—like she'd been the trigger point, the thread tugging loose an entire tapestry, making it unravel.

She pressed her hands against her burning eyes. *Not for the first time am I grateful I escaped Boston...* But at the same time, it was strange to think that the house she'd grown up in was no longer a place she could return to. And her parents were no longer in Boston. Lou's letter proved just how little her parents cared. *They couldn't even be bothered to come out and find me.*

It's for the best, Violet told herself. But it stung when she watched Martha with her father, or Gabriel and his mother. These people had loved ones—families. And she was alone. Utterly alone. Except for Lou, of course. Still...it made her ache deep inside.

Violet took a walk to town that morning, excited to see Carol. Benjie had informed her on his visit last night that "Gabriel's ma" wanted to tell her something.

When she finally rapped on Carol's door, Carol looked almost shocked to see her. "Oh, dear," she sighed. "You look exhausted."

I am. Preparing lessons was proving an even bigger task than Violet had anticipated.

But she managed a bright smile, letting Carol usher her inside and up the stairs for a piece of cake and some tea. At the table, Carol turned to her with a wide smile. "Guess what? The Miles City Second Club is gonna host a town fair."

"A town fair?" Violet could hardly believe it. She'd been to a few fairs and exhibitions growing up, and always enjoyed them. The idea of a fair in Miles City sent her heartbeat skipping.

"Yes! With bakin' contests, and races, and three-legged races, and plenty of other things. And all the money we'd raise would go to the tablets and the pencils for the children. Maybe some paint for the buildings around the town. They need a touch-up."

Violet couldn't help grinning, and Carol wrapped her in a tight hug, blue-gray eyes shining. Clearly, she was just as excited as Violet. "I didn't know if it was possible. But Miles City might get its second chance," she whispered.

"Of course it will," Violet reassured her.

Carol grabbed two plates of cake and two saucers of tea. Just then, they heard a knock on the shop door and the two of them exchanged looks.

Carol smiled. "It might be Gabriel."

I should really go. But Violet refused to back down and avoid him. Something he seemed all too willing to do on his own. Never even coming home to sleep anymore. It was ridiculous. He was such a stubborn man. *Though maybe it makes sense, his father a sheriff and all.* He must have grown up in a controlling kind of home. And it must sting to be following in that same father's footsteps.

Sure enough, heavy footsteps and Gabriel's low voice drifted up the stairs as he greeted his mother, drawing closer. Violet flew to her feet, hurrying over to the mirror above Carol's porcelain commode. Her cheeks were flushed, but her hair wasn't messy, and there wasn't anything on her face.

Oh, why does it matter? She didn't feel much like seeing Gabriel right now—not after everything that had happened between them. He was a maddening man. Gut-wrenching.

Gabriel paused at the top of the stairs when he saw her, his face unreadable, his knuckles tightening around the brim of his hat. Carol circled around him as an awkward silence descended over the room.

Violet could flounce her skirts with annoyance. *Why does he always have to be so unreadable? So closed off?*

She pitied the woman who would be his real wife.

"Violet," was all he said, tilting his head.

She didn't respond—simply gave a stiff smile and curtsied.

"Why don't you sit down for some tea, Gabriel?" Carol nodded to the table.

Violet stared at the lace doily tablecloth, digging her nails into the china surface of her cup.

"I'll go get you a cup." Carol hurried away and began to fuss in the kitchen over her teacups.

Gabriel lowered himself down at the table across from Violet, picking at the edge of his sleeve cuff. "Pardon me for interrupting." Another nod of his head.

Violet scowled. "We were talking about a fair. Miles City having a fair."

"A—a fair?"

"Is there something wrong with that?"

"No—not at all." To Violet's surprise, the corner of Gabriel's mouth curved up. "I never thought Miles City would have a fair."

"Well, that's what we're here for," Carol said as she bustled back into the room. "To turn Miles City into a real city."

Violet played with the edge of the lacy tablecloth. "Do you really think a train will reach out all this way?" She turned to Carol pointedly, hoping Gabriel understood she wasn't addressing him. "You're sure they'll go around us? What with the rivers being there and all."

"The rivers won't be that much of a problem," Gabriel told her, his voice gratingly measured.

Violet hoped hers wouldn't shake. "I didn't know you were a bridge designer."

Gabriel's eyes widened and he flushed brightly. "Well, I didn't know you laid railroad tracks."

Violet rolled her eyes.

Carol spoke up, and it was painfully obvious by her cheery tone that she didn't like hearing them bicker. "The fair is gonna be for Miles City! But I'm sure folks from over in Elk's Crossing will come here to attend. It ain't every day we get fairs out here."

Unfortunately, the veiled barbs between Violet and Gabriel were enough to snuff out any real conversation, and Carol couldn't keep up a dialogue all by herself. In the end, Gabriel bid his farewells, apparently unwilling to stay longer than a few minutes.

After he left, Violet let out a sigh of relief. But Carol turned to her, forehead knitting. "What's going on between the two of you?"

Violet bit her lip. "We fought. Said things we probably shouldn't have. I think I hurt him, bringing up his father..."

"Oh." Carol gave a sad smile, tracing her fingertip around the rim of her cup. "Gabriel's a little touchy about that whole matter."

Violet swallowed. "And I went and threw it in his face." Sudden guilt stabbed at her. She of all people knew what it was like to struggle in the shadow of one's parents.

Carol stepped over, cupping Violet's face with a worn hand. "One thing I know is to never let anger go too long. Find it in your heart to forgive. And Gabriel will forgive you. He's fond of you."

Violet tried to laugh. "You're mistaken. He's not—"

Carol clucked her tongue. "You think I don't know my son in love?"

"Oh...no, I didn't mean...but he's *not* in love!"

Carol waved her hand. "That boy has never given a girl a second glance for as long as I've known him. Except for one—Lucy. Now, that was just calf love, of course, but he was sweet on her, and he could never bring himself to say a word about it. And she went back east, sure as you please, and he was left here, wishin' he said *somethin'*, I'm sure.*"*

"Why didn't he say anything?" Violet whispered.

"Oh, even if he did, it wouldn't have made a difference. That Lucy was set on going out to Chicago and marryin' some kind of millionaire. She was a friend of Martha's. But you see, I think Gabriel knew deep down it wouldn't have worked. I think deep down, he was waitin' for you."

"For me?" Violet's cheeks were too warm. She shook her head. "Carol..."

"I know that sounds foolish. But it's true."

"Well, what happened with his father—your husband?"

Carol's smile faded, and she let out a long breath. "Gabriel's pa was a good, *good* man. Oh yes. The best man I've known. But he had demons of his own, and he and I..." She blinked, her eyes damp. "We just couldn't ever seem to see eye to eye, though we loved each other fiercely. He just got so caught up in his work, obsessive about it. It was just his nature. And Gabriel—he could see how it affected me, how it hurt me that Michael never came home. And that was one reason he said no when Michael asked him to be his deputy. Gabriel refused, and Michael was *furious*. Real hurt. He just didn't understand why Gabriel wouldn't want to. He didn't see how he'd abandoned his son, in a manner of speaking, what with him never at home, never around, always putting his duty first. I'll forgive him for loving his work more than me, but I'll never forgive him for all but abandoning our son."

"Gabriel seems to take his duty very seriously," Violet whispered bitterly.

"It's his way of mourning his pa," Carol explained softly. "Michael passed before they could make up, and Gabriel...it broke something in him. He still hasn't forgiven himself. He's so hard on himself. And now, he's making himself pay the penance, throwing himself into this whole sheriff thing. Trying to honor his daddy's name."

Violet's eyes blurred with tears, and she stared down at the tips of her shoes beneath her skirt.

Carol reached over and clasped her hand. "Don't let it go on too long. You need each other."

"Need each other?" Violet repeated, taken off-guard. She couldn't imagine Gabriel needing anything or anyone. But then the image of him standing at his father's grave, hat in his hands, tore at her, and she swallowed down a sob.

And did she really need him?

She could get by until school began when the last of the supplies arrived. And then, once she got paid, she'd check to see if there were any rooms open in the boarding house.

"Violet, will you tell me what you're running from?" Carol's voice broke into her thoughts.

She bit her lip, trying to organize her whirling mind. Never an easy task. *I'm so tired of having to keep all these secrets. Lying to everyone I meet here. It hasn't done me a lick of good.* She was through.

So she told Carol everything. About Boston, about her parents, about the big house on Crabtree Lane. About Isaac Wilson and his saloon girls. But she didn't have the heart to ask Carol about Gabriel and that saloon girl. Not now, at least. *Especially not now.*

She told Carol about the fight with her parents, how her father had slapped her, and how she'd run. And run. And run.

"I'm so tired of running," she breathed.

"Of course you are. But you don't have to run anymore." Carol pulled her into a warm embrace before drawing back, holding her at arm's length.

"Don't I?" Violet smiled sadly, dropping her gaze. "Gabriel seems to think the Green Terror is after me."

"Maybe he is, and maybe he isn't. But wouldn't you rather face him and stand your ground, instead of living your life as prey?" Carol ducked forward, giving her another hug. "Why don't you go home and get some sleep? I'll drive you home."

Their ride back to Gabriel's cabin was quiet, calm, and Violet appreciated the silence. She wasn't sure whether to be disappointed or relieved to find Gabriel nowhere in sight when she went inside.

Chapter Eighteen

Beau had apparently spent the past few weeks camping outside the silver mines, bereft of his home. Gabriel and Benjie found him sitting on the shore of a creek branching off the Tongue, staring glumly into the water. He described the strange man now living in his house, and it matched the Donner kid's description.

"Was he wearing a green bandana, by any chance?" Gabriel asked, trying to sound patient.

Beau's eyes went round. "Do you think he was the Green Terror?"

"Could've been," Gabriel said carefully.

Beau surged to his feet. "That green devil stole my house?" he bellowed.

"Hold on!" Benjie held up his hands. "We'll get it back for you. Don't you worry, Beau."

Gabriel hurried over to Apollo and pulled himself up into the saddle. "Maybe that damned idiot has gone back to Beau's house," he said to Benjie. "It's worth checking."

Benjie nodded. "I'll meet you back at the station. Don't worry, Beau," he called back. "You can go on back home whenever you like."

Gabriel urged Apollo into a gallop, and before long, he was back at Beau's cabin.

Smoke curled in the sky. He thundered into the yard and dismounted as fast as he could, rushing up to the cabin door. He kicked the door in, pistol out. But the cabin was once again empty. No sign of life except a dying fire in the hearth.

He ran outside and looked around, searching every corner, every inch of the little barn behind the cabin. Inside it, he found fresh manure. *Horses?* So, the Green Terror had horses of his own now. *But where'd he find them?* Perhaps bought them from natives? Horse thieves? Maybe even stolen them himself?

Gabriel ran a hand over his face, barely stifling a groan. *I need to get back to town.*

As he approached Miles City on Apollo, he saw clusters of people hurrying to and fro. Signs and banners were already erected for the upcoming fair. It would be the biggest even the town had ever seen, and folks from Elk Crossing would join in the festivities. Ma was always busy these days working on dresses for members of the Second Chance Club and a big quilt—some kind of quilting contest at the fair.

Gabriel headed back to his office first and told George and Hawkins about what he'd found. "He's on the move." He pounded is hand into his fist. "He's bound to pop up somewhere."

"Like a prairie dog," Hawkins supplied. Gabriel tried not to smile.

"Violet was over here earlier, lookin' for you," George said, folding his arms across his stomach as he set his feet on the desk. "Said to tell you to come home."

"Come home?" Gabriel echoed.

"She looked mighty pretty," Hawkins commented, and promptly turned beet red. He coughed, scratching the back of his neck, withering beneath Gabriel's hard look.

"Who looked pretty?" Benjie poked his head into the office. Beside him stood Beau. At Gabriel's raised eyebrows, Benjie explained. "When we catch that Green Terror and bring him to the circuit judge, Beau here says he ain't scared to testify against him."

"Violet told Gabriel to come home," George informed him, grinning.

Benjie chuckled and Gabriel scoffed, hurrying out the door. But inside, everything was tangled. His heart was racing, lodged in his mouth, almost.

What did Violet have to say? *Is this it?* The day she'd tell him she was finally done with their arrangement?

Finally, Apollo was freshly brushed and watered, and Gabriel was on the porch of his own cabin again. He pushed open the door, holding his breath. He expected to see Violet's carpet bag on the table, all her belongings around the cabin gone.

But everything was in its place, her Bible on the mantle, her smell still heavy in the air. It looked like a fresh batch of biscuits had just come out of the oven. "Violet?" he exhaled.

"I'm in here," she called out from her bedroom. She pushed aside the curtain in her doorway, and Hawkins was right. She did look very pretty. No…breathtaking. Her dark eyes shone in a comely way, her lips pinker than usual. Her dark hair, now shoulder length, curled around her cheeks charmingly.

Gabriel's throat suddenly felt tight. "Violet? What's the matter?" He removed his hat, setting it on the table.

Violet took a deep breath, crossing the room to stand right in front of him. "I wanted to apologize. For the things I said. The way I acted. You're right. I was terribly reckless to stay out late. I know you just meant to—to do your duty," and she smiled slightly, a bit sadly. "And also, I wanted to apologize for lying. About where I'm from. Who I am."

She closed her eyes, taking in a deep breath. "I'm not really from St. Louis. As you thought. I'm from—"

"Boston."

Violet's eyes flew open and she blinked, stunned. "How did you know?"

"The post boy," Gabriel admitted. "He was yapping about your letters from Boston the other day."

"Oh," Violet exhaled. Her cheeks darkened. "Well, I suppose you already knew that, then."

"I don't know why you left."

"You're probably wondering why someone like me is all the way out here."

"The question crossed my mind."

Violet bit her lip. "To be truthful, I'm sometimes not sure. All I knew when I decided to come out here was that I wanted to be a part of something bigger. Something good. And what better way to do that than teaching? I wanted to put my education to use. My parents went into enough debt as it was, sending me to the school they'd chosen, just because they wanted to tell their friends their daughter went there." She gave her head a little shake, lowering her eyes to the floor. "So, I went. It was dangerous, yes. But I'd still be back in Boston, married to—" She shuddered.

Gabriel ached to take her hand in his, pull her to him and kiss her. But he doubted she'd appreciate that. Especially after their last argument.

"What is it?" Violet was staring at him, frowning slightly.

"Do you intend to stay here?"

"If I do, will we remain married?"

Gabriel clenched his jaw. *What do you want, Violet? Do you want to remain married to me?*

Without even realizing what he was doing, he lifted his hand to her face. Her eyelashes fluttered against her cheekbones, her mouth falling open in a silent gasp.

"Violet," he began, and then he caught himself, and drew back. His face burned. "Biscuits for dinner tonight?"

Violet shook herself. "It's the only thing I know how to cook now—that, and flapjacks."

Gabriel's knees had gone to mush. He strode to the sink to wash his hands.

***

Two hours later, dinner was finished, and they were sitting together in front of the fireplace on a blanket spread on the floor. Gabriel wasn't sure how it had happened, but he did know that Violet's brown eyes were mesmerizing in the firelight. The glow of the flames gave her a pretty flush that made the string go taut deep down inside him.

She told him all about the fair that Ma's group would be putting on. He liked the way her voice lifted with excitement when she discussed it.

"Lou always loved attending things like fairs and circuses. She and I snuck off to one once. My parents were furious."

"Who is Lou?" he asked her, getting up to light his pipe.

"Lou is my friend. She was a servant in my parents' home, and she helped me to leave." Violet stared into the fire. "She wants to come see Miles City for herself."

"Do you miss her?"

The firelight danced across Violet's features. "Yes. Terribly."

"Well, if she does come out here, maybe she and Benjie would get on."

Violet giggled. "You think so?"

Gabriel couldn't help but laugh along with her. "I don't doubt it."

He lowered himself back down onto the blanket beside her, leaning back on one hand. He couldn't ignore the way that every muscle went tight whenever she was close to him, whenever her eyes curved into a bright smile and her fingers brushed against his on the blanket.

Violet seemed to have a fountain of things to say that night. She told him about more of her favorite books, about a writer named Mark Twain, and Dickens. "I met Charles Dickens once, when I was a child." She tilted her head, studying him. "What do you enjoy doing, besides being sheriff?"

"Riding," Gabriel murmured. "Riding is something that'll always put me at ease. And walking. Looking at the stars."

"The stars?"

"I looked up their names once. I even bought a small telescope."

"What happened to it?"

"My pa knocked it over."

Violet tucked her knees under her chin. "I remember. You said something about the stars…that first night."

"Did I?" Gabriel realized that he was smiling.

"You said you preferred to eat under them."

"I did," Gabriel chuckled.

His eyes flickered to her mouth before he could stop himself. Violet's dark eyes grew darker. Her face was so close to his. She didn't pull away, but instead stayed there, her fingers just barely brushing his.

"I'm sorry—about your parents."

Violet gave a smile that didn't quite reach her eyes. "It doesn't matter anymore. They can do what they like."

Gabriel winced. Here he was, dwelling on losing his father too soon, before ever getting to set things right. But Violet had been neglected by her parents, forced to play their little games, to marry. And she had run to freedom. But he had run the opposite direction, desperate to cling to a piece of his father.

***

The fair launched the next day. Gabriel told Hawkins, George, and Benjie to keep their eyes peeled. Hundreds of people came from the surrounding towns and farms, and Gabriel was restless, uncomfortable with crowds surging into the city for the contests, the food, the spectacles. How his mother and the others found enough money for this, he didn't know. It was more elaborate than he'd expected.

He spent the day watching, just watching, with his three men, but still there was no sign of trouble…no sign of the Green Terror.

"Gabriel?"

He turned to see Violet standing there next to a table full of lemonade, her expression curious. Behind her, couples whirled in a dance. From the looks of it, she'd been watching them.

She stepped closer and asked, "Do you want to dance with me?"

Dance? Gabriel blinked. He didn't know what to say. After a pause, he nodded. As soon as the next dance began, he walked with her to the area where couples were dancing. A reel started, and there was clapping and stomping of feet.

And then they began to dance. The rest of the world melted away as he watched Violet in his arms, saw her laugh, pressing her hand to the back of her eyes, her hair whipping against her cheeks as she circled around him in the dance, her hands in his. He accidentally brushed her hips once or twice, bringing his heart to a stuttering halt.

Once the reel finished, they began a slow dance to the tune of *Away, away, my heart's on fire.*

Violet's dark eyes sparked, her grip tightening subtly, and Gabriel couldn't tear his eyes from her, taking in every detail about her and memorizing it. Someday, when she was gone, he'd cherish this moment.

For the first time in a long time, he didn't feel so lonely.

And then she shifted closer, her eyes lowering to his mouth briefly.

Oh, Violet...

He clenched his teeth, holding himself back from kissing her.

"What are you waiting for?' she murmured, and then she'd raised on her tiptoes, pressed her lips to his. It all happened so fast, and bolts of lightning arced through him, making it impossible to think or breathe.

Her lips lingered against his for several echoing heartbeats, and he found her mouth softer than he'd imagined. She tasted better than he'd dreamed, and he had been dreaming of it every night.

"Violet…" He caught his breath. Her dark eyes were wide, her eyes searching him, pleading almost. He began to lean towards her, to kiss her again. He *needed* to kiss her again.

And then the moment shattered as gunfire rang through the air. Screams and cries echoed through the street, and Gabriel turned to see George tumble forward, his fiddle cracking as it hit the ground.

Chapter Nineteen

"Pick your bride, or your town. You can't have both!" A voice echoed loudly through the crowded streets, tinny and strange. It sounded as if it came from the building rooftops. Gooseflesh erupted on Violet's skin and she nearly pressed her face into Gabriel's chest. Her name? *Who's calling my name? Calling me his* bride?

Her stomach turned and she cast Gabriel a wild look. "What's happening?" *Is that the Green Terror?*

Gabriel grabbed her arm and they rushed towards Benjie, who was checking on George.

"How bad is it?" Gabriel breathed as Hawkins appeared, his face white.

"It's a surface wound. That's all," George wheezed. But his face glistened with sweat.

"Get him back to the office," Gabriel told Hawkins. To Benjie, he ordered, "Take Violet back to the farmhouse. Don't you leave her once."

Benjie grabbed Violet's arm and ran with her to Carol's wagon. Carol joined them, leaping into the bed, and Benjie turned to help Violet up into the seat.

Violet tried to pull away, but Benjie was much stronger, his hand like an iron clasp. "Gabriel knows how to look out for himself," he told her gently.

Violet bit down on her cheek, blinking back tears. *What about George?*

Finally, they reached Gabriel's farmhouse, and Benjie lifted her down from the wagon before turning to help Carol out of the wagon bed. "Get inside," he ordered. He was no longer cheery, joking Benjie, but instead grim, worried Benjie. The two women nodded and ran indoors, shutting the door and locking it.

Carol darted over to the window and peered out, her hand on her chest. The sound of thundering hooves filled the air. There was a shout of "Prairie fire!" Benjie had mounted his horse and was charging into a nearby field, echoing the cry: "Prairie fire!"

Violet's throat went dry, and she walked on shaky legs into her bedroom, sinking down onto the bed. Her vision blurred, her head swimming. *Where is Gabriel?*

Carol followed her.

"Bride? That man thinks I'm his bride?" Violet whispered.

"I think he's a little touched in the head." Carol grabbed her hand and gave it a squeeze. "Don't fret about him. He ain't going to live long enough to come within a yard of you. Not if Gabriel has anything to do with it."

Violet stared off out the window, watching the black smoke rising into the sky. "How many men do you think the Green Terror has with him?"

"There's no telling. By the looks of it, I'd say several."

Violet ground her teeth, closing her eyes. "You don't think he'd really try something like that?"

"Well, if he did, he'd be gone in one second flat. I think he knows it, too."

Violet sagged against Carol. "I know. But why?"

Carol smoothed Violet's mussed hair from her forehead.

"He's the kind that's always looking for something. Something better, bigger…"

"Ma?"

Gabriel's voice. Both women shot to their feet and darted out of Violet's bedroom.

Sure enough, he was standing in the doorway. Staring at Violet. Like he was drinking in the sight of her.

"Gabriel." Carol rushed over, touching his arm, and led him further inside the cabin. "What's the matter?

Gabriel sank into one of the chairs. "George. His back—it's bad." He rubbed at his face.

Not George! Violet batted back tears. "Where'd Benjie go?" she asked softly.

Gabriel looked grim. "Prairie fire, just north of here. We might need to evacuate if it gets worse." He rubbed his face in his hands. "I have to go. Stay here. Stay safe." He vanished out the door.

Violet turned and flew into her room, collapsing to the floor on weak knees. The thought of Gabriel getting shot like George made her heart pound into her throat. Made her shudder.

Soft footsteps sounded behind, and a gentle hand rested on her shoulder – Carol.

"How many do you think there are?" Violet whispered to Carol.

"There's no telling. Three, maybe four or five." Carol clucked her tongue. "But rest easy. Gabriel and his men will see to it that none of them come near you."

***

The next few hours dragged on, and Violet prayed for Gabriel's safe return. After what seemed like days, it was nightfall, and the only occupants of the cabin were still herself and Carol.

She couldn't eat, just pushed the food around on her plate. When they heard footsteps outside on the steps, both Violet and Carol sprang to their feet.

Benjie pushed open the door, stepping inside. The woman sank back into their seats.

"Well?" Carol asked softly.

"We couldn't ever get him," Benjie sighed. "Though we did put that fire out. He must've set it as a distraction."

Violet's mouth fell open. "You mean he's that close to Miles City? Or, he was?"

Benjie smiled wearily. "Don't worry, Violet. Ain't no one gonna take you again. Promise."

***

Carol slept on Gabriel's bed, and Violet slept on her own. Benjie took up a post outside. At some point that night, Gabriel returned. Violet wasn't sure what time, but when she opened her eyes, she caught a glimpse of Gabriel on the other side of the curtain, dozing in one of the chairs.

She scrambled to her feet, pulling on a shawl, and padded over to him. She touched him and he started awake, his blue eyes hazy with sleep. "Violet," he breathed. And he caught her hand in his, his grip warm and strong. "How are you?"

"I'm fine," she murmured. "Did you see the Green Terror? Did you catch him?"

"No. We didn't catch him. But we will. Soon." Gabriel smiled at her softly. "I've been thinking about you all day."

"You have?" Violet whispered.

He nodded. "About our dance…isn't it the strangest thing? We've been charging all over God's good earth searching for that devil…and all I can think about is—" He broke off, eyes flicking to her lips.

"I keep thinking about George," Violet confessed, her voice shaking. "I don't—"

He looked up at her with those deep blue-gray eyes, waiting, and something inside her fell to pieces.

She threw her arms around his neck and held him tightly. "Gabriel…I don't want you to die." Hot tears stung her eyes.

And then his arms were around her, and he was holding her, stroking her head, her hair, her back. "I swear to you that I'm not gonna die."

She drew back, sniffling, trying to bite back sobs. "How can you promise that?" she demanded softly, searching his face.

He brushed a thumb under her eye, wiping the tears away. "I can't die when I know you're waiting here for me."

And then he leaned up, cradled her face in his hand, and planted a soft kiss on her lips.

Violet's knees nearly buckled beneath her. *Oh, Gabriel…*

Then there was a scuffling sound outside, and Violet drew back. She was breathing heavily, her entire body trembling. "I should—I should go."

Gabriel nodded. His eyes were unbearably soft. "Get some sleep," he whispered.

And then she turned, rushing away from Gabriel, pushing the curtain closed. She sank on to her bed, collapsing sideways, hiding her hot face in her hands. She was dizzy, everything too warm, her skin burning where his lips had been.

***

It took hours of tossing and turning to fall asleep, worrying about Miles City, the townspeople, Carol, Martha and her family...*Gabriel.* When Violet woke again, it was already morning, and when she scrambled out of bed to peer out into the main room, her heart sank. Gabriel was gone.

Carol was at the stove, stirring eggs in a pan. Violet drew back, retreating into her room, her hands fluttering against her skirts. She was still wearing yesterday's clothes.

What would Carol say if she'd seen our moment in the kitchen last night?

She smoothed her hair and dress and stepped out into the room.

Carol turned, beaming, though it didn't quite reach her eyes. "Did you sleep well, dear?"

Violet nodded and gave a sigh.

"I'm so sorry about all of this," Carol said with a compassionate gaze. "But it won't be long now. And then his reign of terror will be over."

Violet joined her at the stove. "What's going to happen?" She hoped her face wasn't too flushed.

"A siege, maybe. Nobody comes or goes from Miles City until they find the Green Terror."

"Where's Gabriel?"

"He's out searching for any sign of the Green Terror. Benjie's out with him."

Violet twisted the fabric of her dress between her fingers, closing her eyes. This was insanity. Falling in love with Gabriel, hearing him promise he'd come back for her... *Lou would say it was just like one of our novels.*

What would she think of last night?

***

After breakfast, Violet wandered onto the porch for a breath of fresh air. She heard something crunch under her foot and looked down to see a piece of paper rolled up beneath her shoe.

Bending, she picked it up to unfurl it. In messy handwriting, a note had been written.

I wanted to pay respects to my lovely bride. Before long, we'll be sending the announcement to your mother and father back East. I'm sure they'll be happy to send a wedding gift.

The Green Terror

Violet dropped the piece of paper, her stomach and heart trading places. She stumbled backwards towards the door. "Carol!" she heard herself cry out. "Carol, come here!"

"What's the matter?" Carol's footsteps sounded on the floor. Violet glanced over her shoulder to see Carol stoop and pick up the note. Then her face drained of color, and she let out a cry. "This was on the porch?" she murmured.

Violet nodded. "I stepped on it. It was right by the door."

"He was here. Right here! What time could it have been?"

"I don't know." Violet tried to steady herself. "But he's somewhere nearby. Planning something."

She clambered to her feet, swaying slightly, and then rushed headlong into Carol's arms, dissolving into tears.

Carol stroked her hair and held her until she'd calmed herself. "He's not going to get you, dear."

"Why does he want me?" Violet choked.

"I'm not sure. To him, you're the fish that got away."

Violet closed her eyes tightly. "Maybe. But if he's just outside, nearby…are we supposed to just sit here and wait?"

Carol sighed. "There's not much else we can do."

She guided Violet inside, and they pushed a chair up to the door, securing the windows of the cabin. Violet sank into a chair at the table, pressing her clasped hands to her mouth.

Carol sat down beside her, grasping her hand firmly, her blue-gray eyes just as certain and steely as her son's. "The important thing now is to just stay calm," she murmured. "Don't you fret, now. We ain't gonna let anything happen to you. You hear?"

Violet nodded, taking in a deep breath. Carol was right. She needed to keep a level head. But all she wanted was to wake up from this terrible nightmare.

Perhaps I should have gone back east with the stagecoach.

But whenever she thought of leaving Miles City, her stomach knotted.

Carol let out a soft chuckle, shaking her head. "You know, I remember when Gabriel was about…oh, ten or so. He's always been careful, but he was bold when he needed to be.

And there was this kid here in town, a bully—he'd pick on the little girls, just to be cruel. And he was much larger than Gabriel, stronger. But that didn't stop Gabriel. He stood up to him, even though it meant he came home with his face all black and blue. I scolded him, and you know what he said? He said, 'Was I supposed to let those kids get hurt and just watch?' The boy's got a heart for justice. Just like his pa. He ain't gonna let the Green Terror escape, mark my words."

Violet's mouth twitched, even as her eyes blurred. "I just...I hope he doesn't get hurt. Maybe...maybe I should have gone back east. And then this wouldn't be happening. George wouldn't be shot, and I—I wouldn't be a burden to you or Gabriel."

"Oh, no, honey," Carol said immediately. "We were bound to reckon with the Green Terror sooner or later. May as well be sooner. Now, why don't you get some more rest? You look peaked." She brushed her thumb over Violet's cheekbones, just under her eyes.

Violet nodded, though she knew she'd probably just toss and turn instead of sleeping.

***

The sound of banging woke Violet with a gasp. She leapt off her bed and stumbled to the doorway to peek out. Carol was already at the door, her ear to the wall. She met Violet's eyes, her face white, her features taut. She held a finger to her lips before stealing over to where Violet hovered behind the doorframe in her room.

"Carol? You in there?" a familiar voice rang out.

Benjie. It was Benjie.

Violet nearly wept. Carol rushed over to the door and shoved the chair away before jerking the door open, and in came Benjie.

"What's happening out there?" Carol clutched Benjie's arm, her eyes wide.

"Gabriel and I parted ways, and he sent me back here to see after you two," Benjie explained. "He went back to town to check on George. The problem is that we don't know if it's just the Green Terror by himself, or if he's got men."

"We found this on the porch this morning." Violet picked up the scrap of paper off the table and handed it to Benjie.

His eyes went wide as he read it, and he shook his head slowly. "He must have been too afraid to try to get in here. Likely thought there was someone in here who could tan his hide."

"Oh, I certainly could." Carol's face darkened.

"I believe it, Mrs. Brooks," Benjie said seriously.

"How's George?" Violet whispered.

"He's gonna be alright. I'm sure the Doc and Martha are takin' good care of him."

Carol squeezed her eyes shut tightly. "Thank the Lord."

"And Gabriel?" Violet blurted.

"Like I said, I ain't seen him since we parted ways." Benjie offered Violet a comforting smile. "Don't you worry, ma'am. Ain't nothin' gonna happen to him."

Chapter Twenty

In just a few hours, Miles City had become a ghost town. Everyone else had bunkered down in their own homes and buildings. The fair had been completely abandoned. Even the tables of food still sat in the street, gathering flies.

Gabriel entered town via one of the side streets, hand on his holster, expecting bullets to whiz past him. But there'd been nothing but eerie silence to greet him. *Maybe the Green Terror retreated. Was he alone?*

He tied Apollo to the hitching post in the alley behind his office and crept up to the door with a rap.

The shuffle of footsteps within his office was just barely distinguishable, and then there was a low voice. "Who's there?" It was Hawkins.

"It's Sheriff Brooks," Gabriel whispered, glancing over his shoulder.

The door creaked open and Gabriel shoved his way in, pushing the door shut behind him. "How's George?" he asked Hawkins.

"Weak, but Doc says he's gonna be fine."

Gabriel exhaled deeply, closing his eyes. He stepped forward to peer into his office, where George lay in the cell. Martha, her husband Jeff, and their son sat in a line along the cell wall.

"Where's Benjie?" Hawkins whispered.

"Back at my cabin, with my ma and Violet."

"Do you think the Green Terror's got himself an army?" Hawkins sounded nervous, and the whites of his eyes were visible even in the dim lighting.

Gabriel glanced towards the cell as Martha stirred, clutching her young son in her arms tightly. He held a finger to his lips to remind Hawkins to keep quiet. "I don't know," he sighed.

He hated having to give that answer. The helplessness left him feeling like he'd been punched in the gut, and there was a chill creeping down his back. *How did everything go so wrong in just a matter of minutes?* One second, he'd been on top of the world, dancing with Violet, circling with her round and round. The next moment, chaos had erupted. This was the first time in hours he'd slowed down enough to think, to try to plan his next steps. He'd caught no glimpse of that Green Terror on his ride.

All he wanted right now was to return to his cabin to see to it that Violet and Ma remained safe. But his first duty was to the town, to keeping it safe.

Whatever happens, the Green Terror wasn't going to get his hands on Violet.

Would any of this have happened if Pa was sheriff? Gabriel didn't think so. He squeezed the bridge of his nose between thumb and forefinger, his head beginning to ache.

"Gabriel Brooks!" A hoarse voice rang through the air, bouncing off the walls of the alley behind the office, causing him to freeze. He exchanged looks with Hawkins before he stepped over to the back door, opening it just a crack. Nobody in sight. He opened it a bit more and stepped outside onto the step.

That Green Terror must be on the roof just above, watching like a hawk from his perch. That meant he had the high ground, and it would be difficult for Gabriel to sneak up there without being noticed. Not to mention, the Green Terror could have men everywhere, watching his every move. One wrong step and Gabriel could get a bullet through his skull.

"What do you want?" he bawled out, so loud that his lungs burned.

"I told you!" the Green Terror screamed back, his voice scratchy and fainter than before. "I want you to hand over that sweet little wife of yours. If you want your town to survive, that is."

"And what makes you think I'd hand her over? For all I know, it could just be you up there, all by yourself! I could come up there and put an end to you real quick!" Rage burned in the pit of Gabriel's stomach. If only he could get his hands around that greasy man's neck—!

"But you *don't* know it, do you? I could have your town surrounded. I could have your precious Miles City ablaze like that prairie in a matter of minutes!" There was a wheezing laugh. "But, alright, alright. I give you my *word*, as a gentleman. And I don't give my word to just anybody." More irritating laughter.

"Why should that mean anythin' to me?" Gabriel balled his hands into fists.

"I'm a good man, that's why! So good that I give you my word I won't touch your precious town if you hand over the pretty lady. But if you don't, Miles City will pay." His whoop split the still air.

Gabriel's chest burned. He gritted his teeth. "Go to hell!" he shouted.

"Just as soon as I get my bride! You have three days to do this the easy way—call your men off, hand her over, and I'll be out of your hair. Send her to the old Johnson mine in the Beartooth Hills. *Alone.* You have three days. Otherwise, I'll burn this place to the ground. And I don't aim to leave any survivors. " He cackled. "I might get impatient. So I'd hurry if I were you."

Gabriel could call his bluff, clamber to the roof and see for himself. Or, he could get himself shot and leave the town defenseless, leave Violet to the mercy of the Green Terror. He had to take this slow, be tactical about it.

"Fine!" he yelled up at the sky, feeling like he was making a deal with a devilish phantom.

He turned to see Jeff and Martha standing behind him, little Georgie in Jeff's arms, the daylight from outside illuminating their pale faces.

Closing the back office door, he walked past them to his desk, sinking down into his chair and running a trembling hand over his face.

"How's George?" he asked softly.

"Weak. Very weak," Martha replied. "But Doc got the bullet out of him—most of at least. He told us to watch out for fever—that can be a sign of infection."

Face pensive, she joined Jeff and Hawkins in front of Gabriel's desk.

"What do you plan to do?" Jeff asked. "You don't mean to hand her over, do you?"

"Of course not," Gabriel snapped. The others recoiled at his tone, and contrition washed over him, forming a lump in his throat. He tried to swallow. "I'm sorry."

Jeff shuffled his feet, clearing his throat. "No, no. Don't worry about it. I know you've got a lot on your plate."

"It sure was generous of him to give us three days," Martha remarked dryly, settling into the spare chair opposite Gabriel's desk. She rested her hand on her swollen belly.

Jeff stepped up to the desk, tapping his fingers on its surface. "Whatever you need, I can help. Hawkins and me, we can help."

Jeff was a notoriously bad shot. Still, he was brave. And Gabriel was down a deputy, and Benjie was tied up guarding his cabin.

So Gabriel managed a faint smile. "Thank you." He'd need to be careful to not raise the Green Terror's suspicions that he was planning something, lest the man decide to douse the rooftop in kerosene and send the town ablaze, or start shooting, trying to pick people off.

He pressed his forehead into his palm, closing his eyes. *What would Pa do?*

Pa wouldn't have this kind of problem to begin with. He would have caught that Green Terror long before this, come hell or high water. *No time for self-pity,* Gabriel told himself sternly.

"Do you think he knows where Violet is?" Martha spoke up, her voice loud in the silent room.

"I—I don't know," Gabriel whispered. *Keep a cool head.* A memory flickered through his mind—Pa training him how to hunt as a kid. They'd been out in the Gallatin forest and stumbled on a mama bear and her cubs. She'd begun to charge, swinging back and forth on all fours, dragging her claws through the dirt as she lumbered towards them, bared teeth glistening in the overhead sunlight. *Keep a cool head,* Pa had said. *No quick moves, or she'll charge.*

The Green Terror was the bear today. Any second, he could charge. He could order his men to start shooting. He could turn Miles City into a pile of ashes on the prairie. He'd already burnt up one of the large fields outside of town. *What's stopping him from killing every last soul to get what he wants? And why does he want Violet?*

White hot anger clenched like a fist around Gabriel's lungs, making it hard to breathe.

Someone rapped on the front door of the office, and he stiffened, lifting his head. Hawkins crept over to the door, calling out in a soft voice, "Who is it?"

"Thomas Lawrence."

Gabriel pushed back his desk chair, standing up and walking over to the window. He hugged the wall and peered out the glass pane. It was indeed Thomas Lawrence standing on the boardwalk.

Gabriel nodded at Hawkins, who pulled the door open, letting the mercantile owner stumble inside. He was pale as a sheet.

"I thought I told everyone to stay indoors," Gabriel muttered.

"I know, I know. But Sylvia is frantic. She wanted me to come down here and ask what you were planning to do." Thomas let out a shaky laugh. "We heard that man's request. Is it really the Green Terror?"

"Sounds like it."

"You think he's alone?"

"He could be. Or he could have fifty men surrounding the town."

"Wouldn't they have shot you earlier, when you was ridin' around?" Hawkins asked.

Gabriel shrugged. "Maybe the Green Terror wanted them to wait until he could bargain with me."

"And he wants your wife?" Thomas furrowed his brows.

Gabriel closed his eyes. "It sounds like it. He's out of his mind if he thinks I'm just going to give her to him."

"People are getting nervous." Thomas shoved his hands into his pockets. "We've got folks holed up in our store, and they're getting restless. If things don't turn around, there could be chaos."

"I know," Gabriel muttered. "Just go back and tell 'em to stay put. And you stay put, too, you hear?"

Thomas took a deep breath. "I should let you know...some of the men are talking about going out to your cabin and handing Violet over themselves. They...they just want to keep their families safe."

Gabriel rolled his jaw. "Tell them we have three days to decide what to do. He gave us his word."

"Mighty naïve of you, Sheriff," Thomas retorted. "He said he might get impatient. And we all know his word means nothing. Are we going to lose our homes, everything we care about, just so you can play the coward? I know she's your wife," he added hurriedly at Gabriel's hard look, "but she's not the only one in danger here."

Gabriel could kick something. He refrained from doing so, digging his nails into his palm. "We're not rushing this."

"But—"

"It's under control," Gabriel bit out. "Now, *go*."

Thomas's mouth thinned, but he dipped his head in assent. Hawkins opened the door just wide enough for him to slip through. Once he was gone and Hawkins shut the door again, the room fell dead silent.

Gabriel let out a deep breath. *Looks like I have less than three days to figure this out.* The last thing he needed was some idiot taking matters into his own hands and trying to hand over Violet in a desperate bid to be a hero.

I'll kill the man who tries. Ma and Violet would probably be horrified if they knew he was thinking in that way, but right now, he didn't particularly care.

He grimaced. *I've got to find out if the Green Terror is alone, or if he's got men to back him up.*

Martha and her husband exchanged glances. "Looks like Mile City's under siege," she murmured.

Her words caused Gabriel's stomach to weave itself into knots. *Under siege.*

He'd need to keep the townspeople calm, first and foremost. He couldn't have them riling each other up. He'd need to go and check on everyone, reassure them, tell them to lay low and not panic. Promise them he'd clean all of this up in no time at all.

But word spread like wildfire around here, and for all he knew, the whole of Miles City had heard of the Green Terror's threat. And he'd learned long ago that when people were scared, they were at their worst.

Chapter Twenty-One

Violet stared into the fire, Gabriel's handkerchief in her hand. The sky outside had just started to pale with dawn's early light. She twisted the handkerchief fabric around her fingers over and over again as she watched the flames dance and leap, pirouetting like blazing dancers at the circus. She kept replaying the words she'd read yesterday in the note from the porch, the taunting threat laced in those messily scribbled words.

Gabriel's bed creaked, and Violet turned her head, listening. Carol was sound asleep in Gabriel's room, probably turning over.

Benjie was dozing at the table, his head resting on his arms. Violet got to her feet and went to her room, picking up her Bible off her bedside table. She flipped to her favorite passage. *Yea, though I walk through the valley of the shadow of death, I will fear no evil...*

The words swam together, and she scooted backwards on her bed until she could lean back against the wall. *Is Gabriel injured? Is he safe?*

She pictured him in her mind's eye—just a boy, his face bruised after defending those little girls. Had he always been so serious, so dutiful? It sounded like it.

Will he always put duty above all else?

Her heart fluttered as she remembered the way he had gazed at her...that night, which seemed like days ago, right in the next room at the table, when his arms were around her. *If anything happens to him...*

A chill ran through her veins, leaving her with a sinking sense in her chest. She picked at the silk bookmark in her

Bible, chewing down on her lip so hard that she tasted the metallic tang of blood. *Where is he?*

Perhaps he'd found the Green Terror already, and was putting him into jail. Any minute now, he'd walk through the door and announce that the danger had passed. *Please, God, let this all be over soon...*

Another shudder ran through her as the Green Terror's raspy voice echoed in her head, the phantom-like way his voice had echoed through the streets after shooting George. The sight of George, eyes wide, plummeting forward, blood blossoming across his shirt.

Bile rose in Violet's throat, and she jumped off her bed, stumbling out of her room, running to the back door. She wrenched it open and leaned over the edge of the porch, emptying her stomach of the breakfast she'd picked over that morning.

Tears rose into her eyes. Then she felt gentle hands grasping her, pulling her back inside, Carol's voice in her ear.

It was already dark out, the sun just setting behind the horizon, and the cool breeze against Violet's fevered skin was refreshing.

She returned inside with Carol's arm around her shoulder to find Benjie already on his feet. He and Carol both looked half-awake but concerned.

"You alright, dear?" Carol asked, helping Violet over to the chair in front of the fireplace.

Violet nodded, lifting Gabriel's handkerchief to dab at her mouth, embarrassed to have succumbed to her nerves.

"You're shaking like a leaf," Carol sighed. "Why don't you lay down and get some rest? How long have you been up?"

"A couple of hours. I can't sleep," Violet murmured.

"Now, we can't have you falling ill, can we? You're terribly exhausted. And a little warm." Carol pressed her hand to Violet's forehead.

Violet nodded, tears leaking from the corners of her eyes no matter how much she willed them to stay put.

Benjie glanced aside, froze, and then dashed to the window. "Lanterns!"

Carol bustled over to him, peering out beside him. Violet's heart climbed into her throat as she gripped the handles of her chair. *Is it the Green Terror, coming to get me?*

Benjie pulled his pistol out of his holster, motioning for Carol to retreat into one of the bedrooms. Carol grabbed Violet's arm and drew her to her feet, walking her into Gabriel's room. It smelled strongly of leather and smoke, the scents Violet had come to associate with the sheriff.

"Oh, thank heavens," Benjie sighed from his station at the window. "It's just a couple of fellows from town. Hold on, I'll step outside." He pocketed his gun and unlatched the door, slipping out onto the porch. Violet hung in the bedroom doorway, clutching the doorjamb for support.

Carol pattered over to the window, peering out. "It's Thomas Lawrence, and...I think that's Doctor Johnson...and the blacksmith, Franz. Maybe they have news of Gabriel." She followed Benjie out on to the porch, leaving Violet alone in the cabin.

Taking a deep breath, Violet walked over to the window and peeked out. Benjie was talking to the three men, who were standing out there with their arms crossed. The lantern light glowed on their unsmiling faces. She heard her name float through the cracks in the door and hurried over, easing it open just a sliver.

"What are you talkin' about? You want me to hand Violet over? For *what?*" Benjie was demanding, his voice raising.

Thomas Lawrence sighed. "To save our families, our wives and children. The Green Terror threatened to burn Miles City to the ground if Gabriel doesn't hand her over within three days."

Violet's stomach dropped. She tightened her hold on the door to keep herself upright.

"We all heard him say it earlier," added Doctor Johnson. "People are going to get hurt if we don't do as he asks. He's got an army hiding everywhere, and it's only a matter of time before they start picking us off like varmints."

Benjie turned to exchange looks with Carol, and Violet stiffened when his eyes flickered back to the house. *Is he considering it? Will he hand me over?*

"How could you even *entertain* the idea of surrendering the girl to that beast?" Carol spat, marching down the porch steps to confront the visitors.

Franz Hansen held up his hands. "I know she's your daughter by marriage, Carol. But we got our own loved ones to think of. And the sheriff hasn't come up with a better plan yet. Seems like we've got to take matters into our own hands."

"That Green Terror is all bluster." Carol glared at them, her body taut with anger.

Violet nearly shrank back when Thomas's eyes flicked to the house, and his face darkened. "She's not one of us. She's an outsider. We got to stick together, protect each other. And if we wait too much longer, our homes and our livelihoods will be burnt down."

"Thomas Lawrence!" Carol stepped forward, grabbing him by the shirtfront. "Do you call raisin' your mercantile prices *sticking together?* You and Sylvia are always trying to gouge money out of the rest of us. And now you've got the *gall* to make this about protecting each other?"

"See here, Carol!" Thomas shook her hand off. "Your *husband* got himself killed in action, facing off those highwaymen terrorizing hero township a few years ago. He couldn't keep order in this town any better than your son! So you can't blame us for being worried. Times like these, we need to step up and make the tough decisions."

"This is just day one. There's still time, ain't there?" Benjie stepped forward, cutting between Carol and Thomas. "You fellows go back home, get some sleep, and do something actually useful. Help Gabriel in any way you can. But there ain't no way I'm letting you leave with Violet." He pulled out the gun from his holster on his hip, and Violet caught her breath.

"You ought to be ashamed, coming out here in the night to turn a young lady over to a criminal," Carol told them, the vitriol in her voice chilling.

I would hate to be on the receiving end of her wrath.

She kept at them, waving her hand. "Go home to your families. Worry about keeping *them* safe. Turning Violet over to the Green Terror won't accomplish anything. Behave like real men and help my son defend our town."

Violet backed away from the door and went to her room. She sank down onto her bed, clutching the mattress so tightly her hands ached.

What if the Green Terror got impatient and set Miles City ablaze early? What if he and his men descended upon Gabriel and the rest of the townsfolk?

She'd never be able to forgive herself if the people she'd come to love got injured—or even worse, killed.

She drew her knees to her chest, hugging them close. *I couldn't forgive myself...especially if Gabriel or Carol or Benjie got hurt because of me.*

Perhaps there was only one way out of this. And that would be to turn herself over to the Green Terror. She could spare Miles City from harm.

A few minutes later, the door creaked, and Carol and Benjie returned inside. They spoke in whispers, too quiet for Violet to hear even though she strained. She wouldn't be surprised if they agreed with Thomas Lawrence and the others. Carol loved her son fiercely, and Violet knew the woman would do anything to keep him safe. She had to be worried sick about him. And Benjie—this was his home too, and he had every right to want to protect it.

The real question was—did Gabriel want to acquiesce to the Green Terror's wishes? *It would make everything simpler for him.* If he delayed too much longer, his own people might turn on him.

The curtain hooks screeched as the cloth in her bedroom doorway was pushed aside. Violet lifted her eyes to see Carol standing there, watching her. Her brow was knitted. "Don't you pay those fellows no mind, you hear?" She walked over and sat down on the bed beside Violet.

Violet nodded, unable to speak.

"We ain't gonna let *nothin'* happen to you." In the dim, flickering firelight, Carol's eyes glistened. "I swear it."

"I don't want anyone to get hurt on account of me," Violet finally managed.

"Gabriel will think of a way around this. He's mighty good at that," Benjie said from the bedroom doorway. "Always has been."

Violet tried to smile but knew that the expression fell flat. "I should have left on that last stagecoach. Miles City wouldn't be in this situation if I had just gone." Her voice cracked and she lowered her face, burying it in her skirt.

"Shhhh, none of that! I for one am delighted that you stuck around. You're the daughter I never had." Carol wrapped her arm around Violet, and Violet nearly said aloud, *You're the mother I've always wanted. The mother I never got.*

"Now, you get some sleep. I for one am worn thin as a dishrag." Carol stood up, yawning. "Goodnight, dear."

"Get some rest," said Benjie with a small smile. Then he went back to the kitchen table. Carol followed him, but not before pausing and turning to smile at Violet. "I meant what I said, Violet."

Violet desperately wanted to believe her.

Chapter Twenty-Two

"George, you're in no condition to come!" Gabriel folded his arms across his chest, fighting an amused smile as he watched his deputy fasten his holster in place around his waist.

It was the first morning of the Green Terror's siege on Miles City. Gabriel needed to ride around, gather a group of men to face off with the Green Terror and his posse.

The only problem was George. He insisted that he could come along with Gabriel, Hawkins, and Jeff to help. But his face was pale and clammy. If it were anyone else, Gabriel wouldn't even consider allowing a wounded man to join them. But this was George. So, Gabriel had reason to hesitate.

As long as Gabriel had known him, George had been a formidable force of nature, stronger than an ox, stubborn as a mule. As steady and sure a shot as Pa. Gabriel sure could use him today to assemble a group, locate the Green Terror and his men, devise a defense plan. But it wouldn't be wise.

"Pa, you were just *shot!*" Martha sat up from where she'd been sleeping on the cot in the cell. Her father had given her the bed the night before, wincing as he took a seat on the floor outside the cell. It had not been a deep bullet wound, but it was still clearly painful.

"Course I'm going to go," George muttered, sliding his pistol into his holster.

"George..." Gabriel ran a hand over his face. "The best thing you can do is stay here and look after your daughter and grandson."

George scowled, but as he took a step towards the door, he winced again. His jaw tightened, and Gabriel watched as pain twisted his features.

"Stay," Gabriel repeated, walking over and setting his hands on his deputy's shoulders. "It's for your own good. And somebody needs to stay here, anyhow. Keep an eye on things."

"Keep an eye on things?" George scoffed.

"Just think of ridin' around. With that wound on your hip, it won't be pleasant a'tall," said Hawkins from his place next to the back door.

George scowled at him, waving his hand. "Fine," he huffed.

Martha rushed over to him, grabbing his arm. "Sit down, Pa. You're gonna pass out if you work yourself up." She guided him over to the desk chair where Gabriel had slept the entire night, helped him lower down onto it.

Gabriel grabbed his hat off the desk and joined Hawkins in front of the door. Jeff set down little Georgie and followed.

Gabriel kept his voice low as he gave instructions to George. "Keep an eye out for any strange activity or behavior. For all we know, the Green Terror could have friends laying low at the saloon. He could have people anywhere."

George nodded, his mouth a thin line.

"We'll be back tonight. After sunset," Gabriel promised.

Then Hawkins opened the back door, and the three men slipped out into the dark alley. The sun had not even risen yet, and they'd be able to escape town hopefully unnoticed under the cover of dark.

Gabriel mounted Apollo, settling his hat onto his head. Hawkins and Jeff trotted on foot alongside him towards the blacksmith shop, where several ready-to-sell horses waited. Their own mounts had run off after the madness at the fair, likely grazing in some field with wild horses.

The blacksmith Hansen was dozing in an empty stall full of hay, but he woke up when they approached. He held up his gun, aiming it at Hawkins. "Who goes there?"

"It's me, Sheriff Brooks," Gabriel called in a hushed tone. "And Hawkins and Woodard. We need to borrow a couple of your horses."

"What for?" Hansen's voice filled with suspicion.

Gabriel clenched his jaw. "We're going on a patrol. I want you to spread the word to all the men in the township. I want everyone gathered at my office tonight, after dusk, in my office. We need as many men as we can get."

Hansen nodded slowly, the lantern light bobbing across his face. "Saddles are in my storeroom," he told Hawkins and Jeff.

They vanished and reappeared with tack a few minutes later, hurrying to their new horses.

Apollo stamped impatiently as Gabriel waited atop him. His thoughts returned, not for the first time, to Violet. *Is she safe?*

He didn't miss Hansen's hard glare in his direction, and his stomach twisted with apprehension. He didn't need people turning on each other to save their own skin. They needed to unify against the threat. That was the only way to survive.

At last, Hawkins and Jeff's horses were ready, and they both mounted, urging their horses into the street to join Gabriel. Gabriel lifted his hand to touch the brim of his hat, a wordless thanks to Hansen, and then the three of them rode down the street towards the edge of town.

Gabriel held his breath as they approached the boarding house on the outskirts. It was dark and quiet for once—either everyone inside was still asleep, or they were cooped up in terror. The entire town was usually stirring at this point, but this morning, there was not a soul to be seen.

Gabriel half-expected a bullet to sing by his head, for the Green Terror or one of his men to take this opportunity. But then again, it was likely too dark for them to hit their mark. Finally, he and the other two men reached a crest overlooking Miles City, not too far from the town's cemetery. "First thing's first," Gabriel muttered. "We got to come up with a way to reach the roofs without him or his men knowing."

"I'll do it," Hawkins said breathlessly. "I'll climb up there from the south side of town. I'll get up on the church and—"

"No!" Gabriel waved his hand.

"Why not?" Hawkins's voice lifted in protest.

"I don't need nobody getting hurt."

"But—but I can do it! Really, I can!" Hawkins' voice cracked, and any other time it would have been humorous—but now Gabriel's patience slipped a notch further.

"Absolutely not, Hawkins."

"Sheriff Brooks—"

"Hawkins, either you shut up, or you go home. I don't need you whining right now. Nobody will be getting on the roof until we are sure of the best location, and the best time to do so. And it certainly won't be you going up there."

Hawkins deflated, his eyes flashing. "You know, you're a coward. You can sit thinking about the best way to do it all day, but ain't nothin' gonna be fixed if you keep waiting for the best time."

Gabriel stepped closer to the young man, glaring down at him. "I said, shut up, or go home. Pull yourself together, Hawkins."

Hawkins' face reddened, and he swallowed and nodded. "Yes sir," he whispered.

Gabriel drew in a deep breath. *Keep it together, Brooks.*

***

Gabriel kept his distance from his cabin that day, fearing that the Green Terror might track him straight to Violet. Instead, he focused on devising an ambush. He interviewed passersby to see if they'd noticed any suspicious activity. He sent Hawkins to scout for any signs of gathering forces…though deep down, he doubted it. For all he knew, the Green Terror could be acting entirely on his own. Reckless, taunting, enough to make Gabriel's blood boil.

For a moment, his concentration slipped, and the memory of Violet, her mouth against his, flickered through his mind. Then he shook his head. *Far too distracting.* He couldn't afford to lose focus.

Late afternoon, Gabriel wound up balanced on his heels, peering through the prairie grass at Miles City from his position at the bottom of the slope. Apollo grazed nearby, clearly grateful for the rest.

The odd thing was that he couldn't spot anybody on the rooves of the building at the moment—at least, not from where he stood. Either the Green Terror and his men had fled already, or they were hiding out somewhere nearby.

Gabriel began to calculate his next move. If he approached from the north side of town, he'd have some cover behind the church's brand new, white-painted steeple. Get a good view of the buildings running down the main street, and perhaps get an idea of where the Green Terror was.

"Sheriff," Hawkins called softly, urgency in his tone.

Gabriel turned, scrambling to his feet.

"Got some news, but you ain't gonna like it."

Gabriel's stomach knotted. "Go on."

"There's a group of men I just saw heading towards your place. Hansen and Lawrence are among them. About twenty or so fellows."

"What?" Gabriel tore past Hawkins. Swinging himself up into the saddle, he urged Apollo into a punishing pace across the fields, down the road, till he reached his farm. Hawkins barely managed to keep pace with him. Finally, he drew Apollo to a halt at the top of the hill overlooking his farm, and his stomach plunged into a pit as he took in the sight of the crowd in front of his cabin.

Swearing, he dug his heels into his horse's sides and flew down the hill.

There was no time to waste. He could hear the shouts from far off between Benjie and Thomas Lawrence, both red-faced and seconds from grappling. It was strange seeing the usually cheerful, unflappable Benjie so flustered.

As he came into the yard, he saw Violet, and his heart lurched. She was shrinking behind his mother and Benjie, her eyes huge in her small, pale face. He leapt off Apollo, stalking over to Hansen and Thomas Lawrence, who looked to be leading this little group. "What is going on?" he demanded, stepping in front of them.

"We've waited long enough, Brooks," Thomas Lawrence declared. "I'm not going to lose an entire store-full of surprise to that Green Terror's insanity. We are all not waiting on you to solve this."

Gabriel grabbed him by his fine silk shirtfront. "Go home," he told Lawrence in a low, shaking voice. *"Go."*

The mercantile owner tore his arm out of Gabriel's grip. "I've got a store-full back in town, and I don't aim to let it all go to ash!"

Gabriel gripped Lawrence's shirt harder, ready to thrust him into Apollo's water trough. He was clearly spiraling into full-on panic, yoking the others into his hysteria. "For all we know, the Green Terror is bluffing. He could set fire to the town anyway. He could have done it now. But if we hand him Violet, he'll—"

To Gabriel's exasperation, Hawkins started to tussle with one of the younger men in the group. Benjie stalked over and yanked him away by the back of his shirt.

"Gabriel." A small hand slid onto his arm, and it took a moment for his brain to catch up. He looked down into Violet's large brown eyes and saw her face. Pale, but drawn with resolution. "Gabriel, come inside. I need to talk to you." Time slowed. His pulse thudded heavily in his ears.

He forgot all about Lawrence for a brief moment, his attention caught by her warm skin against his. He gave a curt nod, trying to swallow. Then he turned to the men, seeing their wild eyes, their mouths flat with impatience. "Go back to town. And lay low, stay with your families. They need you."

"Don't tell me what my family needs," Lawrence bit out.

"I'm *telling* you not to use an innocent young woman as your bargaining chip."

Violet's hold on his arm tightened, as if warning him, steadying him. G took a deep breath. "Go," he repeated to the crowd.

Gabriel ordered Hawkins to return to town, get Jeff, and meet them here at the farm before dawn tomorrow. And then he let Violet lead him indoors, her touch sending a strange thrill through him. He came to a standstill in front of the fireplace.

Ma rushed up to him, grasping his arm. "You're not hurt, are you?"

"I'm fine," he reassured her. "Are the two of you alright?"

Benjie hurried in, shutting the door behind him and barring it with the broom. "Good thing you came when you did. Things was gettin' a bit out of hand there." He scowled. "That idiot Lawrence is riling the town up."

"This is the second time they've come out here to harass us," Ma added, "trying to turn Violet over to that devil."

Gabriel nearly groaned. Things were escalating quickly. And before long, he'd lose control of the town. There could be looting, a full-on shoot-out. *Or worse.* He could see it in the eyes of the men just outside his cabin door.

"Gabriel," Violet said breathlessly. She grabbed his arm, catching his attention, sending him into a daze. "I can turn myself over to the Green Terror."

HANNAH LEE DAVIS

Chapter Twenty-Three

Carol gasped, and Benjie gave a surprised sputter. But Gabriel...Gabriel stared at Violet, his face draining of color. Then he let out a dry, harsh laugh that caused her to draw back. *"What?"*

"I can turn myself in," Violet repeated, drawing herself up as far as she could. It was difficult, of course, since she happened to be short.

Gabriel's eyebrows lifted nearly into his hairline. "Violet, you—" He let out a soft chuckle that for sent a flare of anger through Violet.

"What, you don't think I can do anything but sit about and be pampered?" she whispered, trembling.

"Violet, what you're saying is—is crazy. It's not about that, anyhow—"

"Isn't it?" Violet's eyes blurred with tears. "He knows I come from money. My parents don't have any, but he doesn't have to know that. Use me to draw him out, and all of this can be put to rest."

"It's too dangerous." Gabriel's jaw tightened.

"No, it's dangerous to let this go on. And besides, it's the least I can do. After everything that you and your mother and the rest of the town have done for me...taking me in, after..." *After I realized I never had a family or a home in Boston.* She swallowed and went on. "He wouldn't really take me—or at least, not for long. You'd find me. Please, Gabriel. Otherwise, there will be madness."

Gabriel grimaced, pulling his gaze from hers. "I can't let you do that."

"I survived the Green Terror last time, didn't I?" Violet tried to laugh, to somehow lighten the mood. It didn't work. She turned to step towards the door, already prepared to call after the men, tell them they could take her to the Green Terror. But Gabriel grabbed her arm, giving her a slight shake and causing her to freeze.

"You can't," he insisted in a low, taut voice.

Violet jerked her arm away. "Yes, I can."

His whispered words came out in a rush. "I couldn't live with myself if something happened to you."

Violet drew back, her heart in her throat. "I don't want anyone getting hurt on account of me. Please, Gabriel. It's the least I can do. If the Green Terror sets fire to Miles City, it would be over. And—and you've spent your life here, losing your father to Miles City. And after all his hard work, and your hard work defending this town...for it all to go up in flames because of me? I couldn't live with *myself*."

Gabriel's eyes widened. He recoiled slightly, clearly stunned.

Violet stared at him pleadingly. "Please, Gabriel. Just...trust me. That's all I ask."

"So...you're thinking of using yourself as *bait*?"

Violet's heart lifted, even as her stomach turned into a small, hard knot. "Yes."

Gabriel gave his head a small shake.

She watched him insistently, hoped he could see that she was not to be swayed.

"Very well," he exhaled after a long beat.

"No!" Carol stepped between them. She grasped Gabriel by the arm. "You don't mean you're considering it?"

"She's right. We're running out of time, Ma, and—I'll make sure nothing happens to her."

"You can't be sure of that." Carol let out a humorless laugh. "And would the Green Terror even fall for it?"

"He's not in a right state of mind these days," Gabriel said slowly. "He's desperate, grasping at straws. We'll get him this time. And if we play this right, he won't even set hands on her."

Carol ran a hand over her face, letting out a shuddering breath. "She's going to get killed," she said in a shattered voice.

"Please, Carol," Violet pleaded. "It's the least I can do for Miles City. You have done so much for me, and I'd hate to see him burn down your shop, or the mercantile, or the new church. This is your home."

"And it's yours too, if you'll stop trying to get yourself killed!" Carol touched Violet's face, such a tender, motherly caress that Violet's throat closed.

"I'll be fine. I promise," she whispered, nearly choking.

Carol's eyes glistened, and she stepped back. "You've got your mind set on this, don't you?"

"I do." Violet let out a watery laugh. "I don't want anyone to get hurt. And, like I said, I made it out before alive."

Benjie cleared his throat, stepping towards them. "They're getting riled up out there. Talkin' of finding the Green Terror themselves."

"Tell them I'll go," Violet grasped Gabriel's hand, and a shiver ran through her as his large hand closed around hers.

He dipped his chin and turned. "I'll tell them we'll turn you over tomorrow morning. Tonight, we've got to come up with a plan. And another plan, if the first goes wrong."

Violet's stomach churned. *What if everything goes wrong? What if the Green Terror manages to get away with me?* She straightened her shoulders, clenching her jaw so hard it ached. *I'll make him regret it.*

Gabriel and Benjie stepped out onto the porch, and when the door clicked shut behind them, Carol grasped Violet firmly by the arms. "You don't have to do this. Nobody would blame you."

"I would blame *myself* if the Green Terror hurt someone because I was a coward."

Carol huffed. "You're anything but a coward, little lady."

"Thank you." Violet could hardly breathe. She and Carol crossed the room to look out the cabin window, where Gabriel and Benjie conversed with the crowd of men in heated voices.

Thomas Lawrence muttered something, prompting Gabriel to bark out, "Tomorrow morning." Thomas flinched, and Violet couldn't help but giggle, earning an amused glance from Carol.

Gabriel was certainly good at putting people in their place. Despite his quiet demeanor, he could have a voice of steel when he needed to.

A few minutes later, the last of the posse had cleared out, and Gabriel and Benjie returned inside the cabin.

Then Violet remembered the Green Terror's letter. She darted into her room to grab it, and came back to where he stood. He was leaning against the mantle, staring into the fire.

She quietly approached him, said his name in a soft voice. "Gabriel, we found this." She pressed it into his hand, the rough callouses on his fingers sending shivers through her.

Gabriel blinked, as if coming out of a daze. He frowned at the paper in his hand as he unfurled it. Read it, and then crumpled it up, swearing under his breath. "Of course he knows where you live," he muttered. "This is all a game to him."

"Then let's play his game." Violet stepped even closer, so close that she could see the faint scattering of freckles on his nose and cheekbones, the curl of his light eyelashes. The way his throat moved up and down.

Benjie sat down at the kitchen table. "I say we let him think Violet's all alone. Then, when he's running off with her, we grab him."

"I just don't want him or his men to do something desperate, like kill—" Gabriel abruptly cut himself off, casting his eyes to the floor. The room fell silent, and Violet's heart sank like a stone in water.

Like kill me. She internally finished Gabriel's sentence. *Which could very well happen. I could be killed tomorrow morning. The Green Terror could slice my throat, like that wicked Frenchman Blandois in* Little Dorrit.

Carol joined Benjie at the table slowly, and lowered her face into her hands.

"We need to make him think he's got her," Benjie said quietly.

"And what if you lose him?" Carol demanded, slamming her hand on the table. "What if you do? What then? You've lost Violet, and when he finds that her family isn't good for the money—"

"He *won't*," Gabriel insisted. "I'll track him, and Hawkins and Benjie and any volunteers will ambush him and whoever's with him. But we'll be careful, so the Green Terror doesn't suspect a thing. That way he doesn't get jumpy and do something desperate."

Violet glanced out the window and caught her breath. It was already dark out. She probably wouldn't get a bit of sleep tonight. She was restless as it was, trying to not pace back and forth across the cabin. But a little bit of her could relax, now that she knew Gabriel was safe, at least.

"Are you returnin' to the office?" Benjie asked.

Gabriel shook his head. "Not tonight. We'll leave tomorrow soon as the sun rises."

"Well in the meantime, you all need to get something in your stomachs," Carol said. "I'm thinkin' fried chicken and buttermilk biscuits."

"I'll go get a chicken or two, Mrs. B." Benjie smiled, though it didn't quite reach his eyes. He placed his hat back on and strode out towards the chicken coop.

"I'll come with you to show you the one I've got my eye on."

And suddenly, Violet was alone again with Gabriel, for the first time in over a day.

"Violet..."

Her body went stiff as he stepped closer to her, bringing a hand up to cup her cheek. "You don't have to do this. We can think of another way," he whispered.

"There's no time for that," she whispered. "They're going to turn on you if you don't act soon." In his eyes, she could see he agreed with her. She managed a shaky smile. "Don't worry about me, Gabriel. I beg you. Don't."

"I can't help it." His voice was hoarse, barely audible.

Then he leaned down suddenly and kissed her, a soft peck that sent her heart racing. A moment later, he pulled away.

"I worry about you too, you know," Violet blurted. "I've been terrified you've been hurt. I haven't been able to sleep."

"I know," he murmured, his eyes darkening. "Believe me, I know. But I'll be sure you make it out of this just fine. I swear that man won't hurt you." His tone was vehement.

Violet knew that he meant every word. He couldn't really promise that, of course...but her heart ached at his surety, the desperate, trembling resolution in his features.

"Thank you," she whispered.

The back door opened, and Carol and Benjie returned with a headless, mostly de-feathered chicken.

Gabriel pulled away from Violet and walked over to the mantle to lean against it. Violet's face burned and she hurried over to the sink to distract herself, washing up so she could help Carol with dinner.

She scrubbed her hands as Carol chattered blithely in an attempt to break the somber mood. But she was only half-listening, trying to pick up on Gabriel as he spoke to Benjie in a low tone.

"I don't think the Green Terror has anybody fighting with him. I think it's just him, all by himself," Gabriel murmured. Violet glanced over her shoulder cautiously, observing.

Benjie nodded, rubbing his neck thoughtfully. "If that's true, it'll make things easy. But if it's not...?"

"His men all turned on him months ago," Gabriel argued. "Unless he's bribed them back, I doubt they'd help him ambush Miles City for the heck of it."

"'Course," Benjie agreed.

Please let Gabriel be right. Violet realized her hands were shaking. *Please let it just be the Green Terror by himself. He won't stand a chance alone.*

A voice taunted her. *It's very likely I don't stand a chance.*

"You ought to lay down, get some rest." Carol's gentle voice sent Violet's dark thoughts scattering.

She gulped and shook her head. "I want to help," she insisted.

Carol nodded, the cornering of her mouth curling up. "If you're worried about betterin' your cookin', you don't need to worry. You've been improvin' by leaps and bounds."

Violet couldn't help the laugh that bubbled up in her throat. "Thank you."

"Now, you can go ahead and finish up plucking that bird. And I'll mix up the batter."

Chapter Twenty-Four

After a hearty dinner of fried chicken and biscuits, the evening ended quietly, a welcome respite from the exhausting day.

Gabriel drew on his pipe, leaning against the supporting porch beam as he watched Violet entered the barn. She approached Apollo's stall and stroked the horse's forehead, scratching under his chin, just the way he liked it.

Perhaps she'd like a horse of her own. Gabriel pulled his pipe from between his lips, breathing out a puff of smoke.

"She's a magnificent girl, ain't she?" Ma commented behind him.

He stiffened, his face heating. Unable to find the words, he placed his pipe back in his mouth and took another puff.

Ma stepped up beside him, leaning against the neighboring beam. "Why don't you just ask her to stay for good?" she asked softly.

Gabriel shot her a hard look. "Ma..."

"You love her, and she loves you. It's simple."

"She doesn't—" he sputtered. "She doesn't *love* me. She cares for me, and that's enough."

Ma let out a soft laugh. "You know what I think? I think you're afraid to let her in."

Gabriel blinked. He truly did wish he could believe his mother. Wished he could read more into Violet's looks, the words she spoke. What she'd said about wanting to save Miles City...he could see she meant it. *But that doesn't mean...*and regardless...it didn't matter. All that mattered now was that he wasn't going to let the Green Terror take even one step with Violet in his grasp.

The door squeaked on the hinges behind him. Ma had returned inside. With a deep breath, Gabriel climbed down the porch steps and crossed the yard to pause in the barn door. He lingered there, watching Violet feed some oats to Apollo from his feed bucket. Her short, dark hair tumbled loosely down to her shoulders. She was talking to Apollo, asking him how he liked his food in a sing-songy voice that was nothing but charming.

Gabriel cleared his throat, shifting his weight from one foot to the other, and Violet turned, startled.

"Oh, good evening," she smiled softly. Her eyes were somber, though. She seemed years older than she had just a few days ago.

Gabriel smothered his pipe and set it down on the edge of a stall door. He joined her in front of Apollo, managing a smile of his own. "How are you?" he asked in an undertone.

"I'm fine." She let out a quiet, humorless laugh. "I just wish it was tomorrow morning already."

"I'm glad it isn't." Gabriel dug his boot through the dirt.

They both fell silent for a few long moments before Violet spoke up again. "I feel as though I've caused you and everyone here nothing but trouble, since the second I arrived."

"Violet, don't think of yourself that way," he said softly. "Please. You shouldn't."

She swallowed. "I can't help it."

He grasped her hand, drawing her closer to him. His heart lodged in his throat, mouth dry. "Let me figure out another way," he whispered. "I will. And you don't have to do this."

"I know. But...I feel as though I should." She stared back at him, that same resolute look from earlier appearing in her face.

He squeezed his eyes shut. "Let's go for a walk. You've been cooped up in here for days."

Violet's eyes widened, and then she nodded. "I'd love to."

***

They only went a short way, to Gabriel's favorite field on his farm. It rose steeply to a grassy crest in one corner. It was the perfect place to see the distant hills, and Gabriel would often retreat out there.

Now, he sat beside Violet in the tall grasses, gazing down at the cabin they shared, its lights twinkling like a firefly hovering in the field.

Violet leaned back on her arms, and he gazed at her. Her profile was mesmerizing, from her porcelain skin to those fathomless eyes that took his breath away.

"Do you miss it? Boston?" he asked, reluctantly drawing his gaze from her to stare at the cabin.

To his surprise, Violet shook her head. "Not one bit."

"What was it like?"

Violet thought for a long moment before answering. "It was a gilded cage. It was like being a doll in a display. I was just there to...be what my parents needed."

"I'm sorry."

"Don't be. I just wish I'd left much sooner than I did."

"Do you know if your parents are lookin' for you?"

"They aren't." Violet's smile turned sad, and anger bubbled in Gabriel's stomach. "At least, I don't think they are. Lou tells me they're separated. My mother ran to Cape Cod, and Father went to New York." She frowned down into her lap. "But they're no different from most other socialites in Boston. People like my parents are all about appearances. But behind closed doors, it's a different matter."

Her shoulders were tense, her teeth digging into her bottom lip.

"You don't have to speak of it if you'd rather not," he said softly.

She looked up at him quickly. "I want to. I don't know why, but ever since I met you…I felt deep down that I could trust you."

"You can," Gabriel said quietly. "You can trust me."

Violet plucked a blade of grass and began to play with it, rolling it between her fingertips. "I must have been a sight that day." She giggled, a musical sound.

Gabriel couldn't help but smile. "You were."

Violet gave yelp. She swatted his arm lightly, and the two of them dissolved into laughter. He meant it, though. She'd been dazzling, ever since that first night she ran headlong into his arms.

Once their laughter subsided, Violet snapped the blade of grass in two. "My parents married young—my mother always said that they rushed into it. Her family wanted her to snatch up my father, because he was a Boston Thompson."

Gabriel frowned in bewilderment, and Violet must have noticed. "His family is nearly as big as the Cabots," she attempted to explain, but that only confused him further.

She turned her head as if to hide a smile. "Well, let's just say that they're a prestigious family in New England. My mother's family thought the Thompsons were made of money, and it turned out that the Thompsons held a similar belief about my mother's family. And when they learned that they'd made a mistake and married their son to a girl with only her name but no fortune, they were furious."

Violet plucked another blade of grass and fidgeted with it. "Because they disapproved of my mother, my father didn't get as large a portion of his grandfather's fortune as he'd hoped. I think he resents my mother for it. It really was all just a silly misunderstanding." Her tone hardened, and she shook her head. "All they did was fight about money. I became their hope to secure a better fortune."

She closed her eyes, scoffing. "Then, they tried to marry me off. And I refused." She opened her eyes and gazed at Gabriel, sorrow written vividly across her features in the pale dusk.

"Why?"

"Do you remember me...ah...accusing you of being with that saloon girl?"

Gabriel winced, nodding. "I seem to recall it." He managed a small smile.

"I followed my would-be suitor to a brothel. He didn't know. But I—I watched him go in. It was just hours after he'd been in my parlor, courting me, telling me how I had his whole heart. It was all just...talk. He didn't really care about anyone but himself. My—my father enjoyed visiting those places as well. My mother hated it."

Gabriel could sympathize. His own father had played the hero to a dozen damsels in distress, all in the name of acting as sheriff of Miles City. And it had hurt Ma deeply. "To tell you the truth, I despise those places," he sighed.

"You do?" Violet's eyes glistened in the fading light of sunset.

"Always have. My pa..." Gabriel's gut twisted. "He visited them, too. Or at least, to act as if he was protecting them. And sure, he was helping them. But he was just...lying to himself about *why* he was doing it. He and my ma fought. It was always strained. Over how much he worked, how being a sheriff was his everything."

To his surprise, Violet reached over and grasped his hand in hers tightly. "It appears that our families are more similar than we thought."

Gabriel chuckled, blinking away the dampness in his eyes. *For heaven's sake.* He detested crying. He'd rather remain numb.

But something about Violet left him raw, cut wide open. She got under his skin somehow, past all his barriers. He lifted her hand to his lips and kissed it, a silly impulse. "Thank you."

Her eyes widened. His face warmed and he released her hand, but to his relief, she laughed again, and he watched her as the sun finally dropped below the horizon.

Please, let this not be our last time together...

***

The next morning, Gabriel and Benjie readied their horses while Carol and Violet stood nearby, saying goodbye. Out of the corner of his eye, Gabriel watched Ma take Violet's hands in hers. "I'll be prayin' for you, dear," he heard her say tearfully. "The good Lord will be watchin' over you."

"Thank you, Carol." Violet hugged her. Gabriel checked Apollo's girth and then pulled himself into his saddle, and Benjie mounted his own horse. Hawkins and Jeff and hopefully a few others should be here any minute, and then they'd decide where everyone should be stationed for the next part of the plan.

Then Gabriel called to Violet, holding out a hand. She took his hand in hers and he pulled her up behind him into the saddle. *Just like the night we met.* She grasped onto his shirt before winding her arms around him, and he forgot how to breathe for a moment.

Ma wiped her eyes and hurried over to the barn door. "Looks like Hawkins and Jeff gathered a small army," she chuckled.

Gabriel steered Apollo into the yard, Benjie following suit. Hawkins waved from the road, cantering up to greet them. "We got plenty of volunteers for this."

"Good. We'll need them to lay low while Violet meets the Green Terror. I'll send Benjie as a relay to let everyone know what direction they're headed."

"Yes, sir," Hawkins cried. He didn't even bother hiding his exhilaration. Gabriel nearly rolled his eyes.

Well, the kid did as he'd been asked. He'd brought more men than Gabriel had expected, to say the least.

Gabriel snapped his reins, nudging Apollo into motion, and he and Violet cantered down the road towards the hills. Benjie rode alongside them.

They entered the thick woods clustered at the base of the Beartooth Hills and began winding up the switchback trails of a hill that Gabriel had known since boyhood. It overlooked the entrance of the Johnson silver mine. The hill afforded them a clear view of that entrance, even from this distance across the gulley. Gabriel would just have to hope they didn't run into any of the Green Terror's men along the way.

It was rough territory out there, with lots of big boulders and high grass, tree roots jutting out everywhere they looked. A beautiful fertile country that Gabriel had once loved to wander through. But today, every sound sent his heart racing, his head turning; he expected to see the Green Terror's men waiting to attack around every bend in the road. Even the birdsong overhead couldn't be trusted – the Green Terror had been known to use birdcalls as signals during his stagecoach robbing days.

Finally, they reached the crest of the hill. Gabriel and Benjie dismounted first, and Gabriel lifted Violet to the ground.

Benjie's eyes met his, and a silent understanding passed between them. Benjie turned, walking a yard away to survey the town.

Then Gabriel gathered Violet into his arms tightly, breath catching in his throat. *Thank you, Benjie.*

He drew back slightly. "You don't have to do this," he told her for what felt like the hundredth time.

"I want to, Gabriel."

"Let's get going before it gets too light out," Benjie called quietly. "Don't want the Green Terror mad as a hornet about us not following his *stupid* rules."

Violet lifted her chin, her eyes flashing, and she began to descend the slope towards the entrance of the mine. Halfway down, she paused and turned, and Gabriel's throat closed. Her glance said a world of things, and the ground fell away from his feet. He tried to keep his breathing as he locked eyes with her.

Then she turned back and kept going. Gabriel traced her steps the entire way across the gulley.

This was wrong, all wrong. *She shouldn't be doing this...I shouldn't be letting her.* But deep down, he knew that if he'd refused, she would have tried anyway. She was delightfully stubborn. At least this way, he could do everything in his power to be sure it would go the way he needed.

She faded into the trees, and a chill ran down Gabriel's spine. Mouth dry, he kept his eyes glued on the mine entrance. Finally, he spotted her again. "There," he whispered to Benjie. "There she is."

Benjie let out a soft whistle of relief.

Part one of the plan done. Now for part two.

Squinting, Gabriel watched as Violet stopped at the mine entrance, a small, bright figure in stark relief against the dark, gaping tunnel mouth behind her.

He didn't dare blink. The Green Terror could whisk her away in a mere second, and he couldn't lose track of them.

Gabriel doubted the man was staying in this mine. He was wiser than to corner himself. He must have chosen the place only because it was a well-known but remote site outside of Miles City.

Then a man emerged from the cave's shadows, prowling around Violet. Gabriel's chest went tight. "There—there he is!" he breathed

The man grabbed Violet roughly. Gabriel ground his teeth together as her shriek echoed off the surrounding hills.

And then the Green Terror screamed "Quiet!" and slapped Violet across the face, so hard that it sent her to the ground, a small, motionless heap. Gabriel saw red. He surged to his feet, lunging forwards to run across the gulley. He'd beat that bastard senseless.

But Benjie grabbed him. "He'll kill her if sees you, or even hears you," he hissed.

Chapter Twenty-Five

Violet stiffened her muscles as Hank held her tight. His breath reeked of whiskey, just like last time. If she wasn't pretending to be knocked unconscious, she'd retch.

Hank kept muttering to himself, all kind of foul things, rambling on nonsensically. *He's out of his mind.*

"Wake up, you little—" he wheezed, nearly stumbling as he tried to heave her down the steep incline, deeper into the gulley. Somewhere in the distance, she thought she could hear footsteps, the rustle of leaves, just barely audible over the birdsong lifting around them.

Hank paused and knelt, easing her onto his back as best he could, draping Violet over his shoulder like a rag doll. She couldn't help but smile into his greasy shirt. She'd make this as cumbersome for him as possible.

Finally he stopped, cursing again, dropping to his knees. Then he began to cough violently, letting Violet crash to the ground with a thud. She nearly cried out as sharp pain shot through her arm and up her shoulder. The forest floor might be thick with leaves and pine needles, but not soft enough to cushion her landing. She gritted her teeth to keep from moaning.

"Just a little further…and…I'll be in hearin' distance of Jake soon." Hank's voice was faint through her haze of pain.

Jake? Who is Jake?

Hank began to cackle again. He hauled Violet back up onto his shoulder, and his dirty nails dug into her wrist, trapping her in place.

He went on, still muttering to himself, weaving slightly, as if he was growing weary. Each step he took sent more pain arcing through her. They went on about another mile like that, Hank plodding along at a grueling pace. Finally, he stopped. "Oh, to hell with it." He gave a shrill whistle. A signal of some kind..

A signal for what? What does he want Jake to do?

Hank's wheeze turned into guttural coughs, and it sounded like he was about to hack up his lungs. He began spitting onto the ground again, and Violet's stomach turned as she smelled blood.

When the coughing passed, he paused and sent out a series of short whistles that sounded remarkably like a bird chirruping. Somewhere, far away, Violet heard someone whistle in reply, the exact same way Hank had done.

He chuckled. "Now, you and me, we're gonna go make ourselves a nice little home." Violet almost cringed. Apparently, he seemed to be addressing her, even though she was supposedly unconscious. "And your me and pa are going to send their daughter and her new husband a bit of money. A little wedding present."

She blinked again, her vision growing hazy, blurry. *Oh, no. What's happening?*

I'm passing out, she realized, as the world plunged into darkness. *Blasted arm.*

***

Lou—Lou hovered over her, smiling. Violet couldn't count how many mornings she'd woken up to the sigh of Lou's grin, her green eyes crinkling as she told Violet, *Good morning, ma'am.* And this morning was no different. Violet stretched, the room hazy and warm, the bed beneath her soft, but somehow damp.

And then the door opened, and in strode Mother, her face smothered in rouge, her lips smeared with bright lipstick. She jerked the curtains open. "Today is your wedding day," she cried, whirling to face Violet.

Then Mother's face morphed into Hank's, and Violet's heart dropped.

She blinked rapidly, trying to scramble backwards. The bedroom faded around her, replaced by darkness—plain darkness, a clammy heaviness in the air. She must be in a cave. When she moved her uninjured arm, her fingertips brushed a heap of wet, damp blankets. It smelled of rot in there.

Beside her sat Hank, his face shiny with sweat and wan, blood staining his lips as he held a lantern up to study her.

"Well, good morning, sweetheart," he smirked. "We had to go underground for a bit. We were bein' followed."

Violet tried to swallow, but her throat was tight, like something had gotten stuck in it, and her head whirled too fast. A greasy piece of cloth was wound about her shoulder, haphazardly supporting her injured arm. Hank's bandanna.

"Get up," he hissed, looming over her. He reached down and grabbed her by her wounded arm, and black spots exploded in her vision. "We can't stick around here all day." And then his voice turned sweet. Saccharine sweet. "Don't want to miss our wedding day, do we?"

Violet shook her head, biting down on her tongue. *Stay calm. Whatever you do, stay calm.* The thought floated through her head in Gabriel's voice, low and reassuring. Tears stung behind her eyes. *What if I never see him again...?*

"What time is it?" she stammered. "And—and where are we?"

"No questions," Hank spat. "We're gonna wait in here for a little while your friends are distracted. And then we'll get started again."

"Distracted? What do you mean?" A chill ran through her.

Hank grabbed her face so tightly that she nearly cried out, but she swallowed it back for fear of being hit again.

"I said, no questions," he whispered. And then he lunged away from her. "Get up. We've got to get moving soon, or that sheriff is gonna try to find us again. He already did, but that nearly got *you* killed."

"Gabriel," Violet whispered. Hank stalked back over to her, jerking her to her feet. And he traced his finger over a tender spot on her neck that made her flinch.

"It's all burned down. Down...down...down," he ranted, grinning wide. *"It's all burned down."*

He continued chanting it, over and over, until Violet spat at him, right in his blood-shot eyes. He sent her sprawling again, and again the world faded away into the ether.

***

She was draped on a horse when she woke up. Her body was bent at an uncomfortable angle across the saddle, and her face bumping into the horse's lathered side. The air was still heavy and clammy, and there was nothing but dead silence all around. She could hear her own heartbeat over the jangle of the horse's reins and Hank's wheezing.

Violet didn't dare move. Hank might notice and knock her unconscious once again, and after that happened enough times, she might never wake up again. And she needed to remain as clear-headed as possible. At least, as much as her throbbing arm would allow. Her eyes stung, salt mixing with that tang of blood on her tongue as she listened to the creak of leather, the clip of the horse's hooves.

Where is Gabriel? A hopeless pit yawned inside her.

Hank had chosen a cavernous route to wherever he intended to take her. And it was clear he knew it like the back of his hand down here. *What if Gabriel never manages to find me?* She quietly inhaled and exhaled, trying calm herself. One of the stirrups spun into her eye, and she gulped down another cry.

Hank began to hum softly in a horrible nasal voice. Violet shuddered. The man did not have an ear for music.

The minutes turned to hours, and the hours into day. And she had no idea how much time had really passed, down here in the depths of hades, this damp, dripping cavern, as silent as she imagined the catacombs under Paris would be. She'd been fascinated reading about those as a girl, but this was nothing beyond horrifying.

The horse stumbled, jarring Violet from her haze. She nearly slipped off the saddle, and above her, Hank let loose a string of expletives. "This just ain't my day, now, is it? Here, there's a nice little pond just ahead for you to drink." He wheezed, slapping the horse's rump.

At last, the swaying motion stopped, and Violet listened, her dry mouth aching, as the horse lapped at water.

"Guess we'll set up camp here now." And Hank grabbed her by the waist, pulling her off the saddle and hauling her down like she was nothing more than a bag of flour, sitting her against a wet wall. Jagged rocks dug into her cheek as she slumped over, the eerie silence around them swallowing her whole.

"Ain't she pretty?" Hank seemed to address the horse drinking water nearby. He brushed his hand against Violet's face, and she barely stopped herself from jerking her head away. A shudder went down her spine.

Hank released Violet and limped away, slumping down beside the lantern he'd been carrying. This must be his haunt, his refuge. He kept right on rambling. "No matter what, she'll fetch a fair price, whether that's from her parents or any lucky fellow who might want her for a night."

Violent went stiff and cold with horror. *Does he mean...?*

Bile rose in her throat. *He can't mean that. He just can't.* A scream burnt in her chest, and she dug her fingernails into her palm. Sobs bubbled in her throat, and her body began to tremble. She'd never felt this kind of paralyzing fear before, not even the first time he'd kidnapped her. This was a whole new kind of dread, a realization that the man beside her was not only a lunatic, but an evil wretch as well. *Gabriel, please find me...*

A fist closed around her throat, and she squeezed her eyes shut. *Please find me...before you lose me forever.*

Chapter Twenty-Six

Hank kept cackling to himself, imagining Miles City burning to the ground. That Sheriff Brooks was likely losing his mind over it, too. *The fool.* And he thought he'd be able to pull a fast one on Hank Logan. Well, he'd certainly learned better. Learned that he shouldn't test the Green Terror. *If he persisted, he would have had to watch me bury my knife in the pretty little lady's throat.*

That also earned a throaty chuckle from Hank. He shook his head as he sat back, listening to the repetitive *drip* of water on the stony floor, the echoes that resounded with every scrape of his shoe, every rasp he took. The humid air around him seemed to swallow all sound, muffling it strangely.

He knew this cave system as well as his blood knew the veins in his arm. Sheriff Brooks would never find him. There were paths in here that led all over the Beartooth hills. He'd just wait it out until the coast was clear.

Jake, the old devil, was probably long gone before the sheriff ever reached town. He'd been all too eager to accept the silver in exchange for waiting for Hank's cue to burn down Miles City.

Hank cackled again. He'd never forget the sheriff's expression when he'd gathered Violet into his arms, teasing the blade against her soft neck.

"The sheriff takin' orders from little old me," Hank snickered. "Imagine."

Where do I want to go? Denver? Once we're there, the girl will telegraph her parents, and they'll wire that money just as smart as you please. And if they don't pay, she *will.* Then

Hank paused. He'd just said all that out loud... *Well, no matter.* If the girl heard, so be it. She'd find out soon enough anyway.

Hank had worked it all out in his head thoroughly. Now all that was left was to find his way out of this cavern. Everything was beginning to look the same, and he was pretty sure he'd passed this little pond twice already.

Wheezing again, he crawled over to the water, splashing some in his face and mouth. It tasted strange, but water was water. And his mouth was dry.

With a groan, he sat on his rear, watching the flickering lanternlight dance on the ceiling above. "Least there's no bats in here." No blinking eyes peering down at him. Just water, sparkling light, like diamonds. Maybe there *were* diamonds up there, and he just needed to chisel them out—like Michelangelo with his statues.

He'd read about Michelangelo once upon a time—seen pictures of that big statue, the David. "Yes, the *David*. That was that big feller's name," Hank cried aloud. *Still got a little of that learning from those Quebec nuns.* He drummed his crooked forefinger against his temple, unable to help another laugh. He seemed to be doing a lot of laughing these days. At least, that's what old Jake said earlier.

Good old Jake. Hank hadn't seen him in *years*. Seemed like once, he'd slammed Jake's head into a bar in Miles City, years and years ago. Maybe that explained Jake's foolery.

Hank yawned. He needed to get some sleep, gather the strength to find his way out of this maze of twists and turns. *I could be stuck in here, for all I know*, and this earned another burst of wheezing. *Stuck in here. Wandering and wandering, like Moses in the desert. Moses in the cave.*

He held his side—it had begun to ache from all the laughing. Laying back, he gripped the handle of his knife in one hand, and the butt of his pistol in the other. He'd bound the girl's feet up anyway. She couldn't run for it. Maybe he should get her hands. But that arm of hers shouldn't be working too well, the way it was all crooked-like. She must've broken it.

***

When Hank awoke again, it was still dark. Still dark, still dripping. Diamonds glittered across the black ceiling over him. Like stars. He began to sit up, but his gut cramped, and he fell sideways, sputtering out nothing but bile and water. *Something's wrong.* But wasn't something always wrong? He was coughing up blood every day now, every other minute. It was a wonder he still had any blood left inside.

He gritted his teeth and pushed himself to his feet with all the strength he could summon, which wasn't much. His knees knocked together and he nearly stumbled back onto the ground. He grabbed wildly for something to hold onto to keep himself standing.

He glanced around wildly. Violet lay in a motionless huddle against the wall. The kerosene in his lamp had been burnt halfway. Half left. Probably about a half a day's worth of kerosene left. If he delayed in here much longer, they'd be plunged into darkness. Something like fear stirred in his chest. He turned around in a circle and froze, noticing his horse, the one the Crow tribe had given him—a real beauty. She lay on her side, on the floor.

Swearing, Hank hobbled over, his legs barely holding him up. He kicked the beast, hoping to rouse it. But it didn't move. *It's dead.*

He cursed again, and Violet awoke with a gasp that bounced off the walls of the cave. The sound grated on his nerves, and he stalked over to her, grabbing her by the hair. She let out a cry and he smacked her hard across the face. *Stupid girl.* She'd poisoned him. But how had she managed it?

He jabbed his finger in her face, pushing her into a sitting position against the wall. "You poisoned me," he chanted.

"N-no, I didn't," she choked out.

"Yes, you did, and you poisoned my horse too. Look at 'im." He grabbed her face and twisted it in the direction of the poor old paint, lying lifeless nearby.

"I didn't," she repeated, her voice breaking. "I promise you I didn't." She shook like a leaf in his grasp, her teeth chattering. "It must be—it must be the water. Did you drink some?"

"You expect me to believe some fool nonsense like that? You *poisoned* me!" he shouted. "Put something in my flask. See, it's empty." He yanked his little flask out of his pocket, unscrewing it. Tipped it upside down to demonstrate. He could just barely make out the whites of her eyes in the dim lantern light.

Terrified out of her mind, ain't she? Hank sucked in a sharp breath, trying to ease the tight fury bottling up behind his ribcage. He relaxed his grip on her hair, cupping the back of her head. She just needed a little tenderness. "Shhh, shhhh," he breathed, sinking to his knees, easing her around so that her head rested on his lap. But her chattering teeth didn't stop. It was worse than nails on rough wood.

"Stop that!" he hissed, pressing a finger to her bruised cheek, but her shuddering worsened.

Suddenly, she lurched upward, slamming her hand up into Hank's chin. He went sprawling backwards, feeling her nails rake over his cheek. She tore herself from his grasp as best she could, but her feet were still bound.

Then he heard a shattering sound, and everything went black. Pitch black.

He screamed. "You—!" He clambered back to his knees. "You little—!" He let loose a string of expletives, none enough to capture the rage and desolation building inside him. He heard Violet's trembling breaths, her scuffling, and he got to his feet, ignoring the stinging pain raking across his face.

It was a miracle he didn't fall right back down. His knees were more useless than ever. Must be the poison she'd given him, working its way through his system. Shaking with fury, he staggered across the cave, trying to find her in the dark. He heard her panting and sobbing, the shuffling sounds getting louder. *She's tryin' to free herself.*

He lunged forward with another cry, grasping for her—for anything. Her hair, her neck...

But you need her. She's your ticket out of this hell. His last bid for the life he deserved, the life he'd always yearned for. She was his currency, his godsend. *His.*

Sheriff Brooks would live to regret the day he or his daddy ever tried to lay hands on Hank Logan.

And yet Violet still evaded him, stumbling across the cave, away from his grasp.

He heard her cry out, imagined that she'd nearly tumbled into the water. *Hope she did.* It would give him a good chance to catch her again. He just needed to grab her and then get her out of here. Liquid dripped on his cheek and ran down his jaw. Blood? Or maybe that was the dripping water. The water that never *stopped dripping.* If only it were possible to tear off his ears...

"Come here," he sang out. "Come here, sweetheart."

His toe caught on something, and he tripped, slamming his face into the ground. Pain splintered up his chin, and just like that, he couldn't move anymore, mouth stretched in a silent yell.

And then something hard and wet slammed into his temple. The dripping finally stopped.

***

When Hank at last came to, excruciating and slow, the cavern had fallen so silent that he could've heard a pin drop. He groaned, pressing the back of his arm over his aching eyes. He couldn't move—he could only lay still, waiting for the spinning to stop.

And then he realized. It was silent. *Does that mean...does that mean that little rich girl ran off, and left me...?*

No—no, of course she hadn't. She'd never find her way out. The passages leading out of here were twisting, complex. Perhaps she'd step in a shaft—that would keep her in one place for the time being. Hank stared up into the darkness, as black as tar. The back of his head throbbed, as did his chin.

"Miss Violet?" he hummed, squirming until he could sit up. "Miss Violet?" He enjoyed saying her name. It flowed off the tongue like water. *Water.* The very thing that had landed him here, vulnerable. One reason he'd sworn if off years ago, in favor of whiskey. Whiskey never turned rotten on him like that water. Whiskey never killed his *horse.*

Hank paused again to listen. For anything...the quick intake of breath, a soft cry, the scrape of a shoe against the rock. "Miss Violet," he drawled again, twisting onto his knees so he could crawl across the floor. If he tried walking, he'd surely trip. Or worse, plummet into the water. He couldn't afford to lose any more of his strength. *Have to find that girl.* But how?

Furious tears stung his eyes. *Not like anyone can see them*, a voice laughed somewhere in his head. It echoed too loudly in his ears, and he flinched. He continued crawling until he reached a wall. He felt his way up it until he could stand, and then he sagged against it, pressing his forehead into his palm. And he continued to strain for just the faintest sound.

There. Hank froze, squeezing his eyes shut. There it was again. A shuffling sound. *Violet.* Clenching his teeth, he lurched forward, feeling his way along the wall until he reached a gap. The darkness was almost dizzying. For all he knew, he was about to walk into a chasm. That blasted girl. She'd extinguished his lamp.

Well, if this cavern finally claimed his life, at least he wouldn't be alone.

That thought earned a loud laugh from him, and then he cursed. The shuffling had stopped.

"Miss Violet?" he crooned. "Wherever have you gone?"

A shuddering exhale. Not too far from him, from the sound of it. He slid along the corridor, turning into what seemed like a smaller space than the previous cavern.

He followed the sounds to the center of the room, a giant formation protruding from the floor here. He'd have to maneuver his way around it. With every step, he was certain he'd have his hands on the girl in no time.

Chapter Twenty-Seven

How could they just be...*gone*? In a matter of seconds?

Gabriel couldn't breathe. His lungs were burning. He tore through the trees in an endless search, for just a glimpse of Violet, somewhere in the trees. Or the Green Terror. *They couldn't have just disappeared...*

But sure enough, they were gone. Gabriel couldn't stop replaying it in his mind's eye. They'd leapt out at the Green Terror. Gabriel was close enough to snatch him – but he'd held a knife to Violet's throat.

Go save your town. I'm doin' you a favor here. No need to choose between this pretty little thing and Miles City

Then he'd dug the tip of his blade into Violet's jugular, and Gabriel's heart had plummeted. At last, Gabriel forced himself to rest, perching on a fallen tree. His closed his eyes, pinching the bridge of his nose. *How did it all go so wrong?* Every time he thought about it was like a stone dropping into a pit in his belly as each second dragged on and he pushed himself on and on around the foothills, praying he'd find her.

If the Green Terror had taken her into the caves...he shuddered at the idea. The cave system intertwined with the silver mine shafts, creating an intricate maze that would be difficult to escape or navigate.

*If he hurts her...*Gabriel surged to his feet, ignoring the fog of exhaustion that hung over his vision. He'd push on until he found her.

But he'd been hunting for what must've been hours, his hand cramping as he clutched his drawn pistol, and he still hadn't caught any trace of the Green Terror or Violet. All it had taken was a few seconds, and he'd lost them. *I promised her I wouldn't let anything happen...*

And as much as he knew these foothills backwards and forwards, it made no difference. His imagination kept conjuring images of Violet. Violet, that blade digging into her skin... He swallowed convulsively, focusing on placing one foot in front of the other, ignoring his burning muscles.

"Sheriff Brooks!" Someone's frantic yelling brought Gabriel up short, and he wheeled around to see Hawkins running towards him. The boy was white-faced, and he grabbed Gabriel's arm, his eyes wide and frantic. "Miles City—it's burning."

"Burning?" Gabriel echoed in disbelief. "What do you mean?"

"The—the Green Terror signaled it somehow! I don't know!" Hawkins shook his head vigorously. "His men set it when we was all out here waiting to pounce..."

Gabriel's knees locked. *Should it even surprise me that he didn't keep his word?* No, it shouldn't. "Is it still burning?" he whispered.

Hawkins nodded. "When I left, the church was afire."

Gabriel let out a curse, leaning heavily against a tree nearby. He wanted to cry out, beat a branch against a tree 'until it fell apart. He covered his face in his hands, trying to keep his breathing even. He'd need to go back to town, check that everything was alright. But he couldn't leave.

One thing he knew for certain. He'd never known defeat as all-consuming as this.

What if he's killed her by now?

"You lost 'em?" Hawkins whispered somewhere beside him.

Gabriel nodded, pressing his lips together. "I didn't follow. He threatened to—" He couldn't finish the sentence, or even the thought. "For all I know, they're in the mines," he whispered at last.

"Seems like he'd be trappin' himself in there," Hawkins sighed.

Gabriel nodded. *And Violet with him. She has to know I'll never stop looking for her...*

Hawkins shot him a wary glance. "Well, I reckon we'd better get a search party together back in town."

Gritting his teeth, Gabriel shoved his pistol back into the holster on his hip. It was a first, but he was willing to admit that Hawkins was right. They needed more men, more eyes. More help with this search. He couldn't do it alone, and the town... *Will there be anything but rubble when I return?*

"We'll find her, Sheriff Brooks." Hawkins clapped him on the back. "We will."

Gabriel nodded, numb. *How did it all go so wrong?*

Deep down, he wondered if anyone would even agree to come along and help. They'd all be occupied with the chaos of the fire overtaking Miles City. And he should be, too.

But how could he? He'd lost Violet.

Feet heavy as millstones, he followed Hawkins back up the slope.

***

The town was in total chaos when they arrived at the crest of the nearby hill. Several of the buildings were burning, filling the sky with black smoke that clouded out the sun.

Gabriel drew Apollo to a halt on the ridge overlooking the town, framed between the Tongue and Yellowstone.

He couldn't breathe. He dismounted blindly and staggered to the edge of the crest, watching it all unfold. The church—the same church that Violet had labored to turn into a school. It was gone.

Gone. And there was the post office, up in flames, along with the boarding house. The smoke was darkening even now, drifting up to the hillside where he stood. He mounted Apollo again and dug his heels into Apollo's side. They flew down the hill, right into main street. Everyone was scattered, running to and fro with buckets, desperately dousing the flames that crackled and blazed, relentless.

Women's cries filled the air, along with the sound of children crying. Sylvia Lawrence clutched her husband, watching as the flames overtook their mercantile. The rest of the town rushed around them, working feverishly to toss water upon the fire as it ate away at the buildings.

"It's coming down!" Gabriel heard someone cry as he slung water onto the smoldering boardwalk.

He turned just in time to see the saloon's second floor cave in, plummeting down into the saloon's first floor. Shattering glass tinkled in the air, a strangely delicate sound in the devastation around him.

"My baby!" Gabriel spun to see a woman in front of the burning boarding house up the street. She crumpled to her knees.

Gabriel dropped his bucket and raced over, grabbing her arm. "Where?"

"She's in there," she wailed, pointing towards the second floor of the boarding house.

Gabriel took the steps two at a time, pausing a moment to jerk a handkerchief out of his pocket and tie it around his mouth, keep the smoke out. He shoved open the door and charged inside. All he could see was smoke and the crimson glow of the flames. A wood beam crashed down, and he leapt out of the way before it could hit him.

There. A child crying.

He stumbled forward, hissing in pain as embers dripped down from the ceiling, grazing his arm. Shaking his hand, he pressed on, finding the stairs at last and climbing them. The crying grew louder, a little more audible now over the roar of the fire blazing around him.

At last, he stumbled nearly headfirst over something, and turned to find the child, a little girl in a dirty dress, sitting at the top of the steps, her face buried in her knees.

He grabbed her, hauling her up into his arms, and started down the steps. Just as he reached the bottom, the stairway collapsed with a crash. The fire whirred on, almost deafening.

Violet, where are you? The thought shivered through him as he burst out the doorway, right as the second floor crashed down into the first.

He staggered down the steps in the nick of time, sparks and debris flying behind him, the girl locked in his arms.

"Susie!" the mother screamed, meeting Gabriel in the middle of the street. She wrenched the girl from Gabriel's arm, squeezing her tightly.

"Thank you, thank you...thank you," she choked out, sinking to the ground with the child in her arms.

Gabriel only let himself rest a moment. Then he forced himself back to his feet, rushing for Ma's store down the road. It was ablaze like many of the buildings, but he realized that only half the buildings on Main Street were burning. Perhaps he could stop the fire in time...

***

Putting out the Miles City fire took hours. Days, perhaps—at least, that was how it seemed to Gabriel, stamping out the last of the flames that consumed Main Street. The entire town was in disarray, displaced residents lining the boardwalk steps, clearly unsure of where to go, what to do next.

So far as Gabriel knew, only two people had been taken by the boarding house fire. Up the street, he could see them, bundled up in a wagon. They'd be buried in the cemetery tonight or tomorrow, he imagined. But he wouldn't rest. He needed to still find Violet. That was the most important thing in the world right now.

He sank down onto some empty steps, where Hawkins and Benjie found him a few minutes later. Benjie handed him a water canteen with water, and Gabriel took it gratefully, letting the sweet liquid trickle down his jaw as he drank.

"You didn't find her," Benjie whispered. It wasn't a question.

Gabriel shook his head. "We need to gather men...go and find her."

"I'll help!" George's voice rang out through the smoky air. Gabriel turned, surprised to see his deputy, leaning against the wall. George was paler than usual, thanks to the wound in his side. Clearly still not his old self.

Nevertheless, gratitude swelled in Gabriel, and he smiled at him. "Thank you. You sure? You were just shot."

"It's the least I can do," George shrugged. "And I'll manage."

"I'll help too." It was Jeff. He and Martha had joined George on the boardwalk behind Gabriel.

He massaged his temples. "My guess is that he's taken her into the caves. He must know all the entrances and exits. If he's been staying out there for a while, he's got plenty of supplies to sustain him out there. We've got to flush him out."

"Flush him out?"

"Scare him? I don't know. Or just find him..." Gabriel's mind moved sluggishly, and he stared down at the pink welt that had appeared on his arm. The ember that had landed on him earlier had left quite the mark.

He tipped his head back and closed his eyes. Far overhead, thunder cracked, and the sky went bright with lightning.

Rain. Blessed rain. It would dampen what was left of the fire.

Too little, too late.

"Gabriel!"

Ma. He rose, craning his neck to see down the street. Ma was charging towards him full-speed, not stopping until she grabbed his arm, cupped his face with her hand, hugged him several times. "Oh, praise heavens," she wept. "You're alive."

"Ma." He hugged her before stepping back.

She grasped his shirt, her eyes wide. "Where's Violet?"

A rock must have been lodged in Gabriel's throat. He drew in a deep breath. "He took her," he whispered. "He took her. Where, I don't know. But I'm thinking it's the mines…"

Ma's eyes flooded with tears. "Oh, Gabriel," she choked.

"He's not going to kill her," he reassured her.

"She's never been in the mines, though. Nor those caves in the Beartooth. What if—?"

"Ma. She *will* make it," he hissed.

Ma's face crumpled, but she nodded.

Martha approached and pulled Ma into a tight hug. "How are you doing, Carol?" She guided her over to the steps and they sat down together.

***

Devastation lurked everywhere Gabriel looked as he rode out of town on Apollo. Behind him on horseback were Benjie, Hawkins, and George.

The Green Terror had kept his word. He'd sent someone else to set fire to the town. All because Gabriel had tried to go the offensive route…

But if I didn't, he would have hurt Violet even more…

Or, he could have followed the man's strange rules exactly. Spared everyone the horror of a burning town, homes blotted from the map. Could have stood by and watched the Green Terror hurt he woman he…

It's only temporary, for heaven's sake.

The woman he loved.

I love her. The thought hovered traitorously in his head, echoing louder and louder. *And what if I'm about to lose her?*

"Let's stop at the mercantile, grab some lamps. We'll need them," he told the others, before urging poor Apollo into a gallop. The sunlight slanted down through the trees, the warm peace of mid-morning disturbed by the crying and shouting raising through the town. Something grim and heavy hung over everything. Hopelessness, Gabriel realized.

Chapter Twenty-Eight

"Answer me!" Hank's cry bounced off the cavern walls, and Violet shrunk back, too close to the invisible precipice for her comfort. But she didn't dare budge. This had been going on for what must have been hours. Perhaps days. That wouldn't be surprising. Or maybe she had died, and now she was locked into some kind of horrible limbo with Hank's phantom voice always hovering nearby.

She covered her face with her hands, forcing down the urge to scream. She just wanted it to be over. *Over.* To never see Hank ever again. Or hear his voice.

Violet shifted, and a rock under her foot slid off the edge. She heard it thud somewhere below. How deep could it be? Deep enough that if she fell in, she'd die there?

"Answer me!" Hank's voice shifted abruptly into a more sing-song tone. The way he'd been carrying on told Violet that he was hardly in a right state of mind. The muttering to himself, the singing, the taunting edge in his tone. His erratic movements...he was frail and fading. His mind, especially. Most of what he said didn't even make sense, and he kept on spitting blood.

He's weak. I could take him. But every time Violet had tried, it never ended well. Already her entire body hurt, tender in almost every spot. Especially her arm. Something serious must have happened there, but she didn't know exactly what. Everything ran together in a blur.

Weariness weighed down her limbs, and she was hardly experienced in such matters as fighting one's captor. She and Lou might have read countless stories about situations just like this. But now, living through it, Violet decided she would never fault a heroine for crying too much when getting seized by the villain, or for the measures she'd take to escape.

"Violet!" Hank's voice resounded through the air again, much too close this time. Heart thudding, Violet shrank backwards as far as she dared, more rocks and gravel sliding loose under her.

"There you are," Hank purred, just a few feet away now. Violet's heart lurched, and she dove forward in a desperate bid to somehow pass him. Here in the pitch-black cave, she was blind, helpless.

But as she rushed forward, something grabbed her around the arm. She screamed, flailing out, and then she was on her back, Hank holding her down. His hands were bruising, pinning her down into place. "Gotcha," he gasped.

Violet thrashed, trying to fight off his hands, but he was stronger, despite sickly he was. "Let me *go*!" she screamed, her throat burning, and she sent her uninjured arm flailing, striking something hard. Hopefully his face.

And sure enough, he let out a cry, and his grasp loosened. Violet yanked free of his grasp, crawling forward blindly, away from him.

Hank called her a crude name, the word reverberating around her as she scrambled to her feet. She'd lost track of where that precipice was. All she could do was pray she didn't walk off it and tumble to her death.

One step, another step. She kept placing one foot in front of the other until she met a wall, and then she followed it along for what seemed like forever. Somewhere behind her, Hank moaned and muttered to himself. More foul words. She imagined him lying flat on his back, holding his face.

Then, she glimpsed a sliver of light just ahead. *At last!* Her knees almost buckled.

She pressed on, everything else falling away. Perhaps Hank was inches behind her—in this fever dream, she wouldn't be surprised. She just needed to keep going. She ignored the way her entire body protested with every step, a throbbing ache spreading out over her from her shoulder.

The light ahead grew larger as she drew towards it, until at last, at last she stood in the small entrance of another room in the cavern, this one opening out on the side of the hill. Blessed daylight—she drank it in, eyes stinging, her throat closed.

The ground fell away from her rather steeply. She leaned heavily against the wall, peering out the entrance. A glance over her shoulder showed her that Hank was not behind her—at least not yet. She needed to get out of here, somehow. She'd have to climb down the steep incline into the ravine below.

"Wait!" Hank's voice rasped from the depths of the cave. "You sure you want to go that way?"

Violet started and stumbled around, and then she saw him. He was dragging himself slowly towards her. He must have also felt his way here against the wall. In the faint outside light, she could see his skin glistening, the white of his one opened eye, the other one bruised and swelling.

He was still several yards away when Violet turned back around and began to slide forward, rocks tumbling out beneath her, cascading down into the ravine.

Her stomach dropped. *I can do this.* She'd just have to turn over on her belly and slide down that way. The ground wasn't more than ten feet below.

"Stupid girl," Hank growled, now almost above her. Violet closed her eyes, breathed a prayer, and pushed herself off. Down she careened, heart in her throat, until she was falling through the air. She landed on the ground more gently than she'd hoped.

Above her, Hank let out an enraged roar, sounding like some kind of beast.

She managed to stumble backwards just in time before he followed her down the incline. But he didn't land as gracefully as she did—instead, he crumbled to the ground with a thud.

Violet scrambled away from him and began to skitter her way through the dead leaves littering the slope. She needed to get away from him, get as far as possible. *At least I escaped that horrible cave.* She thought she'd be stuck in there forever. Maybe even truly die in there.

She attempted to run, but the world spun beneath her feet, and she sagged against a tree, holding onto it tightly. It would be hard to run, with her head whirling like that.

Go. Keep going. Don't stop or he will catch you. And you'll die if he catches you.

Peeling herself from the tree, Violet continued to slide down the steep slope until she reached the bottom. Far above, Hank muttered as he scrambled as quickly as he dared down the side of the ravine after her.

Violet scanned her surroundings wildly, fighting to remain alert. But her body begged her to just lay down, rest. Sleep.

Sleep sounds wonderful right now. But she pressed forward, weaving amongst the trees. Several yards behind, leaves crackled and twigs snapped. Hank was still pursuing.

"Where do you think you're goin'?" A deep voice brought Violet to a standstill, and she whirled on her heel to see an older man—maybe around George's age—standing just behind a large tree, pistol in his hand.

She let out a cry, backing away. *If I run, he might shoot—*

"Got her, Hank!" the man hollered. He lowered his gun, taking a step towards Violet.

She took her chances. She turned and began to run. Pain arced out through her body with each step, but she kept going, forcing herself faster and faster through the trees. Then she tripped, crashing into the leaf-covered ground.

You can do this. You'll escape. You have to escape. The words played on repeat in her head, louder and louder until they were deafening. Her lungs and throat burned, and she staggered to her feet again.

Just then, strong arms caught her. She screamed, sobbing, and fought with what little strength was left.

It wasn't enough. The man didn't budge an inch. His grip was like iron around her wrists. He just laughed at her attempts to extricate herself from his arms.

"Stop that," he sneered. "Hank, I got her!"

Violet's head rang as he shouted in her ear.

Then, out of the corner of her eye, she glimpsed Hank. He was holding onto a tree trunk to keep himself on his feet. His face was a mess, covered in blood and bruises. She hardly recognized him...then again, everything was fading in and out of focus in her vision...

"She's a feisty one, ain't she?" The man who was holding her gave a cackle.

"I've got half a mind to kill her." Hank let out another one of those chilling laughs, the laughs that had echoed around the cave that Violet would never forget.

"Looks like she got you pretty good." The man's grip tightened on Violet's wrists.

"Shut up," Hank spat. And then, after a pause, "Didn't think you'd come back."

"Well, you're not out of silver, are you?" her captor accused. "I've got half a mind to keep this little girl for myself if you don't tell me where the rest of your stash is."

Violet's stomach turned. Hank swore, called the man a crude name.

But he only laughed, unfazed. "Rest assured, Miles City lit up like the Fourth of July. I kept that end of my deal. But if I'm going to put a bounty on my head for setting a town afire, I am to make it worth my while."

Miles City on fire... A chill went through Violet as she pictured Miles City, burning to the ground. The man who'd caught her must be Jake, the one Hank had been rattling on about earlier.

The news about Miles City earned a slow grin from Hank, but then his face crumpled into a grimace. He sank to the ground.

"We need to get out of here. They could come back, lookin' for her," Jake said, his fingers digging into Violet's forearm.

"Naw, they're gonna be busy tryin' to keep their precious town from turning to ash," Hank's coughs dissolved into a fit of laughter. "Hell, that's worth all the silver in the world. Just picture that fool sheriff cryin' over his little lady here *and* Miles City as it burns."

"You're goin' to pay me more, though—don't think you won't," Jake said in a hard tone. He joined Hank in laughing, but his chuckle was humorless, cold.

A pit of defeat yawned inside Violet. *I'll never see Gabriel again. Or Carol. Or Benjie, or any of them.* For the first time in what felt like days, her will to fight, to survive, drained completely out of her. She couldn't do anything with her wounded arm, and her legs might give out at any moment. And her head—pain splintered through it.

More than anything in the world, she just wanted to hear Gabriel's voice again, to feel his arms around her. To know that she was safe. With him, she'd always felt safe. But now, he was miles and miles away, likely putting out the fire in Miles City. *Gabriel, where are you...?*

"Violet there," and Hank pointed at her, "she's going to fetch me a pretty penny in Denver, I'm sure of it."

"Is she, now? Not if you don't let me in on your little deal."

"Only if you don't want to see another bar of silver," Hank snapped.

Violet felt Jake stiffen. "How much money do you think she's worth?" he shot back.

"That's for me to know and you to never find out," Hank cackled, but his laughter faded when Jake held up his pistol. Violet froze, heart hammering against her ribs.

"How much do you think she's worth?" he repeated, each word taut with impatience.

Hank scowled. "She's from a fine family back east. Boston, weren't it?" For the first time in the entire conversation, he addressed Violet directly.

She clenched her jaw, battling back the drowsy haze that wanted to take over her mind. "I told you, I'm not—"

"Oh, stop tryin' to fool me! I know a New England socialite when I see one. Plenty enough come out here for those bogus newspaper jobs."

Violet's stomach dropped. Hank must have had some hand in the schemes that Mr. Laramore had attempted to lure her into.

"Let's just camp here for the night. Get going come the morning." Hank sat right down in the underbrush. His head sagged as he swiped his arm across his face. "I need to rest," he muttered.

"Fine," Jake hissed. "But we leave at first light. We stick around here too much longer, and they'll catch up with us."

Hank waved his hand. "Like I said, they're too busy with Miles City. You got any whiskey? Also, if I were you, I'd tie Miss Violet up. Can't have her tryin' to escape us."

Chapter Twenty-Nine

"We'll find her, Gabe. Don't you worry." Benjie's voice broke through the haze in Gabriel's head.

He nodded automatically, trying and failing to smile.

"We will," Benjie insisted. "She's strong, and smart, and she's a fighter on top of it." They stood with George, Jeff, and Hawkins, in the entrance of the. Gabriel could only hope it was where the Green Terror had taken Violet earlier.

It was the best place they could hope to begin their search. George and Jeff had agreed to search the surrounding woods, while Hawkins, Benjie, and Gabe would enter the mines to look for the Green Terror and Violet.

"We'll find her," George spoke up, offering Gabriel a smile that didn't entirely disguise pain. He was still sore and weak from his gunshot wound, but he'd insisted on coming out to help.

Gabriel, Benjie, and Hawkins lit their lanterns with an old piece of flint in Benjie's pocket. It was late afternoon, almost dusk, and it would be dark before long. But Gabriel wouldn't return home until he'd found Violet.

He wouldn't ever sleep again until he did.

Benjie clapped him on the shoulder. "Ready?"

Swallowing around the lump in his throat, Gabriel gave another curt nod. With their lanterns lifted, the three men entered the silver mines, while George and Jeff took off down the slope to scour the woods.

As they moved deeper into the cave, the daylight behind them faded with each footstep, and the air changed. It turned heavy and wet, and Gabriel moved carefully, not wanting to slip on the wet stone beneath his feet.

None of them spoke. Their lantern light danced on the walls, sending shadows quivering around them. Gabriel had never cared much for caves He preferred the forests and prairies around Miles City. Caves were an entirely different matter—they could kill even the most experienced woodsman in just a few seconds flat. One wrong step, one wrong turn, and a person would never see the light of day again. Or worse, the whole place could collapse if too much noise was made. The mines had destroyed the integrity of the hill above them, and it wasn't unusual for a mineshaft to cave in, trap aspiring silver miners inside.

The caverns kept going on and on, water trickling down the walls and from the ceilings, stalagmites and stalactites everywhere he looked.

Hawkins shuddered. "You don't think there's spiders in here, do you?"

Gabriel shot the boy an annoyed look, and he let out a sheepish chuckle.

Of all the things he could be thinking of right now... Gabriel's patience was thinning with each passing second. If they didn't find Violet by nightfall...it was more than likely he'd never see her again.

Too much time would've passed, and she'd be far from his grasp.

I don't care. I'll never stop searching for her.

Please, God. Let her still be alive.

They entered another room of the cavern, descending deeper into the hill. Gabriel paused, a foul smell filling his nose. Something dead, surely. His stomach turned, and he glanced at Benjie. Benjie grimaced, and the three of them forged onward.

Then they entered the next section of the cavern, and the smell grew worse. Gabriel tugged the handkerchief around his neck up over his nose. They came to a pause, peering ahead as far as the dim lantern light would allow.

The lights were thinning, alerting Gabriel that the air would continue waning the deeper they went.

"Something sure is dead in here. Some animal, probably," Benjie muttered beside him.

It can't be Violet. Don't let it be Violet.

Gabriel's eyes watered. His handkerchief was unable to keep out the stench.

Hawkins swore with disgust.

Turning in a circle, Gabriel scanned the area and glimpsed something large and dark in the lantern light. It was a horse, lying on the ground on its side, eyes rolled back. It was a beautiful paint—at least, it had been.

Gabriel paused at the edge of a pool that ran along one side of the cave. "It must have drunk this water."

"Do you think it's the Green Terror's?" Benjie asked in a hushed voice.

"It's got to be. It ain't been here for long."

The smell caused bile to rise in the back of Gabriel's throat, but he swallowed it down. He began to tread cautiously about the outer edge of the cave, scanning the ground for any signs, anything that might be a sign of Violet. Perhaps they were still in here, somewhere. Wandering the bowels of this mountain.

He paused, taking in several deep breaths to calm his churning stomach, peering around the shadows. "Quiet," he whispered to Benjie and Hawkins, who were scuffling too loudly as they walked. Their footsteps sent echoes bouncing off the walls of the cavern. "We don't want them to hear us."

"Course," Benjie whispered apologetically.

Gabriel strained for a sound, any sound. Nothing. It was as if Gabriel had wrapped a scarf tightly about his ears.

Either the Green Terror was keeping quiet somewhere in here, desperate to hide, or he had somehow escaped the place entirely. Gabriel forced one foot in front of the other, careful not to trip on any jutting rocks in his path. Behind him, Benjie and Hawkins continued to scan the floor of the cavern for any sign or hint of Violet.

Shadows danced on the wall, and the lantern light in Gabriel's hand cast glints of gold against the wet walls around them. He held it up higher, squinting into the darkness. Nothing.

"Here!" Benjie pointed to something on the ground nearby. Gabriel hurried over, bending to examine what looked like vomit. The Green Terror and Violet must have lingered here...

"Looks like either the Green Terror or Violet tasted that water," Hawkins murmured.

Gabriel's heart dropped. Had Violet really drunk it? What if she was ill, suffering? And nobody to help her, nobody to comfort her but that devil... She'd need a doctor. Or perhaps he'd stumble upon her, unconscious, somewhere in the darkness.

He inhaled and exhaled in an effort to steady himself. *Pull yourself together, Brooks.* At last, he moved forward, into the next cavern. Benjie and Hawkins followed as quietly as they could behind him.

A pinprick of light caught his eye, and he froze. *Is that daylight?* He pressed on, when suddenly the toe of his boot caught on a ridge of rock and he toppled forward, landing so hard it knocked the wind from his chest. He swallowed a groan, gritting his teeth, and shoved himself back to his feet. "Looks like there's an opening ahead," he hissed to the two men behind him.

"They might've left the cave," Benjie said in a hushed tone.

But there was no way of knowing for sure – the stone floor probably wouldn't show signs of footprints. The Green Terror and his captive could still be in the caves somewhere.

At last, they emerged into the cave opening and spotted a remote hole in the wall that opened onto a steep hillside. Gabriel grabbed Hawkins by the arm before he plummeted down the gulley on loose gravel.

"Careful, boy," he sighed.

Hawkins staggered back, pressing himself against the cave wall. He swore in a shaky voice.

Leaning out as far as he dared, Gabriel peered down. The sun had just set below the horizon, and a bat soared over the nearby treetops. He could hardly see the forest floor in the shadowy dusk.

"Do you think they went down *that*?" Hawkins asked in a whisper.

"I don't know." Gabriel sagged against the edge of the cave, rubbing his eyes. Even the fading daylight made his eyes smart as they tried to adjust after the pitch black within the cave.

"Hey, I see George and Jeff!" Benjie pointed down the slope towards a ridge that rose over the gulley. And sure enough, Gabriel could just make out the two of them. They weren't even that far away, but the climb was too precarious from the shelf where they stood, unless they were willing to inch their way around the edge of the basin-like wall.

Jeff cupped his hands around his mouth and called, "I'm gonna take George home. His wound opened back up."

Gabriel nodded, waving his hand. "Go on! Get him back to town and find the doctor," he replied as quietly as he could.

Two men down. But he would manage. He needed to. He needed to find Violet as soon as he could. He needed to know she was safe.

Turning, he and Benjie and Hawkins returned into the clammy cave. "Let's go down this way," he said, and he turned towards the remainder of the corridor that wound deeper into the hill.

The three of them started forward, slowly but surely. At every echo ,they paused and listened. The corridor they walked opened onto a mine shaft, and Gabriel tugged off his handkerchief, tying it around one of the supporting posts in the mine. It would be a good way to mark their route.

"Too bad we don't got a map of this place," Hawkins murmured.

Gabriel inwardly agreed. After walking for what seemed like hours, they came to a pause. In the silence, Gabriel could hear the other two struggling for breath like he was. His chest was tight, his lungs burning as he fought to swallow a mouthful of air. They must be deep in the mines by now, so deep that the air had begun to thin. Even the flame in the lantern began to sputter and dwindle.

Benjie, usually unfazed by heavy labor, asked if they could pause for a moment, catch their breath.

"'Course," Gabriel agreed. He wasn't sure he'd ever be able to express his gratitude for Benjie, and Hawkins, too. For staying at his side in this waking nightmare. For doing everything in their power to help him find Violet.

Around them, the supporting beams groaned, as if ready to give beneath the weight of the hill. It was an eerie sound that caused the hair on Gabriel's neck to stand on end.

"I don't like the sound of that," he muttered. *No wonder these mines aren't used anymore.* Aside from the gold and silver rushes dying down, some of the mines in these hills were downright dangerous. Unstable. And one wrong step could send it all crashing down.

"Let's slow down a little. Don't want to upset anything," he whispered to the other two men. Above them, more creaking.

The three of them rolled their eyes to the ceiling, holding their breath.

"Do you think he went real deep into the mines?" Hawkins asked in a thready whisper. He drew in a ragged breath as the flame in the lantern let out a sputter. Then he strode on ahead of Gabriel and Benjie, peering into the crevices hidden from them by shadow.

He reached the end of their passage where it fed into the next—an old shaft with a cart inside, from what Gabriel could make out. The walls and ground began to rumble and he and Benjie exchanged glances. *That doesn't sound good.*

Rocks thudded to the ground as the rumble heightened to a roar, and then the horrendous crash of stones crashing to the floor. Gabriel stumbled backwards. In the spitting lantern light, a cloud of dust exploded as the ceiling collapsed mere feet in front of him.

The debris sent Gabriel and Benjie into a fit of coughs, pressing their hands to their mouths. Gabriel gasped, staring at where Hawkins had just stood not a yard away from him. Now, all he could see was crumbling rock, completely blocking the passage. *Was Hawkins crushed?*

He and Benjie surged forward and began to shove aside rocks, calling for the boy as loudly as they dared.

Then, they froze, listening. Nothing. Gabriel couldn't hear anything.

"Probably knocked out," Benjie reassured him. They began to dig, flinging the rubble behind them in their blind rush. At last, at last, Gabriel's fingers met something soft.

He pulled back and lifted his hand into the faint glow from the lantern. Blood soaked his fingers. "Bleeding—he's bleeding," he rasped, and he kept digging until he could grasp Hawkins' shirt. Hauling him from the tumbled stones, he dragged the boy a little ways away, staring down into his pale, bruised face.

Gabriel strained to see, and his heart leapt when he could just barely make out the rise and fall of Hawkins' chest. "He's still alive!" He glanced at Benjie. "Still breathin'."

"The rocks might've crushed his lungs," Benjie sighed, running a hand over his face as he dropped to the ground beside Hawkins. "We got to get him to a doctor. Fast."

Benjie agreed in a shaking whisper. "He gonna be okay?"

"I hope so," Gabriel said quietly. "I sure hope so. Put your arm under his shoulder, and I'll get his other side. We got to get him some air. Can't barely breathe this deep. Don't think that the Green Terror would come this far."

The three of them hobbled back down the shaft, Hawkins sagging between them.

Dismal thoughts ran in a chilling loop through Gabriel's head as they staggered on...thoughts of Violet, entrapped by the Green Terror.

Painstakingly, he led Benjie and Hawkins in a slow hike, retracing their steps until they passed the beam with Gabriel's handkerchief. After what must've been another long hour, they at last reached the entrance of the cave overlooking the gulley.

The sweet night air bloomed in Gabriel's lungs and after fighting through the thin, stale air in the cave, it was a wonderful feeling.

But it didn't last long. Gabriel tried to suppress a shudder at the thought of Violet, her life in the hands of the Green Terror. He turned to Benjie. "Take Hawkins back through the cave. Get him back to town."

"'Course, Gabe," Benjie agreed. He wrapped his arm around Hawkins and hauled him back into the depths.

Gabriel lowered himself onto his rear and slid down the steep hill. Then he pressed into the thicket, tugging his neckerchief back down and lifting his hand, still clutching his lantern, as he shoved aside the vines and branches.

Mosquitoes stung his neck and face in the dense underbrush, buzzing all around in the late summer evening. He kept the lantern lifted high, narrowing his eyes to scan his surroundings.

The sound of voices drifted on the breeze, rustling through the bushes and boughs. Pausing, Gabriel listened.

After another few steps, he stopped again and strained to hear something, anything else. Could it be? *Are they close by?* He stopped, considering his options. He would need to proceed carefully. He needed to remain unheard by whoever was lurking in this gully. He didn't want them jumping him...although for all he knew, they could already be watching him.

He sidestepped to a tree, pressing his back against it and waited, holding his breath. Kept his head on a swivel as he listened for those voices.

And then he heard them again, this time a little louder. Surely, they weren't so foolish as to remain in the area. If the Green Terror knew what was best for him, he'd get far, far away from here.

Gradually, the voices faded, and Gabriel emerged from his place beside the tree. Crouching behind the bushes, he hurried forward, keeping his footsteps muffled like his father had once taught him. Years of hunting the forests and fields around Miles City had taught Gabriel how to move through the land without being seen.

Every few feet he stopped, catching his breath, waiting for their voices to carry through the trees like an echo. At last, the sound of snoring rose into the air just a yard or two ahead, and Gabriel paused again, extinguishing his lantern.

Placing his hand on the gun at his hip, he itched to charge forward, ready to put a bullet in the Green Terror's skull. Instead, he crouched in the bushes, peering through them to search. It was almost too dark now to see anything at all, especially a few feet away.

He could just barely distinguish two figures in the clearing, both sprawled out on the ground. One of them looked like a man, clutching something glistening in his hands.

Across the clearing from him lay the second man, snoring so loud that Gabriel flinched. He scanned the rest of the small clearing, and then the world fell away, and his stomach sprang upside down.

There was a third person, a much smaller person, curled up in a ball at the base of the nearby pine tree.

Either asleep or unconscious, knees drawn up to the chest in a huddled ball.

Violet?

Gabriel bit down on his tongue, the tang of blood leeching through his mouth. His fingers closed around the butt of his gun, and he glanced back towards the two men. One of them was the Green Terror, and Gabriel could wring his neck.

Indignation closed like a fist around his throat, and he breathed in raggedly.

Somehow, he'd have to reach her before the two men awoke. He could walk over right now and shoot both of them. He rose stiffly to his feet, legs burning, and squinted, trying to discern if the snoring man had a gun on him. It was difficult to tell in the dusk.

Chapter Thirty

Twigs and leaves poked into Violet's skin as she lay on her side. The scent of pine and damp earth made her head hazy. For the first time in hours, she could just lay here and rest. Sleep. The thick pine needles on the ground beneath her made for a softer bed than the stone in the cave, and every time she closed her eyes, sleep seeped into the corners of her consciousness, threatening to overtake her. She balanced on that precipice just between slumber and alertness. Her captors were sleeping, and this could be her chance.

Except she couldn't move. Her hands were bound tight behind her back, her ankles were wrapped in heavy hemp cord, and squirming did nothing to loosen them. If she hoped to escape, she needed to get them off. As soon as possible.

She twisted her wrist as far as she could without spraining it and began to extricate herself. It might take hours. If it did...they might wake before she could finally free herself.

Focus on getting out of the rope around your ankles. She began to kick, taking care to not rustle the leaves beneath her. But they crackled and snapped with each writhing motion she made, and each time, she had to pause and listen.

Jake's snoring continued, loud enough to be heard from the ridge overhead, Violet imagined.

And the Green Terror—Hank? Jake had given him a bottle of gin, and he'd fallen asleep with the green glass still wedged in his mouth.

Her stomach flipping, Violet at last gained purchase on a part of the rope, and it slid over her heel, off the end of her foot. Her heart began to pound as she kicked it off her other foot.

Skull throbbing, Violet pulled herself into a sitting position, shaking the hair out of her face. Her breath came in short, rapid bursts and she gulped down panicked sobs.

Get to your feet. Now. Gabirel's voice resounded through her head. *Don't stop.*

She scrambled up, grabbing at the tree to steady herself.

If only I could lay a little longer. Sleep a little longer. Drowsiness hit her in another wave, and she closed her eyes. *I can't sleep. Not now. If I do...I'll never escape.*

Lungs burning, she took a step—and froze. Listened for the sound of the men behind her stirring. But she heard nothing except for Jake's deafening snores. Another step. The Green Terror grunted, and rolled onto his side.

Violet's heart sank into her feet. *Heaven help me.* But then his heavy breathing filled the air. He was still fast asleep.

Two more steps, and she'd made it to the other edge of the clearing. She could run back to the caves, hide in there until they gave up looking for her. She could cut through them to the other side of the hill and go from there. She just needed to keep moving.

With a glance over her shoulder at the two men slumbering on the ground, she forged onwards into the bushes. Eyes stinging, chest tightening by the second, she peeked through the boughs to check on her captors. They still hadn't moved.

Her legs were leaden weights, and it felt as if she were wading through mud. Her body ached with each step. *Don't stop now.* But she would faint if she kept walking. She leaned heavily against a tree, scraping her hand against the rough bark, and dug her fingernails into the wood. *I need to run. Run, run, run...*

So she tried. But she didn't get far—she collided with someone's chest. She opened her mouth to scream, but a big hand clamped over her face, smothering the sound.

She reeled backwards, flailing out, raking her nails across someone's skin, thrusting her elbows at him. She would *not* go without a fight. She wouldn't. She refused. She would fight until her last breath to get back to Gabriel Brooks. She would do whatever it took until she was dead. She'd be dead before she let Hank have her as his own. Before he let others use her for his own fortune.

Her elbow connected with something hard, and the person gasped. She nearly lunged out of the tight grasp of those large hands. But then her spine collided against prickly bark, and a powerful forearm pressed across her clavicle. She almost cried out as the craggy shapes of the trees against the nearly black sky beginning to swim across her vision.

"Violet," someone rasped in her ear. She blinked, gulping for air.

Gabriel? It can't be!

The arm against her collarbone eased, and she crumpled forward, into that hard chest she'd bumped into just minutes ago, except this time she breathed in that wonderful, familiar scent, of sweat and smoke and earth. "Violet," he said again, barely audible, his breath tickling her cheek.

"Gabriel," she choked, her knees giving out. His arms went around her, tightening, and he kept her from sinking to the ground.

"You're here. You're here..." She clung to him, wrapping her arms around his neck.

He shushed her quickly before she could speak again, drawing back and placing a finger against her lips. "We need to go. Now," he breathed. "Violet, we've got to run from here."

And she knew he was right.

She nodded, hiccupping on a sob. He grabbed her by the arm and led her away from the clearing. She followed him blindly, stumbling every other step, unable to pick her feet up high enough to keep them from catching on jutting roots or rocks.

"What about—what about Hank?" she whispered, dazed, as they paused after what seemed like hours and hours of walking, stumbling, staggering, Gabriel's pant rasping in her ear as he kept her steady and upright.

"Right now, all that matters is getting you to safety. I don't need you getting caught in the middle of gunfire," he whispered back. "Now, quiet, we can't have them hear us talkin'."

More walking. Time blurred together, and all that she could see was darkness, nothing but darkness. Her temples pounded, and at each step, she worried she wouldn't be able to take another.

"My horse is just ahead," Gabriel whispered to her. And then at last, at last, he was swinging himself up into the saddle, managing to keep one hand on her to ensure she didn't collapse. And then he hauled her up in front of him, wrapping his warm arms around her frame. Violet tried in vain to fight the sleep grasping for a hold of her. Apollo began to trot, and at last, sleep claimed her.

***

Gabriel smoothed back the tangled hair from Violet's pale face, just barely visible in the dim lantern light that filled the barn. They'd stopped for a rest at someone's farm. He was pretty sure it was Hansen's place, and he knew Hansen wouldn't mind if he paused here on his way back to town.

Violet drifted in and out of consciousness, her body utterly worn. His eyes stung as he stared down at her, rage bubbling in his gut.

He hated that Green Terror. Hated him. And maybe it was wrong, and unchristian, as Ma would say. That brute had struck her—the evidence was plain in the purple bruises blooming across her face, her dress torn, her matted hair clinging damply to her cheeks.

Oh, Violet. What did he do to you?

Gabriel clenched his jaw. He would make the man. He would—

But if he were to do anything rash, he would answer to the law. He would be sentenced...once he captured the devil, the Green Terror's fate would rest in the hands of the law. Not in Gabriel's...no matter how much he relished the thought.

He kept his hand on the pistol digging into his side as he squatted in the hay beside Violet. Every sound had him starting, craning his head to check over his shoulder.

It must be midnight—the moon hung high overhead, just a sliver tonight. He should get some sleep. But sleep eluded him. He needed to watch Violet, keep his eyes and ears open.

But at some point, he drifted off, because he awoke with a gasp when he heard a rustling sound. He peeled open his eyes to see Violet toss her head, as if she was having a nightmare.

She began to flail her arms as if beating back some invisible force, and he reached over, grasping her by the forearms. "Violet," he whispered. She awoke with a soft cry and dissolved into sobs. It reminded him of that night he'd startled her in her bedroom, covering her up with his own blanket. "You're safe, Violet. You're safe."

Her eyes were wide and wild, and no recognition flickered behind them. *Well, who wouldn't be terrified after what she's gone through?* He gently shushed her, holding her arms still, until at last her muscles relaxed, and she sagged against him. "It's me, Gabriel," he murmured against her forehead.

"It wasn't just a dream?" she choked.

"No, it wasn't." He cradled the back of her head in his palm. "Not a dream. I'm here. You're safe…you're safe."

He held her as she continued to sob, until at last she calmed down. Sniffling, she leaned back to look up at him, her eyes black in the dim lantern glow.

He brushed his thumb over her cheek, throat closing. *I'll die,* he nearly said aloud, *before I let anything happen to you again.*

Combing his fingers through her hair, he kept whispering words of reassurance, desperate to comfort her somehow. He'd never been good at consoling people. It just didn't come natural. But he did his best tonight, hoping he wasn't repeating himself too much, until her shaky breathing steadied and she drifted back to sleep in his arms.

How long he sat like that, Violet curled against his side, he didn't know. Hours, likely. Until the first light of dawn slanted through the wall slats of the barn, directly into his eyes. He blinked, lifting an arm to cover his eyes.

Against him, Violet stirred. Instead of waking in a panic, she drifted awake slowly, more calmly. Batted her eyes up at him, recognition lighting in her eyes.

"Gabriel," she said hoarsely. A tear ran down her cheek. "Gabriel, you came for me."

He couldn't fight the smile tugging at his lips. "Of course I did." How could she doubt that he would? He couldn't lose her, not now. He couldn't imagine the pain of ever saying goodbye, of never seeing her again.

"Thank you," she whispered. "I would do the same for you."

Gabriel chuckled, shaking his head. "Thank you, Violet." She laughed with him for a moment.

But then, her face crumbled and she lowered her head, pressing her forehead against his chest. "Why are you so good to me?" he heard her choke.

"Because—because I love you."

She sat up then, staring at him. Her eyes were wide, her chest rising and falling as if she'd just taken in a deep breath. "You do?"

"I love you," Gabriel nodded. "I love you more than anything, anyone." He couldn't finish for the lump rising in his throat.

Violet let out a breathless laugh. "I love you." Her words came in a rush. She shook her head.

They sat like that for minutes, or maybe hours. Gabriel didn't want it to end. But they'd need to face reality again. Miles City was in ruin. Half of it had been burnt to the ground by the Green Terror's henchmen.

Reluctantly, he got to his feet, holding out his hand to help her stand. He caught her by the arm before she could sink back down. He couldn't imagine how exhausted she must be. He wasn't even sure how he was still pushing himself. *Necessity, probably.* "We've got to get movin'," he whispered.

"Get back to town. We'll stop by the farm, see if Ma's still there."

Violet nodded, and he slid his arm around her back, helping her over to the stall where Apollo stood, tied up. He'd spent the night munching hay and drinking from a bucket of water Gabriel had found.

Gabriel ignored his muscles protesting from exhaustion and lifted Violet into the saddle. He'd lead her for now, give Apollo a rest.

As he led the horse into the yard, Hansen emerged from his house, his blond wife and tow-headed son watching from the back door.

"You alright there, little lady?" Hansen grunted, his expression full of remorse.

"I will be alright," Violet told him, mouth twisting into a wan smile.

Hansen reached up, scratched the side of his neck. "I wanna ask you to pardon me. For tryin' to hand you over to the Green Terror. I was...a coward. Desperate. And turns out, Miles City..." He lowered his head to the ground, scuffing his foot through the dirt with a sad scowl.

"It was burned...I've heard," Violet murmured, her voice hitching. Hearing the raw emotion in her voice brought Gabriel up short. She truly did love Miles City, as much as he had once thought her to despise and resent it. "Was anyone injured, or—?"

"One of the saloon girls got burnt bad," Hansen said quietly. "That's the last I heard. But it could be more now. Half the town's gone up in smoke, thought from what I've heard, it was put out."

Thank heavens Ma was at my place instead of in town.

Gabriel thanked Hansen for letting him use the barn and then set off, leading Apollo towards his own cabin, not more than a few miles away. He kept turning to see to it that Violet didn't pass out and collapse to the ground. Once she did, and he caught her before she fell.

At last, they reached his farmhouse. It was empty. Nobody in the barn, either. The chickens squawked, hungry for feed.

"Ma must've gone to town."

Violet turned slightly in his arms. "I'm sure she's safe."

Gabriel instinctively curled his arms around her, chest tightening. The gentle comfort in her voice was soothing, sweet.

He urged Apollo onwards towards town. Violet let out a soft cry as he turned onto the main road. In the direction of town, black smoke rose into the sky, marring the otherwise clear sky. "Oh, Gabriel," she whispered in horror.

Gabriel tried to steady himself. He'd seen the town earlier, but he'd been preoccupied with Violet's kidnapping. But now he would have to see the full extent of the damage. The aftermath. He would have to organize the rebuilding, the panic, the devastation. He would have to be the sheriff.

Guilt twinged in him sharply, for leaving Miles City to save the girl he loved. He had been selfish, perhaps, but he couldn't stomach the thought of abandoning her, leaving her to defend herself against the Green Terror. He might lose sleep over riding off to find Violet, but he wouldn't be able to live with himself if he'd chosen the town over her.

Violet's spine stiffened against his chest as they entered Miles City proper. Even early in the morning, people were up and picking through what was left of the town.

Up ahead in front of the remnants of Ma's shop, Gabriel spotted Jeff and George standing on the boardwalk, along with Benjie. He lifted his arm to wave and they waved back.

Urging Apollo up the street, he reached the shop at last, dismounted, and helped Violet down. Everyone on the boardwalk cheered, throwing up their hats. The three men descended the steps to surround them, calling out, "Good to see you again, Violet!" and "Thank the Lord you're safe."

George squinted at Gabriel. "When do we track down the Green Terror, boss?"

Gabriel clenched his jaw. "Wish I could've grabbed him then and there. But I needed to get Violet to safety."

Violet lifted large brown eyes to him, and he softened a bit. "I didn't want to get in a shootout with you right there."

She nodded, chewing her lip.

"How's Hawkins?" he asked Benjie.

"Weak. Broke his arm. But Doc says he'll recover soon enough, long as he keeps it in a sling."

Gabriel exhaled a sigh of relief. "And George? You doin' better?"

George grinned, patted his side where he'd been shot. "Good as new. Doc stitched me up mighty well. I'm ready to hunt down the Green Terror and rebuild Miles City."

Gabriel tried to smile, but now he doubted it would be an easy task to rebuild the town. Half of it had been burned to mere rubble, and the much of the rest was still under construction. It could barely even be called a town now. And after all his effort to be careful, to ensure that the Green Terror wouldn't strike out at Miles City…it had still happened.

And yet—and yet…Violet reached over, touched his arm, as if to pull him from his thoughts. She offered him a soft smile. "Gabriel?"

He blinked. "I'll find him. Drag him back here so he has to face the marshal." Then he glanced around, scanning. "Where's my mother?"

"At her shop," Benjie told him, just as a wild voice rang out, calling his name.

Everyone turned to see Carol standing further down the boardwalk, her face smudged with soot, her hair falling from its bun. Tears streaked her smoke-darkened cheeks.

"Gabriel! Violet! Oh, thank heavens!" she cried, and started running towards them.

At that moment, a gunshot rang through the air.

Chapter Thirty-One

"I've had about enough of you, Gabriel Brooks!" Hank Logan's voice screamed out, ringing through the streets with the same jarring force as the gunshot.

Violet's heart lurched when she recognized it, when she saw who she was looking at. Surely...surely she was asleep, in the middle of a nightmare.

Hank had appeared from seemingly nowhere, one arm tight around Carol's waist, the other raised to point his gun skyward. His face was as grotesque as Violet remembered. It was a wonder that he was able to stand upright. He swayed slightly as he held Carol to him. Her mouth fell open in a silent, panicked cry.

Gabriel's hand was on his holster lightning-fast, although he didn't draw his gun. His jaw was taut, his face pale under his suntanned complexion.

Please, God, don't let that lunatic shoot Carol.

"Give me back the girl, and I'll let your mama live," Hank screeched. "You hear? I don't want no trouble. I'm just about sick of getting' everything messed up by you."

"I can't believe he showed his face here," Benjie hissed, pulling his own pistol from his belt. George and Jeff did the same, and up and down the street people cowered, fleeing for cover.

"I got men all over town, waitin' to put an end to Miles City once'n for all. Now, what'll it be?" Hank demanded. "Your ma and your town, or that sweet thing beside you? I told you that you got to choose!"

"He's lying," Violet whispered to Gabriel. "It's just him. And Jake."

"Shut up!" Hank screamed. "Put your gun down and walk Miss Violet over here."

Gabriel's face was tight with anger—an anger Violet had never really seen before. It sent her heart racing. Benjie snapped her out of it. "Come here, ma'am. Get behind this wall." He grasped her arm, trying to draw her towards what was left of the post office.

"You won't get anything," Gabriel called, his voice tight, hard. Cold. "Especially not until you release her. Let her go."

"Like hell I will!"

"Quit hiding behind women you've captured," Gabriel snarled. "If you want a fight, then let's do it the right way. A duel."

"Oh, of course," Hank scoffed. "I let her go, and you'll put a bullet through my head, first chance you get. Nothin' fair about that."

"I'm a man of my word," Gabriel shot back, "but I guess I can't say the same for you."

Hank cackled. "Guess you can't."

Violet caught her breath, glancing over to meet Gabriel's questioning look. "Get back, Violet," he whispered. "I don't need nothin' to happen to you."

She nodded, and Benjie grasped her arm, guiding her into the alley. Jeff and George remained beside Gabriel, their guns drawn and poised.

But Violet watched as Gabriel waved them down. "How about this? We talk? Man to man? Come to an agreement."

"What agreement?" Hank cried out, his voice cracking. "There ain't none. And she—"he jabbed his finger wildly towards Violet—"*she* was my last chance to get a fresh start. To find somethin' better." He laughed boisterously, shaking his head like a dog shaking off water. He swayed again, and his arms must have loosened, because Carol tore from his grasp, stumbling away and crying.

"Ma, run!" Gabriel yelled. And she did, just as Hank reached out for her again. The world stopped as Hank pointed his gun at her back, his finger on the trigger.

Another gunshot rang through the air.

Hank crumpled to the ground. Carol lunged forward, crashing to her knees, her hands over her head.

"Carol!" Violet screamed at the same time Gabriel shouted, "Ma!"

Violet ran forward blindly, eyes fixed on Carol, who was now face-down on the boardwalk. But when she reached her, she found her trembling, without a gunshot wound in sight. She looked up, eyes fixed on the fallen man.

Hank lay motionless just a foot away from her, the wooden planks beneath him turning dark in a pool of crimson.

Carol sat up with a cry, gathering Violet into her arms. Violet closed her eyes against the gruesome scene.

It was all over. Finally. The Green Terror was gone. For good.

But at what cost?

She'd just watched Gabriel shoot someone dead, except…

A whoop rang from the roof above them. Everyone turned, scanning the surviving rooftops, and saw…

Hawkins. Hawkins sat perched atop one of the still-erect buildings, rifle in his uninjured hand raised high above his head. He whooped again, and Benjie and George echoed the sound. Cheering erupted throughout the town as shaken bystanders emerged from their cover. More cheers and whoops built to a crescendo as everyone descended upon the little group in front of Carol's ruined shop.

They'd just lost all their possessions, their homes, their businesses, but they could finally celebrate that their greatest threat was finally gone.

Gone for good.

Carol held Violet close for a few sweet moments, and at last she drew back, her eyes shining. "I knew you'd come back," she beamed. "You just can't seem to leave Miles City, now can you?"

Violet couldn't suppress the laugh that spilled out. "Seems like I can't," she agreed.

Carol drew her thumb over what must be a bruise on Violet's cheek, her blue-gray eyes scanning her face. "Oh, you poor thing. What did that brute do to you?" Her voice hitched.

Gabriel joined them on the ground, kneeling beside Violet. He helped Carol to her feet, and she hugged him tight for a long moment. "Thank the Lord he let my son and daughter-in-law come home to me in one piece."

"And I thank Him that he kept you safe. Now, you sure you're alright?"

"Oh, I'll be fine soon as we get this place lookin' like a town again," Carol huffed.

Violet didn't miss the amused smile Gabriel shot her over his mother's head, a smile meant just for her. Her heart might just burst.

***

"You'll do wonderfully," Violet whispered, peering up at Gabriel as they stood in the back door of his office. Just outside waited the inhabitants of Miles City, ready to hear his plans for rebuilding the town.

Gabriel squared his shoulders, trying to keep his pulse steady. But he'd never been much of one for words, much less giving speeches.

But he needed to do this. The town was looking to him for leadership. For guidance. And he was here to give them that. To lay out the steps of rebuilding, to ask them to stay and give Miles City a second chance. To not give up.

Right now, however, he focused on Violet, on the look in her eyes telling him she believed in him. That she thought he could do this.

"Thank you," he whispered, unconsciously reaching out to cup her cheek. She leaned into his touch, a soft smile tugging at her lips as she closed her eyes.

It took him back to the night he'd met her, stared down at her in the golden glow of the lantern light. She'd just run right into him, right into his chest, and knocked the wind out of him. But that was nothing compared to how exhilarating and alarming it was to fall in love with her.

Everything about Violet was unexpected. From the moment he met her to this second right now, she was an enigma, an unpredictable force that had swept into his life, turning it all upside down. At first, he'd tried to resent that. But now, he believed for a fact that she was exactly who he'd been waiting for all this time.

"You ready?" she whispered to him.

He nodded, trying to not smile as she reached up and straightened the badge on his shirt. "I'll be by your side," she told him, and he knew she meant every word. "Every step of the way."

And she was. She followed him out onto the boardwalk and stood beside him as he addressed the dismal crowd waiting for his guidance.

As soon Gabriel he stepped out, they began to bombard him with questions. "Are you going to rebuild all of Miles City?"

"Which buildings get rebuilt first?"

"Where are we supposed to live? Our home got burnt in the fire."

He held up a hand and the crowd quieted. Scanning the onlookers, he noticed that most of the town was present. Save for a small number who'd moved out in the days after the fire, most of them had stayed behind.

That didn't mean they weren't scared, of course. Gabriel could see it in their eyes, in the way the women hugged their children close and clung to their husbands' arms. The way some of them flung out questions, voices too loud.

He paused, taking in a deep breath, thinking. He didn't see any sort of accusation or anger in the faces before him. Just concern. Worry. Fear.

"We are going to rebuild. I'll do everything in my power to restore this city to what it was."

Excited murmurs rippled through the gathered crowd.

"But we're going to have to depend on each other. We've got Jeff Woodard," and Gabriel gestured to Jeff, standing with his arm around Martha nearby. "He and I will work with all of you to get you back on your feet. We'll only make it by being there for each other."

He drew in a deep breath and drove on. "I know some folks have already left Miles City following that fire, but will everyone here today stay and work to rebuild?"

A cheer arose, followed by whoops and a light applause. It was the best Gabriel could ask for. "Talk to me after this if you've got any questions," he finished.

The tightness in his chest eased as he stepped back for Ma to say her piece. "I'm a member of Miles City's Second Chance Women's Club," she declared. "I know that we just got the church all done up before this fire. But we'll start that over again. In the meantime, though, Violet here's gonna start teachin' your children. Class'll be held on the hill outside of town where the pastor's been holdin' church service on Sundays. And like my son said, we've got to pull together. If we don't, we're letting the Green Terror win. And we don't aim to let that happen, do we?"

A determined *No* arose from the people in the street, and a smile tugged at Gabriel's lips as he glanced at the young woman beside him. Violet, her hair fluttering against her cheek in the warm breeze, was pale, worrying at her lip. She was nervous. He resisted the urge to take her hand in his.

"I got a question," hollered Benjie, from where he perched on the hitching post nearby. "When do we start?"

The cheering built, and Gabriel grinned down at his shoes. Benjie sure did know how to lighten the mood. And Gabriel appreciated it, especially right now.

"Now, if all of you will join us in front of my shop, we've got a big dinner waitin' for us. Let's go on over!" Ma gestured up the street, where several long tables had been set up in the middle of the street, blackened buildings rising all around.

Ma's shop was one of the few buildings with the least damage. Her upstairs only had a big hole in the ceiling, and Gabriel had secured a tarp over it to keep out the weather.

Outside of town, those who lost their homes in the fire had begun to set up a camp to live in while their homes got rebuilt. Tomorrow, a crew would head out to the forest to start chopping wood for materials.

But today, they would feast together as one township. As Miles City.

***

After dinner, Gabriel set his plate down beside Violet's. It had begun to get dark already, and lanterns bobbed on strings from one side of the street to the other.

Violet smiled down into her lap as Gabriel lowered himself down into the seat beside hers, pulling his chair up to the checker-tablecloth covered table. His arm brushed his and she lifted her head, dark eyes flashing into his.

"Sheriff Brooks." A soft laugh lilted in her voice.

"Mrs. Brooks," he returned, unable to stifle a goofy smile. He held up one of the fluffy biscuits on his plate. "I have to say," he said in a whisper, "I'm partial to the charcoal biscuits."

Violet giggled, shaking her head. "Gabriel!" She feigned exasperation, but it didn't reach her brown eyes.

As he picked up his fork, his hand brushed hers and a shiver went through him.

"Look at 'em, blushin' like lovebirds over there!" Benjie's voice rang through the air. He sat just down the table from them, beside Hawkins.

He nudged Hawkins, who groaned. "My arm!"

"Look at 'em," Benjie insisted.

Gabriel straightened in his chair, his face heating even more. Beside him, Violet grinned down at her plate.

"I don't know what you're talkin' about," George told Benjie. "They've been like that since the week Miss Violet got here."

Laughter floated through the air. Gabriel wished they'd quit teasing. But he still couldn't stop smiling.

After supper and cleanup, he set Violet up on Apollo and led her homeward. Outside of town, they paused atop the hill they'd been married on. By now it was dark enough to see the stars stretching out in the heavens above.

Gabriel tilted his head back to look at them, and Violet did the same.

"Do you remember that second night? At your mother's place? The night we decided to get married?"

"Yes," Violet murmured from atop Apollo. "You told me you loved eating under the stars."

"I did, didn't I?"

"And I—I was sitting there, thinking I wouldn't be here for long. That I'd get on to Helena as fast as I could. I was—I was terrified."

"I was, too," Gabriel admitted, rubbing his neck.

"You were?" Disbelief tinged Violet's voice. "You're always so calm. Like nothing scares you."

"Plenty scares me." Gabriel tried to swallow. "You scare me."

"I do?" Violet whispered back.

"Of course. You're beautiful, from a whole different world." Gabriel took in a deep breath. He heard her catch her breath, when he caught her hand in his, pressed his lips in a brief kiss.

His mother had once read form a book of fairy stories, of a giant who had been turned into a prince. How he'd kissed the princess on her hand. He heard Violet's shaky intake of breath in the dark and wished he could see her better.

He closed his eyes tightly, weighing his next words. He'd been putting this off. Shemight have said she loved him, but that was different than wanting to stay married to him.

"And I want you to know, even if you stay here in Miles City, I ain't going to hold you to our agreement. To stay married to me."

"Gabriel—"

"Not that I don't want to be married to you. I do, but that's got nothing to do with it."

"Gabriel. I—I do. I want to be married to you. I love you." Violet's voice was quiet, shaky.

His heart swelled.

"I love you," he whispered back.

Chapter Thirty-Two

"Adam, stay away from the fire. Don't go playing in it." Violet set down her pencil, pushing herself up out of her chair. She paused to catch her breath, resting a hand on her swollen stomach. *Just a little longer.* Then started towards the little boy across the room.

He was only two, but it was incredible how a child so young could get into so much mischief.

"I help," he told her, beginning to reach for the pot hanging over the flames.

"Adam!" Violet hurried as fast as she could across the room. A little too fast, and she gasped for breath, steadying herself on the mantle as she guided Adam away from the hearth. Across the room, she set her hands on his shoulders, smiling into those blue-gray eyes. So much like his father's. "Mama has got to finish grading homework. I can't have you trying to burn yourself." She swept her hand through his auburn hair, kissing his forehead. "Why don't you draw while I grade?"

"Violet?" She straightened and turned at the sound of her husband's voice.

Gabriel hovered in the doorway, grinning as he watched her try to cajole their son. "It's ready." He stepped further into the room, gathering her into his arms. Her protruding, pregnant stomach made it a little difficult, but he always managed. "Ready?" he murmured. She nodded, her face aching from smiling so wide. Gabriel picked up Adam, who squealed as he was swung through the air. Violet held onto her husband's arm as he led her towards the door on the other side of the room.

It had once led to the tiny room she'd used as a bedroom. Back in the early days, when they'd first married. Now, it was a nursery, and Gabriel had expanded it into a larger room, just as he had done for their bedroom a year earlier. He'd built most of it himself, with some help from Jeff and Benjie.

He opened the door and she let out a soft grasp. "Oh Gabriel. It's perfect."

Covering her mouth with her hands, she turned toward him as he set a squirming Adam down. *My heart might explode.* She hugged him tight and began to hurry to and from about the room.

From the beautiful new bed Jeff Woodard had built for Adam, to the polished, gleaming cradle where they'd laid Adam the day he was born, it was everything Violet could have hoped for. The cradle was now set aside for their coming baby. In the bed sat a stack of infant clothes Carol had made, back before Adam had been born.

They still had a photo of him draped in one of the baby gowns. Gabriel had let her get a photo taken of their son when a man with one of those newfangled cameras stopped in Miles City.

"I wish it could be bigger," Gabriel sighed.

Violet whirled to face him. "Gabriel. It's perfect," she told him again, setting her hands on her hips.

His mouth curved in a smile as he reached up and brushed a strand of hair out of her face. It had grown back to its full length long ago, and was now gathered in a loose, rather tousled bun at the nape of her neck.

Violet laughed softly, resting a hand on her stomach.

"How are you feeling today?" he asked.

Violet closed her eyes. "Tired. My back is driving me mad."

"Why don't you lay down?" Gabriel ran his thumb over her cheekbone. "Get some rest?"

"I wish I could. But not even laying down helps. I can't get comfortable."

Gabriel grimaced sympathetically. "I'm sorry. Then how about you sit on the porch, wait for folks to arrive? I'll check the stew and bread." Benjie and Lou would be here soon from their farm just over the hill.

"Thank you." Violet leaned up on tiptoe, pressing a kiss to his lips. "I'll keep Adam with me. He was trying to help me with dinner earlier. Nearly burnt himself. If he's not careful, he'll be covered in burns like I was."

Gabriel's mouth twitched. "He's a stubborn one, ain't he?"

"He sure is," Violet laughed softly.

Gabriel chuckled at this, as he crossed the room to pick up Adam, where he was rolling about on the small, newly-erected bed. Adam protested, reaching for his the teddy bear on the pillow beside his head.

Violet watched in admiration as her husband lifted the child with so little effort, carrying him to the door. She followed them, but not before pausing for a moment to enjoy the view of the brand new nursery.

Violet retired to the porch where she sank into one of the rocking chairs, watching the road for a glimpse of Lou and Benjie. She couldn't wait for everyone to see the new nursery. Gabriel set little Adam down at her feet and he toddled into the yard at once, chasing the roaming chickens.

Carol and George arrived first in her wagon, which she parked in the yard. She waved as George helped her down.

Adam toddled up to them, waving a stick in the air and babbling, and Violet couldn't help but smile as Carol scooped him up and covered his face in kisses. "If it isn't my grandson," she declared as Adam began to giggle.

Behind her, George grinned, hands set on his hips. "He's the spitting image of Gabriel at that age," he commented. Violet tried to picture her serious husband as a babbling two-year-old, and it caused her to laugh softly.

"The nursery's done," she told Carol.

Carol's eyes went wide. "It is?"

The front door of the cabin swung open and Gabriel stepped out, resting a hand on the back of Violet's rocking chair.

Carol and George ascended the porch steps, Adam in tow, and Carol stepped up to give her son a peck on the cheek. "I must see the new nursery," she declared, setting down the squirming boy in her arms.

Gabriel stepped aside for her to enter, but George seated himself on the porch steps to watch Adam run across the yard and climb on the haybales next to the barn.

"What was Gabriel like, as a little boy?" Violet asked him. Gabriel had known George all his life, and it was sweet to see how their relationship had shifted into that of a step-father and son ever since George and Carol married.

"Oh, let's see..." George leaned himself back against the porch railing. "He was always moving, I'll say that. He loved ridin' horses, and his pa started him from an early age learnin' how to ride. He's been a good shot long as I can remember. Me and his pa, we took him hunting when he was seven. And boy, he was a sharpshooter even then. He's always been serious, careful, but that's just Gabriel."

Violet smiled to herself, now trying to envision Gabriel as a boy. Intense, thoughtful, eager to prove himself to his father.

The sound of another wagon rumbling down the road drew her attention and she turned to see Benjie and Lou's wagon. Lou held a small bundle in her arms—little Lucy, her and Benjie's first child. She'd just given birth a few months earlier, and Violet had been there to help Carol with the birth.

Benjie took the baby from Lou's arms and helped her down from the wagon. Once that was done, he handed her Lucy and fetched a cake from the bed of the wagon.

Violet clambered to her feet as gracefully as she could in her condition, waving to the young couple. Her heart squeezed joyfully as once again it sank in that her dear friend and former maid, Lou Allis, now Lou Fisher and wife of Benjie, lived just over the next hill. *At last.*

It was surreal to realize that after a year of writing letters back to Boston, Lou had at last taken the leap and moved out here to Miles City. She had started working as a seamstress for Carol, which she still did, though in a limited capacity. She tended to be kept busy with her and Benjie's daughter.

Lou hurried up the steps and gave Violet a tight but careful hug. "How are you feeling today, Vi-Vi?"

"Ready to have this baby," Violet joked.

Little Lucy in Lou's arms blinked big blue eyes up at Violet. The same shade of blue as Benjie's eyes, the same whorl of red hair. She'd inherited Lou's delicate features.

Adam toddled up and Benjie stooped to show him Lucy, and he babbled at her incoherently. Everyone laughed when Lucy cooed back.

Lou and Violet exchanged smiles. Lou was of the firm belief that Lucy and Adam would fall in love someday and marry. And Violet was inclined to believe it.

"The nursery's done," she told the Fishers.

Lou's eyes went wide. "I've got to see it!" she cried. Violet sank back down into her chair as Benjie and Lou hurried inside to see Gabriel's work.

She kept watching the road for a glimpse of the Woodards. Martha and Jeff had four children now, two boys and two girls. Not for the first time, Violet smoothed her hand over her own belly, wondering if she'd have a girl, too. If she did, she and Gabriel had decided on the name Caroline. If it was a boy, they'd name him Michael. After Gabriel's father.

It wasn't long before the Woodards' wagon rolled up as well, four children in tow. Their youngest was a newborn still; their oldest, Georgie, taller each time Violet saw him. They hurried inside to see the finished nursery, but not before Martha gave Violet a hug.

Gradually, their guests returned out to the porch after seeing the new nursery. "Thank you for all your help," Violet told Jeff as he settled himself beside George on the steps.

"Gabriel's getting good at building," he replied with a smile.

Woodworking was something Gabriel had picked up as an escape from the stresses of maintaining law and order in Miles City. With the immediate threat of the Green Terror long since dead, Miles City had rebuilt and improved. If one were to stand on the hill behind the house, it was easy to see the train tracks being laid far off in the distance.

The builders estimated another six months before the train would be able to start coming through Miles City. Every day the workmen built the rails closer and closer to town, closer to the now-finished train station. Before long, a train would be running through Miles City, and it would be just what the town needed to fully get back on its feet.

Gabriel appeared in front of Violet, holding out his arm for her to take. She was grateful that he always remembered to help her stand these days. It was a wonder she even managed to get out of bed these days.

"Ready for supper?" he asked her, blue-gray eyes piercing into her, and her heart fluttered for a moment, as it was wont to do, even two years into marriage.

"I sure am," she murmured.

"Let me go get that son of ours before he disappears into all that hay."

Both of them paused when the sound of rumbling wagon wheels filled the air. "Didn't think we were expecting anyone else," Gabriel commented. "Except for Hawkins. But I thought he'd come by horse a little late tonight. He's on patrol."

They exchanged frowns.

"Well, maybe it's some folks comin' to wish you happy birthday, Violet," Carol said behind them. They turned to see her smiling like she knew something they didn't.

Violet glanced at Lou and Benjie and George to find they all wore the same expression.

Gabriel put a rather protective arm around her, barking out Adam's name as a wagon rolled into view. At once, Adam toddled over to the house and up the steps to watch with them from the porch.

Violet's mouth fell open as she made out what looked like a crowd of children in the wagon bed. The children were her students, and Hawkins sat in the driver's seat holding the reins, and beside him sat his young daughter Betsy. His wife, Melanie, must be at home with their infant boy.

"Hawkins?" Gabriel exclaimed, keeping a steadying arm around Violet's shoulders.

Hawkins drew the wagon to a stop in the yard and the children began to call out, "Happy birthday, Mrs. Brooks!" They all held up a big piece of paper with the words "Best Teacher" written on it. "Happy birthday to the best teacher, Mrs. Brooks."

Violet covered her mouth, overcome by the gesture.

Hawkins climbed down from the wagon and lifted Betsy down. Violet noticed then that she was holding a package. It was small and wrapped in purple paper. Betsy carried it up the steps and held it up to Violet.

"What's this?" Violet asked Hawkins.

He was grinning. "All the kids chipped in and got you something for your birthday. Only the best for Miles City's best teacher."

Violet's eyes blurred as she took the package from little Betsy and unwrapped it. Inside was a bottle of lemon verbena perfume. The children must have noticed it was her favorite kind of perfume. And it looked exactly like the one she'd brought out here from Boston.

"Thank you," Violet cried, unable to wipe away the two tears that slipped down her cheeks. To think that she'd almost left this town behind as soon as she'd been given the chance.

Gabriel helped her down the steps and she hugged each of the children who'd come out in the wagon. She loved teaching more than she'd ever expected to. And she loved these children almost as much as she loved her own.

Hawkins tipped his hat to Violet, grinning. "Melanie organized this, but she couldn't be here today. She couldn't leave the baby. She sent you birthday wishes, though."

Violet hugged him before stepping back to run her hand over Betsy's light brown head. She was nearly Adam's age, and Violet knew that in no time, she'd be teaching them both, along with Lucy and the baby she was carrying.

"Thank you," she called to the children again, throat tight. She didn't even know how to express her gratitude for each of them. They were the best students she could ask for.

Hawkins picked up Betsy, who squealed as she sailed through the air. "Mrs. Lawrence put in an express order for that lemon verbena. But don't let her tell you it was her own children's idea." Laughter ran through the group.

"Of course she'd do that," Gabriel murmured, chuckling. Everyone waved as Hawkins settled back on his wagon and drove it back down the road to town.

Now it was dinner time. The group entered the cabin and the room was filled with laughter and conversation as people took their seats around the table. Gabriel had built a bigger table last year, along with several more chairs for guests.

Violet peeked at the cake under the cloth, covered in frosting with the words, *Happy Birthday Violet* written across it.

"You should open a bakery, Lou," she said. Lou, already seated with Lucy on her lap, beamed. "I do enjoy it. But I've got my hands full with mothering and working at Carol's shop."

"Well, if you ever change your mind, I wouldn't be hurt if you chose to open a bakery," Carol said from the other end of the table. "It's a shame that we lost our bakery in the fire. A real pity. Shame Miss Hetty didn't stay, either. But back then, I suppose, it was easier to just head over to Helena and start fresh."

"As long as we have Lou's cakes, I don't miss it," Benjie declared.

Everyone nodded their agreement. Gabriel carried the bowl of stew from its hook over the fire to the table, and dinner began.

Close to the end of the meal, everyone paused again when they heard another set of wagon wheels on the road.

Probably just one of the new neighbors headed into town. Though it was headed in the wrong direction, from the sound of it, coming towards the Brooks farm, not away from it.

Gabriel rose, followed by Benjie and George. They opened the front door and stepped onto the porch.

"Who are they?" Carol called.

"Don't know. But they're headed our way," Gabriel replied.

Chapter Thirty-Three

The wagon pulled to a stop in the yard, and Violet remained in her seat, waiting for Gabriel to announce who it was. Leaning forward, she watched him walk down the porch steps towards the newcomers, but she couldn't see anything else from her seat at the table. Carol, Martha, and Lou stood and joined the men in the door, peeking out.

Voices rose from the yard, and Violet frowned. *They sound familiar...*

She began to struggle to her feet, but Carol hastened over to help her up.

"Who are they?" Violet whispered.

"Real fancy folk. They're talkin' to Gabriel."

"Oh." Violet let Carol help her to the door, and then she stopped, unable to believe her eyes.

Mother? Father? She must be asleep, then. Dreaming. Because sure enough, there they stood, in her yard, dressed in all their Boston finery. They stuck out like a sore thumb, as much as Violet must have done when arriving two years earlier. Mother held a parasol.

Carol must have noticed her stricken expression. "Do you know them?"

"They're my—my parents," Violet whispered.

Her eyes went wide. "They are?"

Lou hurried over to her from the doorway, grasping her arm. "Why on earth are they here?" she muttered, shaking her head.

Just then, Gabriel turned back to look at her, as did the well-dressed couple. The woman let out a cry, taking a step forward. "Violet!" she cried.

Yes...it was Mother. Violet would recognize that cry anywhere. It was tearful, full of near-disbelief. And Father was scanning her up and down, his eyebrows knitted, as if the sight of her heavy with child was disturbing to him.

Violet recoiled, and it was a good thing Carol was holding her arm, because she might have sunk to the ground otherwise.

"Oh, Violet." Mother took a step towards her before Gabriel stepped in her path.

"That's my daughter," she cried at him. "My little girl. Are you really married? And are we going to be grandparents?" She pressed her free hand to her face. It was untouched by the sun, the parasol casting dancing lights and shadows across her now-graying raven hair.

Father tried to step around Gabriel, but he was greeted with a hard look as Gabriel grasped his arm. Tight enough that Father flinched.

"See here, what's this about?" he demanded, scowling, trying to shake off Gabriel's hand.

"What do you want with her?" Gabriel's voice was low, firm.

"Didn't you hear my wife? That's our daughter," Father exploded, jabbing his finger into Gabriel's chest. "And it would seem like you defiled her, you—"

Gabriel jaw clenched, and he grabbed Father by his shirtfront. Violet tried and failed to conceal a smile as her husband stared down her father.

She'd wondered for a long while what would happen if her parents ever did try to follow her out here. Now she didn't need to wonder.

"Gabriel." She drew in a deep breath and stepped out onto the porch, George and Benjie moving aside for her. She descended the steps carefully, Carol and Lou still holding onto her arms to support her, in more ways than one.

Gabriel released Father and craned his neck to meet her eyes, his gaze searching.

"Violet!" Mother began to weep. "It's been *years.*"

"How did you find me?" Violet asked, bracing herself.

Father fished in his pocket and withdrew a piece of paper. A closer look told Violet that it was a newspaper clipping. Squinting, she recognized the picture on the front. One that had been taken a year ago, of her and her schoolchildren. A reporter had come out to do a piece on teachers in Montana, and to ask her about Mr. Laurent, the charlatan who had tried to lure her out to Helena.

Violet's heart sank. *They can't possibly take me back to Boston. Now that I'm married, they can't take me anywhere. And even if I wasn't, they couldn't get me to go back to that place.*

"So, it would seem you are a wife now?" Mother scanned the group clustered on the porch just behind Violet. She gave a nervous smile, twisting her parasol handle in her hand anxiously. "A sheriff's wife?" She glanced at Gabriel, who peered down at her with a stony expression, his mouth a flat, humorless line.

She tittered, shaking her head. "You were always so…unprecedented, my dear."

Violet nearly winced. She certainly didn't miss that about Mother. The subtle barbs. The cutting remarks, glazed over with a sweet tone.

Carol's hand on her arm tightened.

"I am married now," Violet nodded, keeping her voice even. "We have a son."

Father crossed his arms, narrowing his eyes as he peered at Gabriel. "I just can't understand how you gave up everything Isaac Wilson had to offer. For this," and he gestured around them, at the cabin Violet loved infinitely more than the big, cold house in Boston.

"Yes, for this." Her throat closed, her eyes stinging. "And I'm always thankful that I did."

Mother glared at Lou. She jabbed her finger out accusingly. "*You.* Of course you've come out here. You're the one who put this harebrained notion of teaching out West, into our little girl's head. I always had a dreadful feeling about you."

Lou shrank back, but Violet tightened her grasp on her friend's hand. "No, Mother. You and Father are the ones who drove me away from Boston. You were the ones who made me feel like a prisoner in my own home. Lou had nothing to do with that."

A large tear rolled down Mother's cheek, which she batted away with a gloved fingertip. "How can you speak so cruelly? After everything we've given you? We were just trying to see to it that you were married off well. And Isaac Wilson has *still* not taken a wife. He was quite charmed by you. He adored you. And you—you threw it all away! For this!"

"He did not adore me," Violet said sternly. "And don't try to fool yourself." She was brought back to that night she'd told her parents about Isaac Wilson; how they'd told her she was imagining things; how they'd insisted he was a decent man worthy of becoming her husband.

Except he wasn't—*Gabriel* was. Gabriel was everything they'd pretended Isaac Wilson was. Violet shook her head. "You only wanted me to marry him so you could keep living the way you wanted to. It was never about finding me a good husband."

Father's eyes went cold. "You little ingrate," he hissed.

"Leave," Gabriel commanded them. "You're not welcome here."

Father stepped back, away from him. Fear flickered across his round face. The last two years had not been kind to him.

"Why did you come here, anyway?" Violet asked them, trying to keep her voice steady.

"Why, to see you, of course!" Mother cried. "Except I hoped we'd be welcomed a bit more civilly."

"Why should she welcome you back with open arms?" Carol cried. "The way you treated her—"

"The way we treated her?" Father snorted. "We gave her everything. We spoiled her rotten. And this is the way she thanks us. Not even trying to do her part."

"Why did you come?" Violet asked again. "Tell me the truth. And last I heard from Lou, the two of you had separated."

Mother and Father exchanged looks. "We did. But then we made up. We're star-crossed," Mother said dreamily.

Violet wanted to roll her eyes. She'd heard that same phrase before, when Mother had used it to describe Violet and Isaac Wilson. Violet had nearly believed her, until she decided to follow her fiancé to the brothel.

Mother went on a little more uncertainly. "And we came because—we wanted to see our daughter again. See if you'd like to come with us to St. Louis."

Violet could laugh at the irony of it all. At their gall. Gabriel's back had gone rigid, his face a carefully set mask that she knew by now meant he was desperately trying to keep his emotions in check.

She stepped forward, grasping his arm. "Well, I'm not going anywhere. I'm married, and I love the family we've started, the home I have here."

"Violet, don't be foolish," Mother rebuked her. "What life do you really have out here? Playing the role of a brood mare to a small-town sheriff? There's a fur baron in St. Louis who wouldn't care if you're divorced—"

"*Cynthia.*" Violet interrupted in the coldest voice she'd ever heard from her own mouth. "I want you and Augustine to leave. Now. You've insulted us enough. And never come back here. Or my husband will put the both of you in jail for the Marshal to take care of."

Mother began to sputter, and then weep anew. Father put his arm around her, consoling her.

Violet didn't budge. Today, more than ever before, she was thankful she'd left them far behind. They were strangers to her. Nothing but strangers. Her true family stood beside and behind her.

Father shot Violet a withering glare before guiding Mother back to the wagon. The tightness in Violet's chest and throat eased as they rolled back down the road towards town. She prayed they'd make it back in time before the stage left. She didn't know if she could bear another week with them. Fortunately, Miles City had grown so quickly that the stagecoach no longer took a month to come through. A new one came through every week.

Gabriel helped Violet up the steps, and everyone clustered around as he guided her back inside. Without a word, he knew exactly what to do. He led her into their bedroom, asking everyone to excuse them for a moment.

Once the door clicked shut, Violet sank into his arms, muffling her sobs against his chest. Gabriel lifted his hands, running them over her back and up her arm. "I'm so sorry, Violet," he said in quiet, broken voice. "I'm so sorry you had to have them as parents."

She nodded, drawing back slightly. Her lip trembled. "I've been wondering what it would be like...if I ever saw them again. I suppose I don't have to wonder anymore."

Gabriel kissed the top of her head before leaning away, lifting her chin with the crook of his finger. "You'd best believe that we are proud to be your family now. You don't need them."

Violet nodded. "I just—I just wish I'd been wrong about them. Or that they would change."

"Some people never change," Gabriel whispered. He was thinking of the Green Terror—she could see it in his eyes.

"But some people do," she sniffled. "I certainly did. I was a spoiled girl when I arrived out here."

"And I was a cold man who hid behind work." Gabriel smiled softly. He kissed her forehead now, and then one of her tear-stained cheeks.

"Let's rejoin our guests," Violet whispered. She leaned up on tiptoe and kissed him before hurrying over to the dresser. She checked her appearance in the looking glass and then splashed her face with water in the porcelain bowl.

Then, she turned, straightening, and Gabriel held out his arm. He led her back out of their room. Their guests were waiting, smiling. Carol held little Adam on her lap, and when he saw them emerge, he cried out, "Ma, Pa!"

The heavy mood in the room lifted as Adam scrambled off his grandpa's lap to toddle over to Violet. He hugged her legs through her skirts. "It's your birthday," he chirped. "Why are you sad?" And then he grinned, pleased with his evident knack for humor as everyone laughed again.

Violet ruffled his auburn hair, bending to kiss his forehead. "Are you ready for Aunt Lou's cake?"

Adam nodded vigorously, and this earned him another ripple of chuckles from the group.

"Me too," crowed Georgie from his place on the floor in front of the fire. His younger sister, Margaret echoed him, along with the youngest two Woodards, Samantha and John.

***

That night, after everyone went home, and after Adam had been put to bed in his newly finished bedroom, Gabriel and Violet sat on the porch together, looking out at the stars.

A white streak flew across the sky, and Violet gasped.

"Did you make a wish?" Gabriel whispered in her ear.

"No, I—I felt something." Violet frowned, placing her hands on her stomach. She recognized that feeling. She remembered it very well. That tightening pain low in her belly—it could be only one thing. A contraction.

"The baby?" Gabriel sprang to his feet. "It's time?"

Violet nodded, grinning. "It's time."

Gabriel stepped inside, grabbed his hat off the hook beside the door. "I'll go tell Jeff to fetch the Doc in town. Let me help you into bed."

Violet barely refrained from giggling at her husband's panic, his desperation to ensure she was comfortable at the very least. He helped her to her feet and guided her into their bedroom, easing her down onto the bed.

"I'll be right back," he told her, kissing her forehead, before darting out the door. The front door clicked shut behind him.

Violet stared up at the ceiling, closing her eyes. Just like last time, she felt nothing but peace and calm. Of course, the pain wasn't pleasant, but as she gazed up at the boards above her, she knew that she was truly home. Here, in the middle of nowhere Montana, she was home.

***

Gabriel paced back and forth, scrubbing his hands over his face. At the table, Adam sat, watching him in fascination. The screams coming from the bedroom had quieted at last. Carol had just gone into the bedroom with a basin of fresh water to bathe Violet's face.

If someone had told Gabriel three years earlier that in three years' time, he'd be waiting with bated breath for his wife to deliver their second child...well, he wouldn't have believed it at all. As it was, everything felt hazy as he stopped in front of the mantel where George leaned, drawing on his pipe.

Gabriel closed his eyes. Hearing Violet in pain was agony. He raked his fingers through his hair, taking in a shuddering breath.

"Your little lady will be fine, no doubt." George smiled, puffing out some of the smoke.

"This wasn't easy when Adam was born, and it still ain't easy now." Gabriel pulled up a chair from the table and dragged it into the fire. Sinking down in it, he lowered his head into his hands, elbows propped on his knees.

"Pa?" Adam slipped out of his chair and hurried up, wrapping his little arms around Gabriel's forearm. "Pa, is Ma gonna be okay?" His pale brows were scrunched up, his eyes welled with tears. Gabriel reached down and pulled the boy into his lap.

"She's going to be fine," he whispered against Adam's forehead.

After what seemed like hours later, well after Adam had dozed off in Gabriel's lap, a thin cry filled the air. Gabriel scrambled to his feet, carrying Adam with him.

Before he reached the bedroom door, his mother had emerged, a damp cloth on one shoulder, her face wet with tears. She beamed at him, wrapping him in a hug before kissing Adam on the cheek.

"You've got another son," she cried.

"Another son?" Gabriel whispered. He hurried forward past his mother and perched on the edge of the bed where Violet lay, flushed and sweaty. She grinned at him. "Gabriel. It's a boy. We had a boy."

Epilogue

Six Years Later

Violet stifled a giggle, watching from the kitchen window as little Lucy Fisher, red hair tied in two little braids, followed Adam and Michael across the yard. They were playing in a bale of hay, taking turns leaping off of it.

Drying her hands on a rag, Violet drew in a deep breath, hoping her stomach would stop churning eventually.

"Feeling unwell?" Lou asked her with a smile. She ran her hand over her own stomach. Her pregnancy had just begun to show.

Violet closed her eyes and nodded. "Just a little dizzy." The room had begun to tilt, and she broke out in a cold sweat. But after a couple deep breaths, the feeling passed.

"You might want to get a checkup with Doc, then." Lou shrugged.

"Oh, you don't think—?" Violet stopped herself, not daring to believe it. Two years earlier, she'd given up on the dream that she'd have a third baby—hopefully a girl. It would seem that God didn't intend for her and Gabriel to have another child. And she could accept that. She had accepted it.

But lately, she'd been feeling poorly every day, and Lou was sure it could mean only one thing.

Violet didn't want to get her hopes up.

She walked over to the table where Lou sat, lowering into one of the chairs. Tilting her head back, she sighed. "The last time we lost—" She stopped herself, shaking her head. "It hurt us so deeply."

"I know," Lou said softly, but then she offered Violet a smile. "I have a good feeling about this. The baby boy I'm carrying is going to marry the baby girl you're carrying."

"How do you know you're carrying a boy?" Violet chortled.

She and Lou dissolved into a fit of laughter before Lou spread her hands, exclaiming, "I just know! Speaking of, my little girl is in love with Adam," and she waved towards the window. "All she does is talk about Adam. It's Adam this and Adam that."

Violet snorted. "I think Adam's a little frightened of her."

"Oh, yes. She's very persistent, isn't she? Benjie is so proud of her. She's his pride and joy."

"I love watching him carry her around town on his shoulders." Violet rose up slightly to peer out the window at their children. They weren't in sight—they'd probably run off into the neighbor's corn fields.

"He'd spoil her if he could." Lou rolled her eyes to the ceiling. "And what's even funnier is that I think Martha's son is sweet on her."

They dissolved into more laughter.

"So, do you think you'll be up for the ribbon-cutting ceremony?" Lou asked eagerly. "George has been talking about it nonstop. I think he's truly embracing his role as mayor, isn't he?"

Violet agreed. She was more thankful than ever that George had stepped up as the Miles City mayor. He'd been voted in unanimously by the town, and she was thankful that Gabriel wouldn't be overwhelmed by trying to be both the temporary mayor and the sheriff. "I think I should be feeling better. At least, I hope. I don't know…maybe I'll stop by the doctor's beforehand."

"You should come if you're up to it. There is going to be a luncheon after."

"Well, I'm sure the children would love to attend with me. Gabriel won't, I don't think. He's riding out to meet the marshal about some camps set up near the mines."

Lou blew out her breath. "Never a dull moment out here, is there?" she grinned.

"Certainly not."

***

Violet stood, stunned on the step of the doctor's office. She shook her head, placing a hand on her stomach.

I'm…pregnant?

Her first thought was Gabriel. *Will he be afraid to believe it?* She herself certainly was.

She walked down the front steps and headed up the street towards *Carol's Bows*. Miles City was no longer the one-road town she'd found eight years ago by pure happenstance in the form of a stagecoach crash and a man wearing a green bandana.

It was now a bustling, multi-road city, true to its name at last, with a railroad station, theater, schoolhouse, church, and boarding house. There was the Lawrence Mercantile, *Carol's Bows*, and now *Lou's Bakery*. Miles City sprawled out miles further than it used to, so the drive to town was brief nowadays. And in the eight years since the great fire of '85, it had grown increasingly difficult to spot the marks of soot on the buildings that had survived. They'd been freshly painted for the most part.

And although the road wasn't paved yet, telephone poles rose up everywhere, strung with wire, so that the place lit up at night like any city back east. Almost everyone had a phone in their home or business, in addition to the telegraph at the post office.

Violet ascended the steps onto the boardwalk in front of *Carol's Bows*. Inside, she found Lou and Carol working together on a dress for Sylvia Lawrence. They were measuring her for it, and from what could tell of the bolt of cloth lying on the counter nearby, Sylvia had ordered a beautiful wine-red gown made of silk. "Isn't it the perfect *night at the opera* dress?" Sylvia demanded.

Violet hid a smile. She wouldn't exactly call the Miles City Performance Hall an *opera*, but it certainly was the finest Montana had ever seen. It was a two-story building on Hawkins Street, named after Hawkins, of course, for having put an end once and for all to the Green Terror's reign.

"It truly is, Mrs. Lawrence," she smiled.

"Now, where are those little boys of yours?"

"They're playing down by the school, with Lucy and Martha's children."

"Oh, well, they're just the finest little men, aren't they?" Sylvia beamed. Violet wondered if she was actually still in a fuss about Michael throwing ink on her son's clothes. Well, the Lawrence boy had earned it, teasing others cruelly at school.

She offered Mrs. Lawrence a polite smile and took a seat in one of the chairs by the stairs, watching as Lou and Carol finished taking Sylvia's measurements.

"Oh, Lou. Once upon a time I was as slight and slender as you," Sylvia sighed, turning this way and that in the mirror. "You're in a motherly way, and yet you're still as thin as a pin."

Lou stifled a smile behind the mercantile wife. "I haven't been able to keep anything down this time around," she shrugged. "I can't seem to keep any weight on me."

Violet caught a glimpse of her own reflection in the mirror from where she sat. Having two children had certainly not been easy on her body, but she didn't mind. Years of her mother telling her over and over that she needed to keep her waist small had never mattered in the kind of world Violet now lived in. In Miles City, it was less about appearances and more about proving yourself with hard work. And Violet didn't mind that she was perhaps rounder than was fashionable. She had borne two healthy baby boys with this body...*and perhaps a third now.*

Once Sylvia left, Violet turned to Carol and Lou. "The doctor says I'm pregnant," she said, earning excited cries from both of them.

"I told you!" said Lou triumphantly.

Violet couldn't quite manage a smile. "But—I'm afraid to believe it. That it'll last, I mean. After last time...I don't want to get Gabriel's hopes up and—"

"If you're asking us if you should tell him or not, you should." Carol marched over, cupped Violet's cheek in her hand. "He's your husband. Let him be by your side through this, regardless of what happens. He wants to protect you as much as you want to protect him."

Violet would never tire of Carol's straightforward, warm way of saying things. She was the mother Violet had always wished for growing up. A mother who didn't only care about the latest ball, the richest eligible bachelors, or social appearances.

"I know," she sighed. "You're right. I do want to tell him...it's just—"

Carol clucked her tongue. "No, no. You let him comfort you through this. Whether it lasts or not, and I'll pray that it does—you let him be there for you. Support you. You hear?"

Violet nodded, chewing her lip. *Maybe I could tell him tonight...if he makes it back in time for the ribbon cutting.* He would've hated to miss it—after all, it was George's first town event as a mayor, and Violet knew he wanted to be there for his friend.

***

Violet had been quiet lately, more withdrawn. Gabriel tried to not let it get to him, but he kept mulling it over as he rode Apollo back down the road towards Miles City from the Beartooth foothills.

He'd stood at the mouth of the silver mine he'd stared into eight years ago. *Eight years. Heavens. Has it really been that long?*

Adam and Michael loved hearing the story of how he'd rescued Violet from the clutches of the Green Terror...though he'd always remind them that Violet had truly rescued herself. He'd just been thankful to be there to ensure she made it out unscathed.

And she'd shared a life with him ever since. Joys and sorrows both. But her recent change in mood was sudden, impossible to ignore—she was listless, sad, withdrawn. Almost on the edge of tears most days.

Is it the baby we lost last year? Gabriel winced, urging Apollo into a gallop as they reached the base of the hill. He flew across the prairie towards Miles City. It was already late afternoon. The ceremony would begin in just a couple of hours. If he hurried, he would get there just in time.

He hadn't found anything at the Johnson Silver Mines—nothing telling, anyway. All in all, it had been something of a fruitless effort. But he'd still welcomed it as a chance to clear his head.

The conversation from the night before ran through his head on repeat. It had not gone well. Violet had dissolved into tears when he asked her what was wrong, told him she'd rather not talk about it. He didn't press it, but it worried him. Her failed pregnancies over the past few years since Michael's birth had been very hard on her, especially since many other women around town seemed to have a never-ending train of babies.

One thing Gabriel could say with certainty—Miles City wouldn't have any sort of population drop in the oncoming years. The place had doubled in size over the past few years, and it was everything he'd dreamed it could be that day, so many years ago now, when he'd been riding to find Violet. The night they'd met.

She'd been a wide-eyed, naïve girl, and he'd been set in his ways, hardened to love. Ready to face the rest of his life as a lonely bachelor. But then she'd stormed into his life and thrown asunder all those plans.

The ride passed quickly, and before long, Gabriel was riding onto Miles City's main street, catching glimpses of the river flowing at the end of the road. A crowd had already gathered in front of the new performance center, the theater. Next week, so he'd heard, a moving picture would be shown there. The town was buzzing about it constantly these days.

He tied Apollo to the hitching post and heard Benjie call his name. "Gabriel, there you are! We was hoping you'd make it."

Benjie, Lou under his arm, was on the nearest section of the boardwalk where they could more easily see the stage. George was about to begin the ceremony.

Scanning the crowd, Gabriel spotted Violet, with Michael and Adam beside her. She hadn't seen him yet, and her forehead was knitted slightly as if deep in thought.

"Lou," he murmured, turning to his wife's friend. "Is everything alright with Violet?"

Lou's expression told him everything he needed to know. "You'd best talk to her about it," she said gently.

He nodded, glancing back over towards his wife. She turned her head just then, her eyes meeting his. She offered a small, wan smile, wrapping her arm around Adam's shoulders, nestling her chin atop his little head.

Gabriel raised his eyebrows in a silent question for her. But a conversation would have to wait until later. George ascended the stage steps in a suit Carol had made him especially for ceremonies such as these. Gabriel couldn't help but smile to himself at the sight of his old friend all starched and dressed up.

George gave a brief speech—he was good at those, at keeping them short and effective. Declared that he was excited to see the arts come in a new way to Miles City, which earned a cheer from the crowd. Then he was handed a pair of sparkling scissors by Sylvia Lawrence, on the custom velvet pillow she'd insisted on ordering for the event. "Everyone, we'll be having refreshments inside," she trilled. "Thanks to Lou Fisher for preparing the spread for us."

A SHERIFF FOR VIOLET

Gabriel waited for everyone to filter inside, but Violet sent their sons on ahead and hung back, waiting under the lanterns bobbing along the front of the building. Gabriel strolled forward, watching her like a hawk.

Then he stepped forward, gathering her in his arms, and she let him, a sigh shaking through her. She was warm and soft in his arms, and he closed his eyes, wondering how to ask what was bothering her.

Pulling back slightly, he smiled down at her, reaching up to brush aside some of her hair from her face. "How are you?" he murmured. "Seems like I haven't asked you that lately. And I wanted to ask your forgiveness for that."

"Oh Gabriel," she whispered, her face paling in the lantern glow.

"What is it?" he whispered against her temple.

"It's—" Her voice broke, and his heart dropped. *What's upsetting her so much?* He caught her face in the palm of her hand, tilting her head to look her in the eye.

"What's the matter?" he asked.

Her eyes sparkled with unshed tears, and pulled her chin from his grasp, as if unable to meet his stare. "Oh, Gabriel, it's—I'm pregnant."

"Pregnant?" Gabriel echoed. "You're pregnant? With a baby?"

Violet laughed through her tears. "Yes. With a baby."

Gabriel's heart leapt, even as his stomach clenched with apprehension. Last year, Violet's pregnancy had ended horribly. She had nearly died from it. And they had been careful ever since then. Until about a month ago. They'd been less careful than usual. *And now...and now...*

"That's good. That's good," he told her firmly. He would love another child with her, but at the same time, he desperately didn't want anything to happen to her. And he didn't want to watch her sink into a state of melancholy over losing yet another baby. "It is good," he insisted.

Violet nodded, but her face crumpled. "Oh, Gabriel, I don't think I can go through it again..."

He tightened his grip on her arms. "Violet, no matter what, I'll be here next to you. The whole way through." His own voice hitched, and he drew her to him in a tight embrace. She trembled in his arms, and he pressed a kiss into her soft hair.

Soft music of an orchestra began peal through the air, a rendition of "O Susanna."

"Mrs. Brooks," he murmured, stepping back. "May I have this dance?"

Violet nodded, pressing her cheek against his chest in one small final hug, before stepping back and accepting his hand. They began to slowly dance around the street, a soft autumn breeze rustling past, blowing tendrils of her hair into his face. As he brushed them out of the way they both laughed again, and he spun her, her skirt swirling around her legs and ankles.

"It's going to be fine," he murmured into her hair when he drew her back into him. She nodded, leaning back a little.

"I hope so."

"Pa!" Someone darted up in his peripheral vision, and then Adam barreled into him. "Hi, Pa!"

He grinned, ruffling his son's hair. Then Michael rushed up, his face covered in chocolate. Violet let out a laugh and pulled him close, using her sleeve to clean his face. "Michael," she scolded. "What happened?"

"He ate two pieces of chocolate cake," Adam piped up.

Michael tried to wrestle him into the dirt road.

"Two pieces of cake," Gabriel repeated, shaking his head.

As he and Violet led their sons inside, he met her eye, offered her a comforting smile that she returned.

***

Seven months later, Violet wiped her chalk-covered hands on her skirts, surveying everything she'd written there for tomorrow's lesson. It was a Thursday night, and she could hear Adam and Michael playing outside with Lucy and the Woodard children. They'd all walk home with her as soon as she'd finished up preparing for the next day of school.

She sat down at her desk, her aching legs thanking her. It wasn't necessarily easy to teach while being nearly eight months pregnant with her third child, but she loved teaching too much to give it up just yet. *Though, when this baby is born, I doubt I'll have as much time to give to it.*

However, Sylvia was reluctant to lose Violet as the Miles City schoolmarm. She was certain that Violet would instill in her daughter, Genevieve, a Bostonian refinement if given enough time. She even talked of sending the girl to a finishing school, either in Boston or New York.

But if what Violet had seen between Genevieve and the postmaster's son behind the schoolhouse was anything to go by, Genevieve would be getting married by the end of the year. At least, if her parents found out that she and the boy were sweet on each other.

"Ma?" Adam ran in, stopping at the end of the aisle. "A lady's here, askin' for you."

"A lady?" Violet frowned.

"She's dressed real fancy, like she's goin' to church."

A woman entered behind Adam.

Mother.

Violet's heart dropped into her stomach.

Adam ran back outside to play with the others, leaving her alone with Cynthia Thompson.

"Violet," said the woman from the other end of the schoolhouse. "Violet, I'm so sorry. To come back here, like this."

"Mother." Violet braced her hands on the desk, swallowing hard. Watched as the woman who had been her mother in what felt like another life entirely took a step closer. "Why are you here?" She fought to keep her voice level, contained.

"Your father and I are done. For good." Mother's voice trembled.

"But—but why are you here?" Violet clenched her jaw.

"I suppose I—I just got on a train from St. Louis and somehow, here I was. In Montana. I didn't know where else to go."

"Where's Father?" Violet managed.

"I don't know. I don't know," Mother choked. "Last I heard from him, he was on his way to San Francisco. Or New Orleans? I'm not sure…"

Violet closed her eyes for a long moment, trying to compose herself. Then she opened them again. "I'm trying to finish up grading student work," and she gestured at the stack of papers in front of her on the desk.

Mother nodded. "I understand. I just—I was told that Mrs. Brooks teaches at the school by the shop keeper. And I came to tell you—I came to tell you that I'm sorry. I want to ask for your forgiveness. For the way your father and I treated you. The way we tried to set you up with Isaac Wilson. It was wrong. And we were cruel to you. Unfair. Especially the last time we came out here to get you."

Violet lowered her eyes to her desk. She bit her lip, trying to find the words.

Finally, she looked up and spoke. All the things she'd wanted to say…but hadn't known how. Until now. "This whole time, for as long as I remember, I've been used as a pawn by you and Father. Like some piece in a game of chess. But since coming out here, I've been able to choose. I could choose to stay or go. I chose to stay. And you and Father never understood why. It's because you never tried to understand. You never tried to know me."

To Violet's surprise, Mother nodded in agreement. Violet had expected her to try to defend herself, say that Violet was wrong, mistaken. Ungrateful.

She went on regardless. "It doesn't matter. Because I've learned that my family isn't necessarily about blood. It's about who stays by your side, no matter what. Who is there for you on the worst days, and the best days. Who you let yourself let in."

Mother stared down at the floor. "You're right," Violet heard her whisper.

Violet pushed herself to her feet, leaning heavily on the desk in front of her.

Mother gasped. "You're going to have another baby?"

You called me a broodmare, if I remember correctly. If Gabriel heard that Mother had come back to Miles City, he'd be furious. He'd been there in the nights after, when she'd cried herself to sleep as her parents' cruel words flitted through her head again and again.

"Yes," she murmured, perching on the edge of the desk. She set her hand atop her stomach, smiling softly.

"Oh Violet, last time I know I said some unspeakable things." Mother took another step closer till Violet could see the lines fanning around her eyes, around her mouth and across her forehead. Another reminder of how much time had passed since then.

Violet shook her head. "I've forgiven you. I have."

Mother pressed the back of her hand to her mouth and a sob escaped her. "Thank you," she sighed. "I don't deserve it. But, thank you."

She turned as if to go and Violet blurted out before thinking: "Do you want to have dinner with us tonight?"

Perhaps she shouldn't have offered. She'd need to stop by Gabriel's office on the way home, talk to him first. He would likely be upset, but he would understand. She knew that if he had another chance to make amends with his father one last time, he would.

***

Gabriel hung his hat on the peg on the wall, taking a moment to draw in a centering breath before stepping onto the porch where his wife, sons, and mother-in-law sat talking. Cynthia Thompson held Michael in her lap. "Are you my other grandma?" Gabriel heard the boy ask.

"Why, you can just call me Cynthia," she replied.

Gabriel's chest was tight with anger towards the woman, towards all the pain she represented for Violet. As far as he was concerned, she should have never come back here. But Violet had asked him to be civil. It was just dinner. It was the Christian thing to do. And he knew she was right.

He stepped out onto the porch and noticed Cynthia stiffen out of the corner of his eye. He greeted Violet and his sons, who shouted in delight that he was home so early, before dark. About half the time he only made it home after the sun had set, filling out reports to send to the marshal.

"Mrs. Thompson," he said coolly after he'd greeted his family.

"Mr. Brooks," she responded, equally polite. "I must thank you for having me."

"Anything for Violet," he said with a half-shrug.

She nodded, pursing her lips.

"Well, dinner is nearly ready," Violet announced. "Cornbread and a roast. And cookies for dessert, though Michael already had his, didn't he?"

Gabriel leaned down to peer at his son. Sure enough, the boy had chocolate on one cheek. He ruffled Michael's hair, chuckling.

Everyone headed inside for dinner, taking their seats around the table. Gabriel still took pride in the table and chairs—he'd learned from Jeff how to woodwork, and it was something he did weekly in an attempt to soothe his mind, work with his hands for a bit. Right now he was making something for Violet. A chest to put at the end of their bed.

Dinner passed smoothly enough, and then Cynthia bid them goodnight, thanking them for having her. "I should really get back to the hotel now," she explained.

"I'll drive you," Gabriel offered.

"Thank you." Cynthia's expression turned apprehensive, but she managed a polite smile.

Violet remained behind with their sons, too tired to go anywhere else that day. Her pregnancy took a lot of her strength.

Gabriel snapped the reins, urging Apollo along as Cynthia sat beside him, silent, in the driver's seat. He didn't plan to say anything to her. He was content to go the entire ride without a word to the woman who had hurt his wife in more ways than one.

But at last, she broke the silence. "Violet picked a good man," she said, just above a whisper.

"Pardon?" Gabriel grunted.

"She picked a good man. You—you're good. You love her, deeply." Cynthia exhaled heavily. "If only I'd seen that back then, when we tried to set her up with—" She waved her hand. "It doesn't matter. She found you. Someone who truly loves her. Someone who will do everything in his power to make her happy."

Gabriel nodded. "I do, and I plan to."

"Your sons are very intelligent young men," Cynthia continued, folding her hands in her lap. "Very intelligent. Of course, that is the Thompson intellect, I must say." Her laugh grated on his nerves.

"What if I were to ask you and Violet to give me a year with them? We could turn them into Boston's finest. They could marry heiresses, if we play the cards right."

Gabriel slowly turned to gape at her in disbelief. "You don't mean that, do you?"

"But of course I do. They're good boys. And they would be every debutante's ideal suitor. From the west, learned…"

"With all due respect, ma'am, you speak about people as if they were dogs to be bred with one another."

Cynthia gasped. "How could you say such a thing to me?"

"Because it's true."

Cynthia sighed. "Listen, I understand that you are unhappy with me because of my last visit. I do. But if we play our card right, your sons could marry a Rockefeller, or an Astor. Perhaps even a Carnegie. I've inherited a sizable amount of funds from a relative. And I want to see to it that my grandchildren carry on the family name, the wealth."

"I don't think so, ma'am," Gabriel said shortly.

"Well, talk to Violet before you give her answer."

"I will, but I already know her reply to such an idea," he scoffed.

"Just ask her," Cynthia snapped. "If it came from you, she'd listen."

Gabriel's stomach turned at her presumptuous attitude. "I don't think she'd be ready to send our boys off across the nation to stay with you."

"Well, it wouldn't be just me. It would be me *and* Violet. I've got a beautiful brownstone in Boston, and enough for a yearly stay in the Hamptons."

Gabriel's stomach began to knot. He didn't like the way she was talking. As if she was sure Violet would want to listen, go with her.

Take their boys along with her.

And moreover, he didn't want to go home and tell Violet that Cynthia had brought any of it up. *If only she hadn't said anything...*

He dropped Cynthia off in front of the small hotel across from the saloon. Before she stepped off the wagon step, she reminded him one last time, "Speak to Violet of it. Please."

He sat for a long time, staring up at the stars and wishing she'd never spoken a word to him the entire ride.

When he at last made it back home, the house was dark and quiet. A quick peek into the nursery showed him that both his sons were fast asleep. A glance into his room revealed Violet, fast asleep in bed on her side.

He crossed the room, perching on the edge of the bed, and smoothed the hair back from her face. A flicker of a memory passed through his head, of him draping the blanket over her, and waking her up, scaring her. And then, in those moments afterward, he'd held her, unsure of what to do or say, just conscious of how much he cared for her. How much he loved her.

She stirred beneath his hand, batting her eyes drowsily. "Gabriel?"

He hushed her gently, leaning down and pecking her on the lips. "I just got home."

"Is it all just a dream?" she murmured. "Did my mother really come back? And apologize for everything?"

"That is not a dream," he told her, his chest aching.

In the morning. He'd tell her in the morning. "I think she likes the boys," Violet added sleepily.

Gabriel nodded, sighing. "She does. Sure does."

He tossed and turned all night. Perhaps Cynthia was right. Perhaps he was selfish to not want to tell Violet about her offer. After all, as much as Miles City had grown, it wasn't Boston. It wasn't full of finery like she place she'd grown up in. It was small and a bit rough, danger around every corner. And he hoped she loved it as much as she did. Heck, he was sure she did.

***

The next morning, he awoke to the smell of frying eggs, bacon, and coffee. Walking out into the living area of the cabin, he found Violet hovering over the stove, her dark hair tumbling down her back in loose waves. A shawl hung around her shoulders. When she heard his footstep, she turned, her pink lips curving into a smile. "Good morning!" She hurried over, a spatula in one hand. She'd been using it to stir biscuit dough, and her hands were covered in dough, flour smeared across her cheek. He loved her like this.

Kissing his cheek, she returned to the stove. "You won't believe what my mother asked me last night," she told him, flipping over the eggs frying on the skillet.

"What's that?" He leaned his shoulder against the doorjamb.

"She asked me if I'd send Adam or Michael back to Boston. To raise them into gentlemen, marry them off to heiresses. I thought for a second that maybe, maybe she'd changed. That she understood finally." She shook her head, pressing her hand into her back, a position she apparently found comfortable during pregnancy. Her voice lowered, and she sat down the spatula with a clatter. "At least she apologized. But I don't think she'll ever accept me being out here."

"Did you think about it?" Gabriel whispered, that old fear cinching deep in his gut. A fear that haunted him. A fear that Violet would tire of life in the wilderness, that she'd run back home to Boston.

Though she never did. And he knew she never would.

Still, the fear lingered.

"No," Violet laughed, as if the very idea was ridiculous, and Gabriel's heart lifted. "I'd never consider it. I don't want our boys raised in a place like Boston." She closed her eyes, sighing again. "My back pain is abominable."

Without thinking, Gabriel crossed the room to stand before her, looming over her practically.

"So, she talked to you about that yesterday?"

"A little. Before I told her absolutely not. Why? Did she talk to you about it?"

"Somewhat. But I didn't know—I didn't know she'd brought it up to you. I thought—"

Violet shrugged, though he didn't miss the hitch of pain in her voice. "I thought so, too. But that's just...Cynthia Thompson."

"Well, I'm grateful to her, for one thing."

"What's that?"

"You." Gabriel leaned down, kissing her on the lips soundly. Violet giggled, a soft breathless sound.

"I want our boys to grow up out here. To grow up into men. Not men like my father or Isaac Wilson. Who don't know the first thing about anything."

"Well, to be fair...we did have someone like Hank Logan."

Violet threw her head back and laughed again. "That's right. Well...maybe someday they will go out there. But that's their decision. Not mine. Not yours."

Gabriel smiled softly. "I think my pa would say I chose being a sheriff because of him. But that's not it. I chose it because I wanted it. Just like you chose to come out here. And our sons will choose what is right for them."

"Exactly." Suddenly Violet gasped and grabbed his hand. She pulled it to her belly, eyes round. "Do you feel that?"

Gabriel knitted his brow. "What?"

And then he felt it...a soft fluttering started up under his fingertips.

"That's our little girl," Violet whispered.

Gabriel chuckled. "You still believe Lou?"

"Well, we have two boys already. It would be nice to have a little girl!"

"Don't get your hopes up, my dear." Gabriel kissed her hand. "But you're going to anyway, aren't you?"

"Carol sewed a dress for her," Violet protested. "It's purple gingham, like the one she made for me."

Gabriel walked over to the sink, pumping out water to wash his hands. Violet hurried over to the boys' bedroom door and called to them. "Breakfast!"

"Lucy came by for Adam," Violet announced as the boys thundered in and collapsed into their seats.

Adam's shoulders sagged. "She did?"

"I think she's sweet on you," Gabriel spoke up, earning a groan from Adam.

"Pa!" he cried, frantic.

Violet and Gabriel shared a small laugh together.

"No, she ain't." Adam folded his arms, pouting. "She's not sweet on me. 'Sides, even if she was, I don't want to kiss a girl." He made a face.

"Well, I thought the same thing when I was your age," Gabriel told him, lips twitching.

"And now you kiss Ma all the time," Michael exclaimed.

Violet and Gabriel laughed even more this time.

***

Violet colluded with the rest of the town to throw Gabriel a birthday celebration. It would be held at *Carol's Bows* and conclude with fireworks. Courtesy of Hawkins, of course. The night of the celebration, Violet asked Gabriel to meet her in his mother's store.

"Isn't it closed?" he asked. "I think she and George will be having dinner at the restaurant."

But Violet met him outside the shop and grasped his hand in hers. "Everyone is waiting inside," she told him, touching his face. "I know you don't like surprises much, but..."

Gabriel kissed her, and then followed her inside. His heart was warmed more than anything by her consideration. Even better, the crowd didn't cheer. Everyone knew he'd been a little gun-shy since the whole ordeal with the Green Terror.

Violet disliked loud sounds, too. So, instead, the lights flicked on with the flip of a switch, and everyone emerged. People swarmed the shop entry behind them until the street was full. Gabriel hooked his arm through Violet's, placing one hand on Adam's shoulder, and the other on Michael.

"The fireworks are starting soon," Violet whispered.

And sure enough, a brilliant shower of sparks filled the sky in uniform circles and stars, causing their boys to jump up and down, shrieking excitedly.

Together they watched the blue and crimson lights dance across the heavens. Gabriel wrapped his arm around Violet's shoulders, and they stood, just finding comfort in each other's nearness.

The crowd gasped as more fireworks lit the sky in a dazzling array of color.

Gabriel leaned down and whispered in Violet's ear. "I thank God every day for you."

"And I thank Him for you," Violet told him, her laughter tickling his ear. "Imagine if the Green Terror had never crashed that stagecoach. Imagine if he'd never taken me. Do you think I would've met you?"

"I don't know. Don't think so, though. Which is a pity."

As the fireworks continued, Violet leaned back into him. "It is a pity, isn't it?" he heard her murmur. She must have felt another kick in her stomach, because she grasped his hand and pulled it to her belly. Sure enough, he could feel the fluttering sensation again.

"Is that our daughter?" he whispered.

"It sure is." Violet's smile widened. She appreciated that he tried to play along. How strange it was, the ways of Providence…that Hank Logan was the reason they'd even met each other at all. That was one thing that shifted his life entirely.

"I love you, Violet Brooks."

She tilted her head to look at him. "I love you too, *sheriff.*"

THE END

Also by Hannah Lee Davis

Thank you for reading "**A Sheriff for Violet**"!

I hope you enjoyed it! If you did, here are some of my other books!

Also, if you liked this book, you can also check out **my full Amazon Book Catalogue at:**
https://go.norajcallaway.com/bc-authorpage

Thank you for allowing me to keep doing what I love! ❤

Made in United States
Troutdale, OR
05/05/2025

31123258R00179